TROUBLED
BONES

The Crispin Guest Novels by Jeri Westerson

Veil of Lies

Serpent in the Thorns

The Demon's Parchment

TROUBLED BONES

A Crispin Guest Medieval Noir

Jeri Westerson

MINOTAUR BOOKS ☙ NEW YORK

TROUBLED BONES. Copyright © 2011 by Jeri Westerson. All rights reserved. Printed in the United States of America. For information, address St. Martin's Press, 175 Fifth Avenue, New York, N.Y. 10010.

www.minotaurbooks.com

Library of Congress Cataloging-in-Publication Data

Westerson, Jeri.
   Troubled bones : a Crispin Guest medieval noir / Jeri Westerson. — 1st ed.
      p.   cm.
   ISBN 978-0-312-62163-6
   1. Guest, Crispin (Fictitious character)—Fiction.   2. Knights and knighthood—England—Fiction.   3. Theft of relics—Fiction.
4. Murder—Investigation—Fiction.   5. Great Britain—History—14th century—Fiction.   6. London (England)—Fiction.   I. Title.
   PS3623.E8478T76 2011
   813'.6—dc22

                                                              2011018785

First Edition: October 2011

10 9 8 7 6 5 4 3 2 1

To Craig, who keeps my bones untroubled

Acknowledgments

Travel across the pond for every little bit of research? Alas, no. And so I rely on those generous people in archives without whose help I would be lost. One such person I wish to thank is Marion Green from the Canterbury Archaeological Trust who indulged me and sent me all manner of information, floor plans, and other helpful items via air mail. Another thank you goes out to pal Marie Meadows for helping me with Crispin's coat of arms and his motto. Thanks also goes to my stalwart Vicious Circle of Ana Brazil, Bobbie Gosnell, and Laura James; the indefatigable Joshua Bilmes; the incomparable Keith Kahla; and the undefeated and oft long-suffering Craig Westerson.

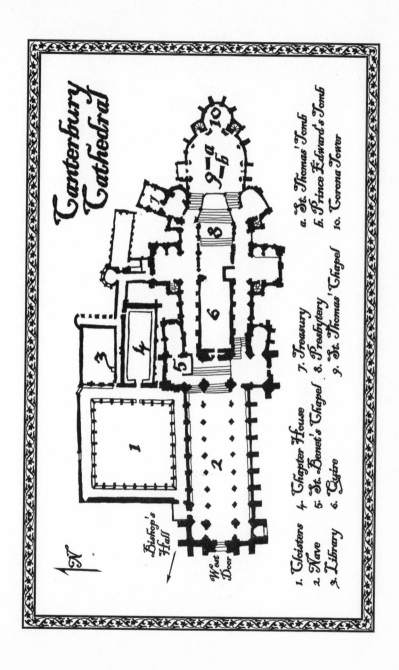

Canterbury Cathedral

N

Bishop's Hall

West Door

1. Cloisters
2. Nave
3. Library
4. Chapter House
5. St. Benet's Chapel
6. Quire
7. Treasury
8. Presbytery
9. St. Thomas' Chapel
a. St. Thomas' Tomb
b. Prince Edward's Tomb
10. Corona Tower

TROUBLED BONES

I

"Mordre wol out, that see we day by day."
—GEOFFREY CHAUCER, *The Canterbury Tales*, "THE NUN'S PRIEST'S TALE"

Canterbury, 1385

"WHY'D YOU HAVE TO take me along, Master Crispin?" complained Jack Tucker, gripping the horse's mane as his body jerked with the rouncey's gait. The boy looked up sorrowfully through a mesh of ginger fringe. "Shouldn't someone keep watch of our lodgings back in London? Shouldn't I have stayed behind?"

"Master Kemp can keep good watch of his own tinker shop, I should think," said Crispin. "And if you ever wish to follow in my footsteps, you must accompany me when I have a paid assignment. As you know, such assignments are few."

"I'd rather follow in your footsteps at that, Master, than ride this beast. If God had wanted Man to have four feet He'd have created Adam with them."

Crispin's left hand lazily held the reins. "Jack, you're fighting him. Roll with the gait. Become as one with him."

"Tell it to the horse."

Chuckling, Crispin raised his eyes to the road. The walls of Canterbury drew closer and rose above the distant copses. It wouldn't be long before they could finally get some food and a warm bed.

Though he appreciated being on a horse once again, the constant drizzle had made their two-day journey from London less than comfortable.

"Why should the archbishop want you to do this thing, sir?" Jack asked.

Crispin gripped the reins. Tension flickered up the muscles in his arm. "The letter delivered to the sheriffs was frustratingly vague. All I know is that it seems to be a matter of Saint Thomas à Becket's bones."

Jack shook his head and whistled. "Saint Thomas the Martyr. It's like a pilgrimage. God blind me! I've never been on a pilgrimage before. And Thomas the Martyr at that. I should very much like to see his bones. They say that Saint Thomas defied a king. A little like you did, Master," he added sheepishly.

Crispin made a sound in his throat but said nothing. He couldn't help but feel a kinship for the martyr. Thomas à Becket had been his own man, to be sure, saint or no.

"But we did leave London rather hastily," Jack went on. "Why, sir, if you hate dealing with relics so much, were you in such a hurry to do this task?"

"I will be paid well for it. I've already received two shillings. Four days' wages isn't bad for work not yet done."

"True. But I've never seen you hurry for no one, let alone a cleric."

Crispin heaved a sigh. He could ignore the boy, tell him to be still and to mind his own business, but after only one short year of knowing the ginger-haired lad, he knew it was pointless. "The sheriffs gave me a choice," he said at last. "Follow the bidding of the archbishop or go to gaol."

"Gaol, sir?"

Crispin adjusted on his saddle. "It seems I might have gotten into a scuffle at the Boar's Tusk."

"Master Crispin!"

"A man was bedeviling Mistress Langton! Should I have stood by while he insulted the tavernkeeper?"

"You were drunk."

Crispin shot him a dark glance. "Careful, Tucker."

"Well . . . were you?"

He pulled his hood down, shivering with a cold wind. "I might have been. The crux of the matter is that the man was a courtier. And I, er, might have . . . struck him."

"God blind me. Then it's a wonder they didn't just hang you."

"Indeed."

They fell silent as they reached the city's gates and then wended their way through narrow lanes, some little wider than the horses' flanks. The late-afternoon light filtered down through the valleys of Canterbury's shops and houses. Their second and third tiers overhung the streets, cutting short the weak light angling through the spring mist.

They found an inn at the end of Mercy Lane, just a bowshot from Canterbury Cathedral, and Crispin left it to Jack to stable both horses and secure a room.

Standing alone at the base of the steps to the great arch of the cathedral's west door, Crispin brushed the mud from his coat. There was little he could do about the state of his stockings with their mud and holes, but surely the archbishop was aware of his situation. After all, he'd asked specifically for Crispin himself.

He climbed the steps and entered the vestibule. Cold stone surrounded him while the stained-glass windows cast rainbows on the floor. The nave opened before him, flanked on either side by a colonnade of impossibly tall stone pillars upholding ribbed vaults. A labyrinth of scaffolding clung to the nave's pillars with spidery fingers of poles and ropes. The church's reconstruction had been under way for years, yet didn't seem any closer to completion since Crispin had last visited nearly a decade ago. While masons worked, showering the nave with stone dust, artisans continued painting the stone runners, spandrels, and corbels in elaborate colors and stripes. The nave was alive in color and gold leaf. Every corner, every inch of every carved bit of stone smelled of new paint and varnish.

He walked across the stone floor, his boots echoing. When he turned at the quire, he made a nod toward the northwest transept archway into Saint Benet's chapel, a miniature church within the large cathedral.

The place where Becket was murdered.

He moved on past the quire on his right and then ascended another set of steps—the pilgrim's steps—to the Chapel of Saint Thomas, its own little parish of occupied tombs and tombs yet to be occupied. *Always room for one more.* He couldn't help but turn his glance to one tomb in particular. It was overhung with a canopy of carved wood covered in gold leaf. He paused and walked forward to study it.

A latten knight lay with hands raised in prayer over his chest. A crown encircled his helm. He did not lie with eyes closed but stared upward at some unseen paradise . . . or possibly a battle, for to the silent knight, Paradise and Battle might very well have been one and the same.

For a long time, Crispin stood and stared at the tomb and at the polished figure of Prince Edward of Woodstock. He crossed himself, studied the face of the man he had known well, and finally turned from the sepulcher.

A drowsy shuffle of monks echoed somewhere in the church.

Crispin turned and stood for a moment, absorbing the sight of

Becket's shrine in the center of the chapel. The chapel's stone pillars created a circle about Crispin and shone golden with the afternoon sun streaming in from the many windows. Raised up on stone steps, the shrine was taller than a man. A stone plinth supported the wooden base, itself resplendent with carved arcades and fine decoration, gold-leafed, painted. As fine as any throne. Set above it all was a finely wrought wooden canopy hiding the gold-and-jewel-encrusted casket in which Becket's remains lay. The canopy was a proud structure of carvings, gold leaf, and bells. Ropes were fastened from the canopy to the center boss on the ceiling. By pulleys and wheels, the canopy could be lifted to reveal the casket's magnificence—for the pilgrims who paid their fee.

Crispin frowned. His eyes searched the shadows. The shrine looked the same as it had probably looked for two centuries.

He turned to go when the sound of voices and scuffing feet stopped him. Pilgrims. Then monks appeared from the shadows and positioned themselves before the ropes and pulleys, ready to reveal Becket's casket. His heart fluttered. How many times had he seen this tomb himself? But he was just as affected as the first time when he was a boy. The archbishop could wait. He wanted a look at Becket's tomb. Just another pilgrim in the crowd.

Steps approached and the voices hushed. The pilgrims, here to see Becket's shrine, moved along the north ambulatory, gawking at the images of Saint Thomas's miracles depicted in the stained-glass windows. They were a varied flock, as Crispin expected. Travelers came from all over the kingdom to see Becket's bones. Some looked to be clerics from other parishes, a priest in rich robes, and two demure nuns in dark habits. A man of wealth was flanked by what appeared to be two tradesmen. A round-bodied woman in a fine gown and cloak stood in the center of the crowd, a look of concentration on her face as she stared at the tomb as if willing it to give up its secrets, while two men, one thin and the other stout, skulked behind the other pilgrims, whispering to each other.

The two monks who stood by the ropes stared suspiciously at Crispin before they set to work cranking the canopy away from the casket. Slowly, with the sound of the rope squealing over the pulley, and with bells tinkling, the canopy lifted higher and the first motes of light struck the casket's gold. The sun revealed it, brushing along its box of carved pillars.

Crispin stood off to the side, waiting in the shadows for the pilgrims to pass. The visitors murmured and were slowly ushered forward one at a time by two monks.

Out of the silence, a sharp voice rang out, incongruous in the silent presence of tombs and the ancient stone chair of Saint Austin standing in a shaft of sunlight. "Well, I'll be damned. Cris Guest!"

It couldn't be. That unmistakable voice. A sinking feeling seized his gut and Crispin slowly turned.

God's blood. Geoffrey Chaucer.

2

CHAUCER CLAPPED CRISPIN ON the shoulder and stood back. "Cris! By God! Let me look at you. I have not seen you in . . . Holy Mother. How long has it been?"

"Eight or so years," he answered stiffly.

"You look very thin."

"Starvation will do that."

Chaucer gave an embarrassed laugh. "Indeed. Well."

Crispin eyed the monks, glaring in their direction. He took Chaucer's arm and directed him out of the chapel area.

"Must you speak so loudly?" Crispin muttered.

"You know me, Cris," said Chaucer, his voice just as loud. "It is my way."

"I remember." He tried to suppress his initial shock. He wasn't successful. He looked at Chaucer, now with a curly beard and mustache. He wore a red ankle-length gown trimmed in dark fur. His belt was dotted with silver studs and held a dagger with a bejeweled pommel. A familiar dagger. One Crispin had gifted to Chaucer too many years ago to count. "What brings you here, Geoffrey?

Shouldn't Lancaster's poet be at court?" He released Geoffrey, though all he wanted to do was clap him in his arms.

"The duke's poet cannot go on a pilgrimage for the sake of his soul?" Chaucer talked in a nervous rush, too jocular, too carefree. "And what brings *you* here, Master Guest? I thought you'd sworn off pilgrimages."

Crispin forced himself back to the present. It had been many a year since he and Chaucer called themselves friends. He weighed how much to reveal. Slowly, he said, "I'm here on a task for the archbishop."

"Task?"

"I must find employment where I can."

If Chaucer was embarrassed, he no longer showed it. "Where are you staying? I am at the Martyrs Inn. I assume there will be ample opportunity to catch up with each other's news. It has been a long time, after all. We've gone our separate ways from those long ago days serving Lancaster, eh? And I . . . well." He paused, his eyes alive and searching every crease and plane of Crispin's face. The rush of words finally hit a stopping point. First he eased back, looking at the long tips of his shoes. Then he edged forward again, raised his face, and said more quietly, "In truth, I would know how you have fared. I remember our days together fondly."

Crispin softened but didn't quite relax. "As do I."

The moment was broken when Chaucer gave a familiar smirk. He stepped back again to boldly appraise his friend. His hat flapped against his back, its long liripipe tail across his chest holding it in place. "Where do you stay? We will meet, will we not?"

"No doubt. I am at the Martyrs, too." His gut roiled with emotions he did his best to tamp down. "I . . . I must go. Later, Geoffrey. Later."

Chaucer tried to speak but Crispin slipped away without looking back. He did not know exactly why he felt so uncomfortable seeing Chaucer again. He reckoned it was mostly because he always felt a certain amount of unease and embarrassment when encountering someone from his former days when he was still a knight and lord. And Chaucer had been one of his best friends; a friend whom Crispin had made certain to abandon.

He strode quickly through the church and out, feeling a sense of relief to walk in the sunshine and leave Chaucer behind. He headed toward the great hall where the archbishop's lodgings were situated and encountered a locked gate at the stair. He pulled the bell rope and soon a monk appeared.

"*Benedicte*," said the monk.

"I have come at the bidding of his Excellency the Archbishop. Tell him Crispin Guest is at the gate."

The monk looked less than inspired with this request, but he turned, trudged back up the stairs, and disappeared around the landing.

Crispin rubbed his chapped hands together and stomped his feet to ward off the chill. He'd met his Excellency William de Courtenay once years ago. How did the archbishop come to think of him for this assignment? It warmed a place in his chest to think that his fame as the Tracker had reached Canterbury, but he squashed the thought just as quickly. If Courtenay remembered him at all, it was as a protégé to John of Gaunt and consequently Courtenay's enemy.

He startled when the monk hurried back down the steps. The monk took a key from a ring at his cincture, unlocked the gate, and pulled it open. He seemed surprised to find himself saying, "His Excellency will see you immediately." He locked the gate again and Crispin followed him up the staircase, through a corner of the great hall, and to a large arched door. The monk knocked, listened a moment, then ushered him through.

Courtenay looked up from his reading with striking blue eyes set in a fleshy but earnest face. A classical nose found on many a Roman statue rose over well-carved lips and a prominent chin. He rose at his place behind a large table and ornate chair. Courtenay wore the long robes of his office. A red cap fit snugly on a head of curled brown hair.

The archbishop pushed the chair aside and strode around the table. He seemed to be a man in his full capacity, fully aware of his role and his position in society. He, like the martyred Becket, had once served as chancellor to a king, but resigned after serving King Richard only four months. Crispin had no reason to suspect that he left the king's services due to any lack of affection for the young king, but he did wonder.

He knelt, kissed Courtenay's ring quickly, and stepped back.

The cleric openly inspected him. Over the years, Crispin expected a certain amount of scrutiny, especially from those who were aware of his history, but knowing this never seemed to dull the sensation that he was a horse at market.

"Crispin Guest," said the archbishop in a clipped and patrician tone. Courtenay hooked his thumbs into his embroidered belt. "We've met before, you know."

"Yes, your Excellency. I thought we might have done."

"But those circumstances are best forgotten."

He agreed. "But if that is so, my lord, then why did you send for me in particular?"

Courtenay smiled. He gestured to a sideboard before he sat in a chair beside the fire. "Pour some wine, Master Guest."

He bowed and moved to the sideboard. He poured wine from a silver flagon into two silver goblets and took them to the fire, giving Courtenay one and keeping the other. Courtenay offered him a wooden chair beside him, and Crispin sat.

"You are well known in certain circles, Master Guest," said Courtenay. His jeweled ring glittered as he turned the goblet in his hand. "And your recent doings at court have made association with you less of a disadvantage than it might have been before."

Crispin raised a brow. Saving the king's life? He supposed that made him less of a pariah, though he was still not welcomed at court. No one forgot treason, he supposed.

"Indeed," Courtenay went on, "your skills investigating crimes make you highly desirable and quite the only one I wished to consider."

Crispin drank in silence.

Courtenay's eyes fixed on him. Suddenly, he offered, "I remember tales of Sir Henry Guest. He was a valorous knight and a devoted baron to the crown as well as servant of Lancaster and the old king."

Crispin straightened at Courtenay's unexpected words. He cleared his throat. "I do not recall much of my father," he said carefully. "He was often gone to war, where he died."

"Yes. And that was when you were fostered into Lancaster's household, I believe."

"Yes, when I was seven. No mother and no father, save Gaunt."

"Your liege lord raised you well, making you a knight."

Crispin moved against the seat, trying to find a comfortable spot. "Lancaster is no longer my liege lord." He wished he could leap to his feet and cast over the chair. Instead, he gripped the arm. "Situations change. Particularly of late." *I came all this way, dammit. Get to the point!*

"Lancaster has staunch views on religious matters. One might even say they lean toward heresy."

"My religious views do not necessarily mirror that of my former mentor."

"Well then. Can I assume that you are a friend of the Church?"

The comfortable spot on the chair still eluded him. He edged forward. "I am neither friend nor foe of the Church."

"Am I mistaken about you, Master Guest? I heard from my brother monk, Abbot Nicholas of Westminster Abbey, of his high regard for you. Of deeds you have performed for the sake of Mother Church."

"He is a friend."

"And the relics?"

He couldn't help cringing. Did it always come to that? The chair proved too uncomfortable. He snapped to his feet, started to pace before the fire, and then thought better of it. He stood before it instead, keeping his back to the flames. "Simply because a holy relic falls into my hands—for whatever reason—does not mean I believe in its power."

Courtenay took a sip of wine, his gaze never leaving Crispin. "Then why *do* these relics come to you?"

He threw up a hand. "I know not. Perhaps it is God's plan. Or jest."

"I suppose a man like you can be trusted, if the Almighty finds you worthy."

"You can trust me. For a shilling you can buy all the trust you desire."

"For money? I don't believe you."

Crispin set the goblet down hard, spilling some of the wine. "You know my history. I have learned that the only thing that can be trusted is gold."

"That is not a godly sentiment. Aren't you a good Christian, Master Guest?"

He raised his chin, staring up at the ribbed ceiling and decorative bosses. "I believe . . . in belief."

"Master Guest—"

He squared on the archbishop. "Forgive me, Excellency. But these niceties get us nowhere. I have come a long way. What do you want with me?"

Courtenay slowly nodded and set his wine aside. He stood. "You are a candid man, so I shall be forthright with you. The Lollard heretics have made threats against the martyr's relics."

At last! Firm ground. "What kind of threats?"

"Letters. Rumors. All indicate that they wish to do harm to Becket's tomb and remains."

"May I see these letters?"

"Alas. I destroyed them. There were only two, and I took them as nothing but the anonymous mischief of a disingenuous rabble. But then there were rumors and incidents. Broken locks and petty thievery. It was only then that I began to take these threats seriously. And as you know, I am no friend to the Lollards."

Crispin remembered. Ten years ago, Courtenay and Lancaster faced off like two cockerels in a barnyard fight. Crispin stood beside Lancaster as he was wont to do. Courtenay no doubt remembered Crispin from that occasion. Courtenay's attempt to suppress the Lollards, and their attacks on papal authority and the doctrines of the Church, outright opposed Lancaster, who took it upon himself to support John Wycliffe, the Oxford theologian and the father of the reform movement, who was also the duke's personal preacher.

"Then you believe it is the Lollards who seek to despoil Becket's tomb?"

"Who else? They dare call the sacred shrine and others like it idolatrous."

"They may hate more the fees charged to the pilgrims."

Courtenay's sharp glare replaced his earlier and more controlled demeanor. "It is just such talk, Master Guest, which produces violent rabbles. Do you suggest that the maintenance of such a holy place be solely on the poor church that is forced to house it?"

"Forced, my lord? Many a monastery would happily go to war to own such a profitable venture."

Courtenay's face reddened. "And you call yourself a son of the Church!"

"Be at ease, my lord. I do not say I approve of such infighting. Can you tell me this does not occur within the Church?"

Courtenay's breathing evened, and he gripped the back of the chair. His rings sparkled in the tinted light of the flames and stained-glass windows. "You are right, of course. Such does occur, and it grieves me to see it."

Crispin sighed and took up his goblet again. "Tell me, then, how do you suggest I protect the bones."

"That, Master Guest, I leave to you."

"Then I propose that you post a guard on them day and night."

"Naturally. But the letters indicated that there would be an attempt made at the beginning of the season. Which is now upon us."

"And so?"

"My hope, Master Guest, is that you would personally guard the tomb."

Crispin choked on the wine. "Me? Sleep alongside Saint Thomas?"

"I trust you, Master Guest. This is my charge to you."

"My lord, I have no wish to play nursemaid to Becket's bones for the rest of my days. I have lodgings in London. I have my life there."

"Certainly I did not expect that you would give up all to spend eternity by a tomb," he said. Except that by his tone, Crispin thought that this was exactly what Courtenay expected. "But I wish it guarded, and I will pay you well."

"You have an entire community of faithful monks, my lord. Surely they can be expected to be obedient in this." Courtenay was silent, and Crispin studied his tightening shoulders. The archbishop left the chair and strode across the room to stand below a large crucifix. He rested his hands behind his back and stared up at the corpus, its limbs carved with care, showing stretched sinews and even scars from flogging.

"A monastery is a wonderful haven, Master Guest. I wonder if the layman can truly appreciate it."

"I have seen it carve great and holy men within its confines."

"As have I. But it can also cripple a weak man."

"Your Excellency?"

"Master Guest, have you ever led an army?"

Crispin's nimble mind tried to keep up with the archbishop's more agile one. "Not an entire army. A garrison."

"But you rely on the competence of your men to win the day."

"Naturally. And their loyalty."

"Their loyalty. Indeed. The battle cannot be won without it."

"My lord, I am at a loss as to your meaning."

He turned. His blue eyes were deep sapphires. "You asked about my monks."

"Yes. The monks of the priory. This is their church." He sensed Courtenay's hesitation. "They *are* faithful monks, my lord, are they not?"

"They call you the Tracker." Courtenay moved from the crucifix and returned to his table. He trailed his fingers along the documents piled there. He picked one up, glanced at it, and set it down again. "My treasurer and his assistant do much of the task of guarding the relics, but I must tell you an unpleasant truth." His hand dropped away from the desk and fell against his robe. He raised those sapphire eyes to Crispin again. They burned with a cold fire. Crispin suddenly had a feeling of raw power emanating from those eyes, reflecting the true heart and soul of the man who owned them. "I believe one of my monks to be a Lollard heretic, Master Guest. I want you to root him out and bring him to me."

3

CRISPIN GRUMBLED TO HIMSELF all the way back to the inn. Tombs, relics, heretical monks. Sixpence a day wasn't enough compensation.

Always better to talk out the problem. Where the hell was Tucker?

He pushed open the inn's door and was stopped short by the press of pilgrims talking, laughing, shouting. The season had most definitely begun.

Crispin recognized most of them as the pilgrims he'd seen at the shrine. There were the two nuns, one older in a black habit and one much younger in a brown veil and gown. They were talking to a priest, the round fellow in prosperous garb. Beside them but not with them was the well-shaped female of the merchant class he recalled from the shrine, talking animatedly to a short, stout fellow hoisting a beaker of ale, who looked to be a tradesman of some sort. He nodded his head and listened to her speech but his shuffling feet seemed to indicate he would rather be skirting away.

The other that Crispin had taken for a tradesman was a tall, lank fellow dressed like a middling merchant. He stood by the shorter man, but on closer examination he appeared to be alone and merely listening to the conversations of the others. He kept a surreptitious eye on two skulking men from the shrine who were still talking secretly to each other in a far corner. One was a tall blond man and the other his shorter, squatter companion.

And there, the wealthy Franklin from Becket's tomb, replete with gold chains over his scarlet robes. He stood before the fire as if he owned it, warming his bejeweled fingers.

"Master Crispin!" Jack rushed forward, a beaker of ale in one hand. His normally pale complexion flushed red from spirits. "Look at the merry folk who are here! All pilgrims, and they have just lately come from London, too!"

Jack had probably never been this far from home, he realized, and he allowed himself a momentary pang of empathy for the boy.

"Cris! What kept you?"

He flinched. He couldn't help it. He turned to see Chaucer bearing down on him. Chaucer clapped him on the back and then left his arm draped lazily over his shoulder. Ears warming, Crispin did his best to shrug him off by pulling Jack forward. "This is Jack Tucker," he said curtly. "My protégé."

Chaucer focused skeptical eyes on Jack. "Protégé?"

"He helps me solve puzzles. Catch criminals. Surely you must have heard—"

"Oh yes! The celebrated 'Tracker.' There's a poem in that, I'll warrant. Like a modern-day Robin Hood."

"Put me in one of your poems and you're a dead man," he growled.

"Now, now Cris. Mustn't lose that famous temper of yours. It does get you into trouble, doesn't it?" He smiled, but not sincerely. He turned from Crispin to study Jack. "And so, Young Jack. Where do you hail from?"

"From London, good sir."

"And pray, what family?" His gaze traveled well over Jack's threadbare tunic with its worn laces.

"No family, sir. Master Crispin took me in from the street. I was little better than a beggar. Taught me to read and write, he did."

"Taught you to read and write?" Chaucer stroked his light brown beard and aimed his eye at Crispin. "How democratic of him."

Crispin put his hands on Jack's shoulders and began to steer him away. "If you'll pardon us, Geoffrey. I have business to attend to." He didn't wait for Chaucer to answer.

"What is it, Master Crispin?" Jack asked softly when they'd moved to a quiet corner. "What have you discovered?"

Near Jack's ear, he said, "The archbishop fears the bones of Saint Thomas are in danger of theft or damage. He wants me to guard them."

"Blind me! What does he take you for? A mastiff?"

"I wondered that myself."

"What will you do?"

"I don't know. There is more—"

"The dinner will be ready anon. Can't it wait till after we've eaten?"

Crispin scanned the room of chattering pilgrims, the warm fire, the inviting aroma drifting in from the kitchens, and considered. Maybe a quick bite would do him good. He could think better on a full stomach.

Just then the innkeeper called for the guests to be seated at a long table in the center of the room. There was a general sound of affirmation before shoes scuffed and garments rustled as they made their way around the table, seating themselves. The pleasant-faced innkeeper scurried from cup to cup, pouring wine from one jug and ale from another.

Crispin sat slightly away from the others while Jack stood behind him, trying for the appearance of a proper servant.

The priest scanned the room before his gaze landed on Crispin and he shuffled into place beside him, scooting closer with his cup in hand. "I am Father Gelfridus le Britton," he said cheerfully. "You seem familiar with our Master Chaucer. He accompanied us from London, you know. Just a pilgrim like the rest of us." He chuckled. "A noteworthy gentleman. A man of wit and good humor. The stories he told! He reminds me fondly of my days as a schoolboy. I read many a tale in those days. The poetry, the histories, the philosophers. Seldom do I get an opportunity to read such like anymore."

"Nor do I," answered Crispin. "Those books are long gone."

"Owned them, did you? What I would not give for a fine library."

"Your parish has no library?"

The priest cut a glance back at the tall nun and then brought up a guilty expression as if he had not meant to look at her. "Well, no. I am the nun's priest, sir. Though the prioress's tastes tend toward the classical, she finds it impractical to own books."

"Perhaps she simply has no stomach for overindulgence. 'A priory in a humble state can only boast in Christ, not in its riches,' so the saying goes."

The priest, a man of Crispin's age though a little shorter and broader, adjusted the collar of his blue robe and straightened his cap. "That sounds dangerously like the opinion of a Lollard, sir."

Jack leaned between them to pour wine. He offered some to the priest. Crispin noticed the boy's cheek bulging with bread, which he was trying to chew quickly. "Not at all, Father Gelfridus. I am no Lollard."

"What's a Lollard?" Jack whispered, mouth still full.

Gelfridus turned toward Jack and tapped the boy's crumb-dusted chest with a finger. "Don't concern yourself with that lot, young man. You just follow your priests as you should."

"Now, now, Father," said Crispin. "'All men by nature desire knowledge.' And Jack is as hungry as the next man."

Jack had managed to down his mouthful. He crooked his thumb in Crispin's direction. "That was Aristotle, that."

Gelfridus seemed surprised and rested an arm on the table.

Jack was proving to be a resilient pupil, but had yet to learn when it was appropriate for him to join a conversation. Still, it was a good excuse to bring the subject into the open. "Lollards, Jack, are those followers of John Wycliffe, a philosopher and theologian at Oxford—"

Gelfridus made a disgusted sound. "So you call him, sir. He does not deserve your charity."

"Nevertheless," he continued, aiming his remarks toward Jack, who had somehow secured an onion and was eating it with relish. "He denounces the influence of clerics and even the pope's authority. He claims that Christ is the only pope and he further argues that the Church owns too much land, too many riches, and has too much power."

Jack eyed Gelfridus in his new robes and rings but said nothing.

"Wycliffe found many supporters," muttered the priest. "His staunchest is his grace the duke of Lancaster."

"Lancaster?" cried Jack.

Crispin kept his eyes on Gelfridus. "Any man may take a long, hard look at the vastness of Church property and perhaps invent philosophies of his own."

"Yes," said the priest. "With one hand these great men pay lip service to the Church and at the same time plot its destruction. All for greed."

"Not all," said another voice.

Crispin turned his head and recognized the wealthy Franklin he'd noticed earlier.

"Master Crispin, may I present Sir Philip Bonefey."

Crispin inclined his head.

"You have something to say, Sir Philip?" asked Gelfridus.

"Only that a man of property may have a better sense of excess, good Father," he said taking a seat. "The Franciscans, for instance, preach poverty. They do not wear fine robes and ride fine horses, for the most part."

Gelfridus rose in his seat. "Sir Philip! Do you presume to ascribe temporal laws to priests and clerics?"

"I presume nothing. I merely state—"

"Gentlemen"—Crispin opened his hands—"I am instructing this lad here on the finer points of Lollardism. Any notes you care to add should be done with a civil tongue. How is he to learn if all questions come to blows?"

Sir Philip looked at Gelfridus, and then they both looked at Jack. The Franklin's face broke into a smile, and he clapped his hand on the table. "Bless me, Master Crispin. But you are right. Instruct!"

"Don't forget pilgrimages," put in Father Gelfridus. "These damnable Lollards declare that pilgrimages are idolatrous."

Jack turned to Crispin.

"That is so."

Frowning, Jack edged forward. "But if his grace the duke was a Lollard supporter, then why aren't you, Master?"

"I was not always in agreement with everything his grace professed. Though I find some of the Lollard doctrine intriguing."

"And Eve found the fruit from the forbidden tree just as 'intriguing,' Master Guest," said Gelfridus. "Remember, only a hairsbreadth lies between rhetoric and heresy."

"I do remember, Father."

They all fell silent. The dinner arrived and the pilgrims readied their eating knives. The prioress and her young chaplain sat opposite Crispin, while Sir Philip Bonefey found a place beside the priest. The round woman with the gat-toothed smile sat beside Crispin to his right.

Jack remained behind Crispin, clutching the wine jug.

One last traveler arrived and fit himself into the bench. "God's wounds," said Crispin, smiling at the round-faced man with the rosy nose. "And what brings you, good sir?"

The man smiled. "Master Crispin!" He leaned over the table and gave the offered hand a hearty shake. "It has been many a day, sir." He gestured toward the rest of the company. "I saw these good pilgrims on their way to Canterbury from my inn and I told the wife it was time I ventured there again myself. And so you see me now."

Crispin turned to Tucker. "Jack. This is Harry Bailey, proprietor of the Tabard Inn in Southwark."

Jack ducked his head in a bow. "A pleasure, good sir. God keep you."

Servants came from the kitchens bearing platters of roasted pullets and haunches of lamb, onions in an almond milk broth, cheese, and loaves stuffed with nuts and meats.

He felt Jack tense behind him. This was possibly the grandest feast Jack had ever partaken of. But Jack appeared determined to play his role, and he served and cut slices of meat for Crispin as Crispin had instructed him—as he had done himself for Lancaster when he started as a page in his household.

With his knife, Crispin jabbed the meat and fed himself the generous slices. The spices and herbs blended together in his mouth. A full bowl of wine sat before him. For the moment, he was content.

The prioress picked delicately at her food, eating as daintily as a bird. The nun beside her did not quite have the same aplomb, but tried to mirror her prioress's table manners. She lifted her horn cup to her lips and reddened upon discovering it empty.

Jack scrambled around the table and quickly offered to pour her beer. She took it without looking up at him. Crispin watched Jack detachedly until he noted the woeful expression on the boy's face when the young nun would not acknowledge him. Jack put down the jug and offered her bread. She shook her head and still would not raise her eyes. Jack lowered himself to the bench beside her and slowly reached for the meat.

Crispin thumbed his wine bowl and edged forward. "Madam Prioress."

The Prioress raised her eyes but kept them carefully shadowed under a canopy of dark lids. "Prioress Eglantine de Mooreville," she announced. "This is my chaplain, Marguerite de Bereham."

"God keep you," he said with a smooth nod of his head. "From which priory do you hail?"

"A small and humble one, Master Guest, not far from London."

"Then you, your nun, and your priest have traveled some distance like the rest of us."

She held a haunch of pullet vertically and sawed down at the flesh as she talked. "Though we have traveled far, it is well worth the journey and expense. I was most impressed by the martyr's shrine today." She sighed. "Such magnificence. Saint Thomas was such a brave and noble man. To stand up as he did against a king, his friend. Such a chivalrous man."

"You speak of him most strangely," said Crispin. "Not as a saint, but as a romantic figure in a minstrel song."

"And why not?" she said, cocking her head. "We love our saints, we cloistered women. And we have no lover but God. 'Let him kiss me with the kisses of his mouth; for thy love is better than wine.' There is no need for outward passion of two vulgar bodies. Let man love from afar and look upward. To Heaven. We must be blind to all else but the love of God."

He flicked his gaze toward Jack whose eyes were glued to the young nun.

"I intend to make a special vigil at the church tonight, later after supper," said the Prioress. "One must make the most of one's outlay."

"The Prioress is very thrifty," said Sir Philip brusquely.

Crispin turned to him but the Prioress went on.

"Thrift is an important trait in a priory. I have my hounds and my garden. What more would I need? Abuses of discipline and money are for the world without. Is that not correct, Dame Marguerite?"

The quiet nun raised her face. Jack no longer appeared to be *his* table servant but the nun's. The boy was quick to drop the food from his hand and fill her cup lest it be empty the next time she touched it.

She lowered her eyes. "My Lady Prioress is correct. I myself was raised under the careful guidance of my lady."

"You were brought to the priory as a child?" asked Crispin.

"No, Master. I was born there. My mother was a servant in the priory. My lady was kind enough to see to my schooling and sponsored me when I begged to take vows." She raised a crust of bread to her lips and carefully took a small bite. Jack pushed another piece of bread toward her, but she shook her head. He munched a pullet leg absently and kept a furtive glance aimed at her beneath his shaded eyes. His lips murmured a sigh.

"By careful discipline tempered by the love of Christ," said the

Prioress, laying a hand gently on the nun's, "we have built a family in proper order. All know their places, have their assignments, and find contentment to do so. We have just enough to sustain us. Fields, crops, animals. We are our own ark, if you will, floating on the seas of iniquity."

"Your own lands, yes," said Sir Philip tightly. He clutched his cup and leaned so far over the table toward the Prioress he was like to lose his balance. "Enough to sustain you, and that should have been quite enough!"

The Prioress showed no signs of distress when she raised her eyes. "Sir Philip and I are acquainted, as you may have supposed, Master Guest. Our dispute, however, has already passed the test of the courts."

"It has not passed my test, madam," said Bonefey.

"Verily, Sir Philip. Is there any point in discussing the matter further? The court decided in our favor. We had use of the lands, they were put to good service in our care, and they were henceforth deeded to the priory."

"They were *my* lands! The Church poaching the land from a faithful man—"

"Faithful, sir, is in the eye of the beholder."

"Do you infer that I am unfaithful merely because I will not willingly give ten acres of useful land to the Church?"

A strident female voice cut a blade between them. "'For what shall it profit a man if he shall gain the whole world and lose his own soul?'" All eyes turned to the lady at Crispin's right. She smiled her crenulated teeth at him. "Greetings. We have not met. I am Alyson de Guernsey, from the great city of Bath. And you are Crispin Guest. A fine name for a fine figure of a man." She punctuated her brisk discourse by eyeing him thoroughly up and down.

Crispin smiled and gave her a nod. "Mistress."

"Oh, it is *madam*. But I'd rather *you* 'mistressed' me than 'madamed' me." And she laughed heartily at her jest. "Five times a wife and five times a widow. Now *that* is discipline well earned," she said, pointing a finger at the Prioress.

Madam Eglantine's thin lips flattened to a line.

"You can have your celibacy," Alyson declared loudly and stabbed her knife into a pullet, lifted it from the platter, and plopped it on her trencher. "But there are some meant for the marriage bed." She winked at Crispin. "Though, back to my point—" She leaned over Crispin to aim her disarming finger at Bonefey. "My lesson is two-fold. First, how much land does a rich man truly need? Recall the story of Dives and Lazarus and take heed. If the court gave it to the priory, then I'll warrant it was land you had no use for. You did not even know that these lands were within your boundary. True?"

Bonefey said nothing. His mouth curled into a snarl.

"And two," she went on, "that charitable use to which the priory no doubt puts this land will serve to send you to Heaven that much quicker, were you to have given it freely."

"Instead," said Bonefey, pushing both Gelfridus and Crispin back to lean closer to Alyson, "the Church stole the property from me like a thief in the night."

"I daresay," said Alyson, "with an attitude like that, there shall be adequate time in Purgatory for you. You'd best speak to Master Chaunticleer here. Bless me, but I believe it will content him to sell you your way out of the purging fires."

"I do not *sell*," said the man identified as Chaunticleer from down the long plank table. He was one of the secretive men Crispin saw earlier. Crispin surmised by the exchange that the man must be a Pardoner, a purveyor of Indulgences. "An Indulgence is a serious matter."

"And an expensive one, too," she said, elbowing Crispin.

Crispin forced his amused glance away from Alyson and continued eating while the arguments raged around him.

A pale young man Crispin had taken for a merchant watched Bonefey with unconcealed concentration, chewing his food with mouth open. The Pardoner, Chaunticleer, and the man with him finished their meal quickly and left the inn. Bonefey's face became increasingly reddened, only occasionally turning an eye toward Alyson and her pointing finger. The priest appeared ready to launch into a sermon. Chaucer, like Crispin, seemed fascinated by merely listening.

Harry Bailey stood up. "Friends! So much discord. Do we forget why we are here?"

A pause followed his statement, and then the noise began again as each one renewed his argument.

Crispin finally had enough of the food as well as the chatter and pushed away from the table. He made his farewells, wiped his knife on the linens, and sheathed it.

Jack finally recalled whose servant he was and scrambled to catch up to him just as Crispin passed over the inn's threshold. Jack wiped his lips with the back of his hand. "What now, Master Crispin?"

"We're going to the cathedral."

HE AND JACK STRODE back up the avenue toward the stone edifice.

"So you're to guard the martyr's bones *and* seek out the heretic amongst the monks?" said Jack.

"One presumably might have to do with the other."

"Ah. And then we can go home."

"Jack, we just arrived."

Tucker fell silent and trailed slightly behind. They passed under the gatehouse and made the long walk down Palace Street to the west door. Chaunticleer and his companion had already set up shop, the Pardoner with his scrolls of papal remissions and the other with his trinkets and pilgrim badges. His table was also spread with an array of relics: cloudy monstrances, curled hair in glass vials, small boxes supposedly containing bones.

The Pardoner, gesturing like a cockerel, admonished passersby with a thundering voice, "Repent and draw near! Do not put off your salvation for another day. For you do not know the day or the hour of His coming, that terrible day of judgment." He aimed a finger at Crispin. "Repent, for 'pride goeth before destruction, and a haughty spirit before a fall!'"

Crispin gazed at him under drawn lids. "'Even a fool, when he holdeth his peace, is counted wise.'" Chaunticleer snapped his jaw closed and Crispin smirked and ducked into the cathedral.

"Was that Aristotle?" asked Jack in a hushed tone.

"No. Proverbs."

He chuckled. "I'll have to remember that one."

Crispin glanced into the falling shadows of the arches and columns. They walked down the long nave past the quire to the other end of the church, ascended the steps to the Chapel of Saint Thomas, and stood before Becket's shrine.

Even after the archbishop's admonitions, no monks stood guard.

"God's blood," Crispin swore softly. He searched in the dimming light but saw no one.

The wooden canopy again covered the casket. Crispin strode up to it unchallenged. Four candle sconces stood at each corner of the shrine. Fat beeswax candles cast a warm glow over the steps and floor. Crispin ran his hand along the carvings of the base, until he noticed Jack was nowhere behind him. "Jack?"

"Here, sir," came the meek voice from behind a pillar.

"What are you doing there? Bring a candle from that chandler."

Jack stretched up on his toes and plucked a candle as instructed. He crept forward and held the candle unsteadily, but the flame never flickered when he brought it up to the shrine. Crispin moved Jack's arm closer so he could better view the wooden base. Nothing amiss. All intact.

He left the shrine and found the pulley system that lifted the canopy. Releasing the lock he pulled on the wheel. "Tucker. Come help me."

Jack trotted over and set the candle upright on the floor. He took hold of the wheel and pulled in rhythm with Crispin.

The rope groaned. With a great, creaking sigh, the canopy rose, bells tinkling. When it rose a foot above the casket, he told Jack to halt. The brake held the wheel in position as he walked back to the shrine, running his hand along its top edge.

He offered a half smile to Jack. "Jack Tucker, meet Thomas à Becket."

Jack swallowed. "He's in there?" he whispered.

"Yes. What remains of him."

Jack's gaze roved over the casket. "Blind me. It's like a palace."

"Very much so."

"That ain't *real* gold, is it?"

"Gold and precious stones. Pearls, carnelian, sapphires."

"'Slud! That's a fortune, that is!"

"Indeed." He ran a finger over a polished red gemstone. Knife marks. "Someone tried to pry out this one."

Jack came closer and brought the candle's light over the spot. He wiped his hand down his tunic before he stretched out his trembling fingers to touch the many scratches.

"A knife blade," said Crispin. "But they are old. See how the polishing compound has accumulated within the scratches?"

"Aye. I *do* see." He looked up at his master's face.

Crispin worked his way around the shrine, inspecting all its precious stones. None were missing. "This is not the work of Lollard sympathizers. The archbishop called it 'petty thievery.' I'm certain he was referring to something else, though he was less than forthcoming on the point."

"You said the archbishop is suspicious of his own monks. I thought they was supposed to be obedient."

"A man's conscience cannot be suppressed, no matter the circumstances." His eyes were drawn to Prince Edward's tomb over his shoulder.

"But to be a holy brother and threaten the relics themselves! That's evil, that."

"Perhaps."

He left the tomb of Saint Thomas for the smaller tomb of Prince Edward and stood before it. He grasped the edge of the sepulcher's lid and lowered himself to his knees. His eyes scanned the prince's tomb and he smiled as he gazed at the latten knight, only the edge of which he could see from his kneeling position.

Jack followed him and carefully read the inscriptions, his eyes screwed up tight with the effort. "This is Prince Edward, Master Crispin."

"Yes. I know."

"You knew him, too, I suppose."

"Yes. He was a fine warrior. He and his brother Lancaster spent much time in each other's company."

Jack ran his hand along the solid stone base with shields decorating its length. "If he'd but lived and been king," he said softly, "you'd still be a knight."

"I might have been many things. But I would not have met you. Leastways . . . not *below* a gibbet."

Jack shivered. "That's true enough. God keep you," he muttered to the latten corpus, then crossed himself before he lowered to his knees beside Crispin and drew silent.

Yes, had you but lived . . . But it was a fruitless thought. He hadn't, and his son had succeeded him to the throne. King Richard was certainly no Prince Edward. Crispin raised his hand and caressed the uneven lid entombing the former heir to the throne, when a shout made him snatch his hand back.

Crispin and Jack rose and turned.

"What are you doing? Come away from there!" Out of the shadows, two dark forms appeared and molded themselves into the shapes of monks. They ran forward, sandals slapping the stone floor, staffs waving in their hands. Jack moved in front of Crispin and drew his short knife. Crispin reached for his sword—an old habit, even though a sword hadn't been there for years.

The monks postured with their weapons. Crispin held up his hands to show they were empty. "I am here under orders from the archbishop."

One monk, the older one, lowered his staff. "You are Crispin Guest."

"Yes."

He tapped the other monk who reluctantly lowered his staff. The older monk's tonsure stopped across his brow, his natural baldness blending with the barber's work.

Crispin gently maneuvered Jack out of the way and the boy backed away into the shadows. "Why is the shrine left alone? Why is no one seeing after it? I walked in here completely unchallenged."

The monk exchanged glances with the younger cleric, a red-nosed boy only a few years older than Jack. "The treasurer is supposed to be here, sir," said the younger. "Look. Here he comes."

The monks bowed to the treasurer as he approached and he swept them all with an arched brow. "What goes on here?"

"I am Crispin Guest. The archbishop—"

"I know what his excellency has done as concerns you, Master Guest. Is it not permitted a man to accede to a call of nature?"

Crispin rubbed the back of his neck. "Of course, Dom."

"Brother Wilfrid," snapped the treasurer, addressing the younger monk. "Where have you been?"

The young monk bowed again to the treasurer. "Dom Martin wished for me to help him with—"

"I remind you that you are *my* assistant, Brother Wilfrid. Not Martin's." He gave Martin a scathing glower.

Martin's face froze and he bowed to the treasurer. "In all obedience," he said stiffly.

"Never mind. Cover that casket, Brother. And take your post. Friend Guest here trusts us not."

"You know my task, my Lord Treasurer."

"Yes, yes. We know it."

Crispin gave the monk a cursory look and made a slow circuit of the chapel, noting windows, archways. He peered far into the dimness, looking for passages. "Brother Wilfrid, will you please stay a moment with my man Jack here?"

Brother Wilfrid's small, dark eyes darted and found Jack in the shadows. He bowed to Crispin while still looking at Jack.

"My lord, will you show me the surrounds?"

The treasurer glared at Martin, who bowed and took his leave. Once his footsteps died and the shadows swallowed him, it was as if he'd never been there.

The treasurer gestured curtly and stomped toward the north

ambulatory, not waiting for Crispin to follow. "The pilgrims enter here by this staircase," he said, sweeping his arm out. "They must come through the nave past the quire gate. When the hours are devoted to the Divine Office, we lock the gate."

"The quire is barred, but what of the aisles?"

They walked back the other way to the steps where the pilgrims exit. "The aisles remain unimpeded. There is a staircase to the roof of the Corona. The northeast transept has a passage, as does the northwest and southwest transepts. Of course there are two entrances for townsfolk, the west door and the southwest porch. After Compline, that way is also barred."

"What of the cloister?"

"A locked door, near Becket's martyrdom at the northwest transept, but only after Compline."

"So the cloister door is open all day?"

"Of course. The monks must have ready access to the church. But it is impossible to get into the cloister from the outside without encountering three locked gates—locked at all times."

"Sounds secure," he muttered. The monk continued to glare at him. "Forgive me, Dom—I do not know your name."

"Thomas Chillenden."

"Dom Thomas." He gave a slight bow. "Since I came at the command of his excellency I wonder why my presence vexes you so."

"He does not need you. We are his monks. We can do his bidding."

"Plainly, that is not so." He didn't know why he took such pleasure in saying it to the lugubrious monk, and he enjoyed the man's enraged reaction kept under careful control. "Tell me," he went on, "why is the priory treasurer assigned to keep guard of the martyr's shrine?"

Dom Thomas tucked his hands beneath his scapular. "You have

seen it. It is a treasure in itself. Besides, I requested this duty years ago."

"Indeed. Why so?"

His eyes narrowed. "Because it is an honor, Master Guest."

"Of course. Dom Thomas, since you know why I am here, can you enlighten me as to why the archbishop should be so concerned for the shrine's welfare?"

"Did he not tell you?"

"I should like you to tell me."

"What can I add to his excellency's fears?"

"Details, Dom. For instance, his excellency spoke of petty thievery."

"His excellency is mistaken. That had nothing to do with the shrine."

"Forgive me, but I'll be the judge of that."

Dom Thomas glared. His mouth twisted as if trying to suppress unpleasant words. The monk inhaled and blew out a foggy breath. "His excellency bade me be obedient in this," he said with obvious resentment. Yet he said nothing more.

Crispin drummed his fingers on his dagger hilt. "Well?"

"It was foolish. I do not know why his excellency even needed to be told. Some overzealous monk trying to worm his way into his good graces, no doubt."

Crispin huffed a breath. "I'm still waiting."

Dom Thomas aimed his gaze directly into Crispin's gray eyes. "I'm coming to it. The keys to the cloister. They went missing a little over a fortnight ago."

"And you didn't find this significant?"

"They were also found." He held them up. "*Ecce signum.*"

"I see only the proof that they were returned. Not to what purpose they were put."

"What purpose? None. How could they be put to a purpose when they were returned and nothing was harmed while they were gone?"

"How long were they missing?"

"Two days. But as I said, nothing was disturbed, nothing was stolen, *nothing* is amiss at all."

"You don't seem to understand, Dom. Someone took them in order to make a copy."

The monk's lips parted. His eyes, so clear and sharp with accusation, suddenly glossed. "That . . . cannot be."

"Such things are not unknown to me." He turned back to look at the shrine. It was going to be a long night and he was already tired from the journey here. He released a sigh that blew a strand of fog into the cold chapel. "Does that key fit all three cloister gates?"

The monk was still lost in his thoughts. He handled the keys with a distant stare.

"Dom Thomas."

The monk awoke, startled, and brought his gaze level with Crispin's, though this time there was no mote of accusation in it. "Yes, *all* gates."

"You shall have to call for a locksmith in the morning and have them changed. It is your only course. And then you must make certain that you do not let the new keys out of your sight."

"No, of course not." He worried at them, his fingers whitening over the metal.

"Tonight, I will stand guard at the shrine. Your monk will relieve me at midnight. Do you understand? When I mean stand guard, I mean directly at the foot of the shrine. And calls of nature are not allowed, I'm afraid. Bring a pot with you."

The monk grabbed his arm. "You are serious?"

"Most serious, Dom Thomas, especially when sleep is concerned.

I am weary, but I will take the first watch. By the time your monk relieves me, I hope I will have thought of a better plan, but for the moment, this is all I have."

"I will have Brother Wilfrid come at midnight, then."

"Very good. Make certain he understands he may not sleep."

The irritation returned to Dom Thomas's voice. "*I* understand it, Master Guest."

"Good." He turned to the shadows. "Jack, you may go along back to the inn." Jack stepped uncertainly across the chapel, casting a glance at Wilfrid when he reached the stairs. "And Dom Thomas," said Crispin, "could you bring me a chair?"

CRISPIN KICKED BACK, LEANING the chair against the wooden base of the shrine. "Just you and me, Saint Thomas." His voice, even as softly as he spoke the words, seemed far too loud. Its echoes rolled into the distant corners, and finally died.

The four candles about the shrine remained lit, and he looked up at the arched ceiling and the demon shadows frolicking there. How were the bones to be protected if the monks could not be relied upon to guard the place themselves? If Dom Thomas and Brother Wilfrid were the only ones to be trusted, they would soon be too exhausted to continue.

He set his jaw. He wasn't about to leave Becket's bones in the hands of scoundrel Lollards who had no respect for the man—

A sound.

He snapped to his feet and cocked his head. Definitely the sound of two people.

He drew his dagger, crept to the edge of the shrine, and peered around the corner.

Shadows. And they were moving. He squinted into the gloom.

The echoes played games with his ears, and it was almost impossible to tell from which direction the sound was coming, but he thought the noise emanated from the quire area. *Damn.* He'd have to leave the shrine to investigate. He looked back at the tomb. Though, should anyone try to interfere with the bones, it would make enough racket to alert him.

He crept down the chapel steps and steeled down the north ambulatory. There were candles burning in the church at all times, but their scant light did little to illumine the vast space. In fact, their small flames did more to confuse the shadows with flickering ghosts of half light. He veered to his right into the northeast transept. The door was shut tight. He proceeded on past the pillars of the quire in the north aisle, shifted around the scaffolding, and saw the shadows thrown against the wall ahead. Someone was at Saint Benet's chapel, the spot of Becket's martyrdom.

He descended the stairs and adjusted his grip on the dagger. He slid his back along the wall toward the archway. Two small figures in black stood silhouetted against a single candle flame. He stepped into the light and the two figures whipped their heads around.

White faces stared at him from wimples and veils. He lowered his knife. He'd forgotten. "Damosel," he said, a little embarrassed.

Prioress Eglantine glided toward him. Dame Marguerite did not move. Her eyes were large with alarm. She lowered her gaze and hid her quaking hands within her cloak.

The Prioress gazed at him with practiced serenity. "Master Crispin. Skulking in the dark?"

"Forgive me. I am here at the bidding of the archbishop. I did not expect anyone else here at this hour." He glanced at the windows. The sky was still pink, ushering in the evening. The late-spring light was only a precursor to the long hours of daylight expected in the summer months.

He remembered the Prioress had said she would return to pray after supper.

"If you are here at the bidding of his excellency," said Madam Eglantine, "then I have no reason to inquire. Pray, do as you are bid. We will remain here."

"Not the shrine?" he asked, looking back, though he could not see it at this distance and around so many obstacles.

"Today I have seen the shrine. But now I wish to spend time here, the site of Saint Thomas's martyrdom. Such a blessed place. A holy man who gave his life for the Church. Do you know that the attack was so vicious, that his murderers sliced off the top of his skull and spilled out his brains upon the floor? Monstrous." She recited as if dictating a shopping list.

Dame Marguerite flinched.

"Of course I feel compelled to be here," the Prioress went on. "Many do not know it, but my ancestor, much to the shame of my family, was one of the murderers."

Crispin's memory clicked into place like cogwheels. He ticked off the names in his head and said aloud, "Hugh de Morville. An ancestor of yours?"

She inclined her head. "It is only mete that I should do penance for his heinous crime, here where it happened."

"The sins of the fathers will be visited upon the sons," he said. "Or in this case, the daughter." He turned to Dame Marguerite, but as usual, she said nothing. "I would not take it quite so to heart, Lady Prioress. These events happened over two hundred years ago."

"Yes, but the blessed heart of Saint Thomas beats as vigorously and courageously today as it did in those long ago days. I do not feel that any time has passed and erased the sin." She said it with a great deal of relish.

"The murderers faced exile in the end and died abroad," he pointed out. "All impoverished penitents, while *you* have made your place in the Church. I do not see that your own penance is mete."

She smiled indulgently at him, as one does when a child says something naïve. "Surely these matters are only of concern to me, Master Guest."

Crispin frowned, then nodded and drew back in an abbreviated bow. "Then I will leave you. I am keeping watch at the martyr's tomb. I shall be at some distance, and so I will not disturb your prayers. I only ask that you tell me when you are leaving so that I may bar the doors."

"As you wish," she said with a slight bow of her head. She turned away from him to kneel on the stone. Dame Marguerite cast a glance back at him and sunk to her knees a little behind the Prioress.

Thus dismissed, Crispin returned to the darkness of the aisle and moved east toward the chapel.

When he took his seat again, the vague sounds of chanting as the nuns recited their prayers shivered along the colonnade below him. The sound played on his ears as a low hum, like the buzz of a hummingbird's wings. He smiled at the notion and leaned back, crossing his cloak over his chest to keep warm.

A faint scent of incense mixed with the painter's varnish tickled his nostrils. He gazed at the tombs around him, dimly lit by the candles, and glanced at the dark windows, their shapes and tracery pattern only discerned by reflections of moon and candlelight.

He didn't recall dozing off. He only realized he had done so when he opened his eyes. Immediately he sat up and cursed himself. He listened. How long had he slept? He checked the windows. Darker than before. The moon's light had moved across the chapel floor. An hour? Maybe more. What woke him?

He heard it. Steps, light, stealthy. And the murmurs. Those nuns were still at it. But it wasn't *their* steps he heard, for the chanting hadn't changed, wasn't moving away or coming closer.

There was a pause, as if the world held its breath. Crispin had just enough time to feel a shiver run over his skin before the scream. It became a horrific shriek and went on and on, its echo rolling and meandering into every crevice of the church. Something metal clanged against the stone floor and footsteps scattered.

Crispin ran.

In seconds he was down the aisle, over the steps. He wound through the forest of scaffolding and careered around the corner where the nuns were. He stopped short, astonished and horrified.

The Prioress lay facedown on the stone. A sword lay on the bloodied floor behind her. Dame Marguerite, spattered with the Prioress's blood, stood stiffly with her fists clenched against her sides, eyes rolled back, an unholy scream issuing from her wide-open mouth.

4

CRISPIN GRABBED DAME MARGUERITE and clapped her to his chest. Her husky screams turned to gasps and she suddenly collapsed in his arms.

He had to get help. His eyes looked down at Prioress Eglantine's dark figure on the stone floor, her glistening black robes and veil encasing her. All around her was the debris from a scattered rosary.

A horrible ache started in his chest and traveled up into his throat. If he had not been careless and fallen asleep he could have prevented this. A nun murdered in a church. Such sacrilege! He clutched the limp woman tighter, as if his touch could eradicate the horrors to which she would soon awaken.

A voice rang out, startling him. "Master Crispin!" It was Brother Wilfrid.

"Here! Come quickly!" cried Crispin, his voice unnaturally piercing.

The young monk dashed around the corner and stopped dead. He stared openmouthed at the prioress crumpled on the stone and the blood pooling beneath her.

"Christ have mercy! What have you done?"

"Wilfrid! Don't be a damned fool. I found them this way. Come help me. Dame Marguerite has swooned."

The monk moved mechanically toward Crispin, though he couldn't take his eyes from the lifeless woman on the ground.

"Take Dame Marguerite to the infirmary."

"But every bed is taken," said Wilfrid, his voice shrill.

"Then take her back to the inn. And get help. I will . . . I will stay with the Prioress until you return." He stared down at the blood-soaked Prioress, his chest heaving.

Even as spare as Wilfrid was, the monk had very little difficulty sweeping the petite nun into his arms. Crispin clenched his hands into tight fists and watched the monk hurry through the darkened church and out the door. Crispin's quickened breath tasted the cold air and flowered into a white cloud around his mouth.

Looking down at Madam Eglantine's crumpled body washed Crispin with an uneasy sense of repetition, a vague memory of a broken body at his feet. Then, as now, he suffered a helpless panic that permeated his being. Yes, it had been very like this twenty-five years ago. No sword had done the damage but a horrifying fall down the stairs. Was it worse because he had heard it, every bump and crunch of bone? Maybe because he was the one to find her, and being six years old he hadn't known what to do. He remembered finally approaching his mother, kneeling, and touching her hand. It was still warm, yet he knew even then that there was no life left in it. He hadn't gone for help. He knew it was useless. He had simply stayed beside her and held her hand until it grew cold in his own.

Crispin knelt and found the Prioress's hand. He curled his fingers into hers—the hand growing steadily colder—and didn't move.

Her dark figure lay like a wounded raven, her thin arms crooked at odd angles only the dead could achieve.

A tiny sound like a step and its residual echo. Crispin froze and his neck hairs stood up. Slowly, he turned his head. He could almost have sworn someone stood behind him, but there was no one there.

Footsteps again. He flicked a glance at the sword still on the ground surrounded by a sprinkling of beads. The sword was there. But that didn't mean the killer didn't have a knife. *I'm a fool! He's still here.*

Crispin rose, huffed a cloud of apology toward the Prioress, and drew his dagger.

Creeping toward the chapel's wall, he threw himself against the stone and slid carefully along the wall until he reached the archway. He peered around the corner and strained to see through the gray darkness.

The night lay heavily over the long nave. Arches gaped into dusky aisles dimly lit by cloudy moonlight. The thicket of pillars stood like oaks marching away to a murky horizon while the mute quire stalls stood guard in the center of the nave. Their intricate spires seemed like shadowy figures standing tall above the floor.

Crispin crept into the north aisle and stopped to search the gloom. The church was menacing in the dark with its many shadows and hiding places. Slowly, he eased forward and winced when his boots crunched on the tiled floor, but there was little he could do about it. The smell of old incense hovered thickly in the air, but it couldn't completely mask the coppery stench of blood. His eyes searched. Neck hairs tingling in anticipation of a blow from behind, he glanced over his shoulder into darkness.

There! He turned his head, straining to listen, to see. A shadow swept past his peripheral vision, and he crouched and raised the dagger. His sweaty grip tightened on the handle, and he trotted forward until he reached the south aisle. Slamming into a crevice between a cluster of pillars, he waited, listening, his own musky sweat rising to his nostrils.

A step. Then a sharp noise sounded somewhere in the gated quire. Crispin hesitated. The sound wasn't right. Not a step. More like the sound of a tossed pebble, trying to send him in the wrong direction.

Cat and mouse, is it? His fingers adjusted their grip on the dagger. Where would the killer try to go? The west door was barred as were the transepts. The cloister door was open, but that was near Saint Benet's chapel, the scene of the nun's awful slaying. If the killer wished to escape after the murder he had already been at the nearest exit. Why then did he need to skulk in the church? What else did he want?

Crispin whipped his head eastward toward Becket's shrine, but he couldn't see it for the surrounding scaffolding, a maze-work of shade and silky shadows cross-hatching the walls and floors.

A loud bang startled him and then the sound of a door closing.

He raced up the south aisle toward the Chapel of Saint Thomas, dodging webs of scaffolding, before he stumbled going up the chapel stairs. Breathless, he stopped before Prince Edward's tomb, his shoulders rising in silent gasps. The figure of the prince lay undisturbed and staring up at the dark arched ceiling. His brassy skin gleamed dully in the aura of candlelight. In contrast, Becket's shrine, planted in the middle of the chapel, gleamed from four bold candles burning brightly at each corner of the rectangular sepulcher.

All at once, one of the candles, hidden by a corner of the shrine, snuffed out. A black thread of smoke wound upward toward the canopy.

Crispin crouched low and tiptoed to the shrine's plinth. He shouldered the wooden base and eased along it toward the edge of the shrine.

He felt it at the back of his neck. Whirling, he thrust his dagger, but in mid-turn something heavy struck his wrist and the knife hit the floor, skidding a few paces. A hooded figure swung a fist upward and caught Crispin's jaw, and then the ground came up to meet him.

CRISPIN RAISED HIMSELF UP on all fours, only vaguely aware that he shouldn't be in this position. Hands took hold of him and he flailed his arms to fend them off. His elbow struck a face, and then he heard a grunt of pain.

"Peace, Master Crispin!" said Dom Thomas, voice muffled by his hand. Crispin stopped and looked up at the monk. Blood ran down the monk's face under his hand.

"Forgive me, Brother. I thought it was my assailant." He regained his feet and leaned against the shrine, rubbing his jaw.

Dom Thomas wiped his nose and chin and looked at the blood on his fingers with a grimace. "You make a good, solid strike, Master Crispin." It wasn't a compliment.

"What happened? Did you catch him?"

The monk looked up at the shrine with a sorrowful expression. "No."

Crispin turned. The angle made him dizzy but what he beheld made his heart seize. The canopy had been pulled away from the casket and the casket's lid shoved aside. "Gone?"

The monk nodded.

"What of the Prioress?"

"I've only just been told. Others are coming. Brother Wilfrid took the young nun to the inn."

"The archbishop—"

"He is on his way."

Against the treasurer's protests, Crispin stumbled back toward Saint Benet's chapel. A monk knelt beside the body of the Prioress, now covered with a sheet blotched with red stains. He touched his sore jaw. The pain did nothing to assuage his growing remorse. "You did not disturb anything?" he said to the monk.

The monk reached forward to catch Crispin as he swayed. "No, Master."

"I am well," he said, not quite believing it himself. He reached down and slipped the sheet away. "Could you bring a candle, Brother?"

"For the love of Christ, leave her in peace!"

"She *is* at peace. An examination is necessary to discover her slayer." He took the candle from the monk and held it above the body, studying her slashed robes. He tread carefully, trying not to step in her blood, but too many feet had already moved around her. The faint hope of finding telltale bloody footprints leading to the murderer was dashed. In the dark, and because of her heavy black robes, it was impossible to see the extent of her wounds, but he could see that she had been struck many times from behind and probably never saw her assailant. Perhaps that was a mercy. He shook his head and smote his thigh with a fist. This never should have happened. None of it.

He took a deep breath and continued his scrutiny of the dark tiles. There were spatters on the floor behind the spot where she had been kneeling and also in front. Each line of blood represented a strike. As the assailant lifted the sword, a line of blood would have splattered before the nun. He wished the light was better, but he didn't suppose it would help.

All along the tiled floor lay the scattered beads of a rosary. A glance at the Prioress told him that hers was still intact on her belt. Then it must belong to the other nun. He gestured for a monk to gather up the beads.

The murder weapon, the sword, lay on the ground, and he picked it up. Drying blood covered the blade as he expected, but the edges were nicked. The fuller bore diagonal slashes in several deep lines. He recognized the look of such a blade. His own sword had received the same kind of blows while fending off an ax. But it was rust and not blood embedded in these marks, and that told him they were aged scars. The sword itself was old and well used, but not cared for as he had cared for his own long-lost blade. No knight would ever have left his sword in such a state. Whose sword was it? He lifted it, feeling that old pang of loss in his chest. But the feeling was quickly replaced by an equally sore ache of guilt; guilt that he enjoyed handling the weapon so much, the weapon that had killed an innocent.

He examined the round pommel that sported enameled arms—red with a muzzled bear head. He didn't recognize them.

The murderer dispatched the Prioress swiftly, so then why didn't he kill her young chaplain?

Or me? Crispin couldn't help but turn again toward Saint Thomas's chapel in the murky distance. Perhaps the assailant did not want to do others harm. The Prioress alone seemed to be the focus of the attack. And soon after, the bones were stolen. Was this all the work of the Lollards? Up until now, the Lollards had used rhetoric to make their case. Had that changed? But if they really only wanted the bones, then why kill the Prioress? She was nowhere near the shrine, whereas Crispin . . .

He rubbed his sore jaw again and hefted the sword before leaning it against the wall, point down. *Curious, that the murderer should leave the weapon behind.* Perhaps he meant it as a warning of some kind. Or was it stolen and left to point blame at another?

A monk stood beside him and held up his cupped hands. They were filled with wooden beads. Crispin opened his nearly empty money pouch and the monk poured them in. The monk bowed, retreating.

Two sets of hurried footsteps approached. Crispin propped himself against the wall and awaited the archbishop.

Courtenay's face was white. He knelt by the Prioress and looked up at no one in particular. "Has she been shriven?"

"There was no time for any confessions," said Crispin. "She was dead when I got to her."

Courtenay rose. "Are you well, Master Guest? My monk tells me you were hurt—"

He grimaced. "Mostly my pride, Excellency. I fear I have failed you. The relics were stolen."

"This is a disaster." He paced, casting anxious looks at the body on the floor. "What's to be done?"

"We must call in the coroner. It may take a week for him to get here. The body must not be disturbed in that time."

Courtenay stopped, whirled, and stared at the body. "No, no. We mustn't. The coroner cannot be called."

"My lord, it is the law."

He turned angry eyes on Crispin. "I do not fear the coroner's fines. This is an ecclesiastical matter. It is not the king's business."

"But a murder—"

"Of a nun in a church! By the mass! It's appalling. Blood has been spilt just as it was in the days of Becket. And his relics . . .

I say it is his blood again spilt on the church floor. I will not have the king's men fouling this holy place."

Crispin shook his head. "I do not agree."

"It is not for you to agree or disagree. You are now charged with discovering the one responsible for these misdeeds and for recovering the relics that I entrusted to you. You and you alone."

"My lord!"

"My purse is at your disposal, Master Guest. This is to be kept quiet. Do you understand me?"

Crispin clamped his lips and curled his fingers around his dagger hilt. By agreeing to work for the archbishop he had indentured himself. But for how long? Who knew if the bones would ever be found and returned? And what of the murderer? Canterbury was a big city.

Courtenay gesticulated over the Prioress. "She is to be removed and readied for burial. I believe she had a chaplain with her."

"Her young companion may not be in a fit state," said Crispin tightly. "She was taken back to the inn. Surely the whole of the inn knows the nature of these circumstances by now."

"Then it is your task, Master Guest, to see that these tidings do not get further than that inn. You have my full authority in this. See to it."

The archbishop turned on his heel. The monks stood around the Prioress, loath to touch her.

Crispin stared at the retreating figure of the archbishop. He cast a glance at the sword and with a deep sigh, turned away from Saint Benet's chapel and said over his shoulder, "I will get you help, Brothers. Leave her for now. Touch nothing."

He suspected the Prioress would not wish for these brothers to handle her remains. He could seek help from the female servants at the inn. Or perhaps Mistress Alyson. No doubt she would have the stomach for tending to Madam Eglantine and preparing her for burial.

He asked the monk for a cloth to cover the sword. When the man returned, Crispin wrapped the bloody blade in the tattered linen, winding it around several times.

Halfway through the dismal march back to the inn, he met Jack running up the dark and silent road.

"Master! God be praised! Brother Wilfrid said only that the Prioress was murdered. He did not say how *you* fared." His obvious relief at Crispin's fate played out in nervous fussing over his person.

Crispin slapped his hands away. "I am as well as can be expected for a man who has miserably failed at his task. The damned relics were stolen."

"Oh!" Jack pressed his hands to his face. "You don't mean it! Not the blessed martyr!"

"I do mean it. Now we must remain in Canterbury for however long it takes to recover them. But I tell you true, Jack. I will not rest until I see that whoreson of a murderer hanged."

"Why'd they do such a terrible thing as to kill the Lady Prioress?"

"I don't know, Jack. It doesn't make sense to me."

Jack shook his head in disbelief. He searched the dark street as if expecting the imminent appearance of devils swooping down upon them. "Are you going to call the hue and cry?"

Crispin clenched his jaw, but the soreness stopped him. "No. The archbishop strictly forbade that. And in fact—" He scanned the quiet street. The houses were dark except for the occasional yellow lines of candlelight etched in the cracks of shutters. "How much was told to those at the inn?"

"When the monk came with the chaplain, all he could blubber was that the Prioress was killed most foully and to beg help for the poor pretty nun."

He eyed Jack. *Poor pretty nun, eh?* "Did anyone leave the inn?"

"No, sir. Not that I could tell. Mistress de Guernsey went up to attend Dame Marguerite. The rest have been sitting in the hall drinking and talking." Jack gestured to the package in Crispin's hand. "What's that?"

"This? The murder weapon." He thrust it into Jack's hands before the boy could protest. They now stood before the inn door and Crispin pushed it open. The pilgrims had indeed assembled as a quiet crowd. They stood when they saw him enter. Without asking, he was given a beaker of wine, and he sat before the fire, surrounded by the anxious pilgrims. He took a quick inventory. Besides Mistress de Guernsey, one other was missing.

Harry Bailey sat beside him and shook his head. "Can you tell us the tidings, Friend Crispin? What we heard cannot be wholly believed."

"Believe it." He drank then wiped his mouth with the back of his hand. His jaw and his head hurt. Vaguely he wondered if a day was allowed to pass without some part of him in pain. "The Lady Prioress was murdered in the church. At the same spot as Saint Thomas the Martyr."

The assembly burst into troubled conversation. "It's an outrage," cried the portly tradesman. "I have never heard of such a thing. Who could have done it?"

Crispin lowered the bowl from his lips. "I intend to find out."

The young, pale merchant shook his head. "I cannot recall a time I heard of such a horrific case. By my life, but the last time such a thing occurred must be when the blessed martyr himself was murdered."

"One of our own," muttered the tradesman. He eased down to the bench beside Crispin and slid his hand to Crispin's shoulder. "I was the last one to talk to her. She and Dame Marguerite were leaving for the church. I bid them good prayers. She touched my hand." He lowered that hand from Crispin's shoulder and looked at it. "She said to me, 'Much thanks, Good Miller. Bless you, sir.' Just that. And then she went. We all traveled for two days together. All of us." He rubbed his hand absently with the other calloused one. "Whatever you need, sir, I am your man. This cannot be allowed. Not in England."

"I thank you, Master," said Crispin wearily. His blood had been hot in pursuit of the killer, but now he felt near to collapse. Cold.

A thump at the stairs made him turn his head. Alyson descended, looking back over her shoulder at the closed room she had just quitted. She ticked her head.

He stood and parted the company to go to her. "How is she? Can she speak?"

"No, alas. She has uttered nothing and does not look as if she will be able to for quite some time."

"She is the only witness," he rasped.

"There is nothing to be done," she said quietly. She turned to the others gathered about them. "Bless me. Such tragedy to befall so temperate a company."

"The tragedy is great," said Crispin. "Before I relate the whole of it," he said to the assembly, "pray tell me . . . where is Master Chaucer?"

They looked around helplessly.

Sir Philip Bonefey shrugged. "I have not seen him since supper."

"Were all here for supper?" asked Crispin. An emptiness inside him reminded that he had missed supper, too.

"All but the nuns," said the merchant. "Bless their souls," he added, crossing himself. Everyone followed suit.

"Nor were Master Maufesour and Master Chaunticleer," said Father Gelfridus with a little too much malice.

Chaunticleer the Pardoner squinted his pale eyes at the priest. "We are here now," he said.

Maufesour, Chaunticleer's stout companion, stroked his greasy beard. "What has that to do with aught?" he snapped. "We have our own business in town. It is not all saints' relics for us."

"Indeed, not," said Bonefey. "It is your stealing the souls from poor folk who fear the Church's wrath, foul Summoner," he said, turning a beady eye on Maufesour, "and the galling fees to be paid to the Pardoner to get them out of Purgatory. You two should always travel together, like Disease and Death, the two partners of Fate."

Maufesour pushed aside the Pardoner and strode up to the Franklin. "You'd best watch your tongue, Bonefey," he shouted. "Or you might find *yourself* slain and not in a fine church, but a back alley as you deserve." Maufesour's tirade left spittle dotting the Franklin's beard.

Bailey and the Miller grabbed Bonefey before he could draw his sword. They wrestled him to a bench. Maufesour huffed and strutted, smoothing out the breast of his gown. Crispin was behind him in an instant and pulled the man's dagger from its sheath before the Summoner knew it happened. He whirled, but without a weapon there was little he could do but glare.

"Have a care," said Crispin in a low voice. "Too much blood has already been spilt this night."

Maufesour calmed, even as he looked at Bonefey, still chomping at the bit. "Very well," he said. "I will if he will."

Crispin turned to Bonefey. "Sir Philip, his threats are groundless, as you might have surmised were you to keep your blood cool. Do you acquiesce?"

Bonefey glanced up at the hearty Miller and the equally solid Harry Bailey flanking him and nodded. "I do."

They released him, and he straightened his houppelande. Crispin approached Maufesour while examining the dagger. The blade was hatched with deep scratches and grooves radiating upward from the point. "Your blade, Master Maufesour, is in poor shape. It looks to me as if you recently tried to pry something open with it."

Maufesour snatched it back and promptly sheathed it. "Those are old scratches."

"Indeed not. The scratches go all the way to the edge of the blade. Were they old the whetstone would have erased them from the edges by now."

Maufesour frowned and glared at the others. "And what if I had? It is of no business of yours."

"We'll see about that." Crispin made a slow circuit of the room, studying the faces glaring back at him. "A heinous murder has been committed." He wondered whether to continue but decided he'd like to see the reaction. "And further . . . there has been a theft in the cathedral."

Gasps erupted. The pilgrims muttered to one another, and invariably, most eyes turned toward the Pardoner and the Summoner. It was not lost on the two. "This is unconscionable!" cried Chaunticleer. "It is plain they mean to accuse us. We are entirely innocent."

"Not entirely, surely," said Crispin.

Maufesour lunged forward, hands clenched. "This is an outrage!"

"No one is accusing you," said Crispin mildly before baring his teeth. "Not yet."

They stepped back and all eyes focused on Crispin. Jack stood guard by the door. He wore an anxious look and clutched the wrapped sword to his chest. Would any of them bolt? Crispin had little reason to suspect the pilgrims of these crimes, though they all seemed to be acting guilty enough. He slid a glance again toward Maufesour and Chaunticleer. Those two certainly seemed in league with each other. What a coup if they managed to snag one of the greatest relics of all. A pretty price it would bring from some lord. He wouldn't mind seeing them hang for it.

"It's my duty to inform you," said Crispin to the assembly, "that no one is allowed to leave Canterbury."

"What? That is quite impossible." It was Father Gelfridus who spoke first, but Bonefey was on his tail.

"You cannot mean to keep us prisoner here," said Bonefey.

"I do not call it 'prisoner,' Sir Philip," said Crispin. "I simply state that you may not leave the city. Further, I advise that you stay close to the inn. I should not like to go searching for you. And lastly . . . you are not to mention the murder or the theft. At all."

"By what authority do you dare this?" cried Bonefey.

Crispin sneered. He pushed Bonefey back until his legs hit a bench, and he sat hard. "I'm not telling you all twice. The archbishop so charged me. I don't like it any better than you do. But if stay we must, then it is to your benefit to assist me in any way you can. The sooner these crimes are resolved the sooner you can leave."

They fell silent, each looking at one another.

"Mistress Alyson," said Crispin. She raised her head. "A word with you."

She stepped from the crowd and came to him. He moved with her into a corner. She tilted her head back and rested her hand at her hip. "Bless me," she said. "I've never been accused of murder and mayhem before. I assure you, I am just as appalled as the rest. More so, after tending to that poor, sweet nun."

His jaw ached. "I have not called you aside to accuse you. There is another matter for which I think you are suited. I believe I read you well, madam, in assuming a little blood will not frighten you."

She nodded solemnly. "You may assume I have a hearty constitution. Do you speak of the Prioress herself?"

He was grateful for her candor. "Yes. The monks are not suited to deal with a woman. The archbishop insists on an expeditious burial. Can I prevail upon you to . . . to prepare the Prioress?"

She nodded gravely. "I would be honored, sir."

"Shall I call upon the assistance of the maids here?"

"They are a hardworking lot, but I do not think it prudent to involve them. I can manage without help, I think. I shall go to the cathedral with you."

He nodded. "It is best it be handled there. The archbishop would prefer it."

"Let me get my cloak."

He turned to Tucker. "Keep watch. Harry Bailey can be relied upon to keep our charges here tonight. But I want you to inform me when Chaucer returns."

Cloaked with her hood raised, Alyson awaited Crispin by the door. In the still of the night, they walked toward the looming cathedral.

5

CRISPIN AND ALYSON ARRIVED at the cathedral's doors where two monks stood at the entrance, their faces shadowed by cowls. Crispin nodded and they let him pass.

He and Alyson walked up the long north aisle to the Saint Benet chapel and turned the corner. Two monks bent to pick up the body. Crispin felt Alyson stiffen with a gasp, and he placed his hand on her arm. She looked up at him and nodded. "I am well."

"Wait," said Crispin. The monks holding the Prioress's shoulders stopped and stared at him. Crispin inspected the scene, trying to etch it into his mind one last time. Many footprints had smeared the spattered blood, but he could still see the initial puddle under the Prioress. A rag and a bucket would soon clear all traces of a life snuffed out.

Someone had thought to bring a bier. "Good Brothers," said Crispin, "can we take her to the infirmary?"

"We must go to the cellar," said one of the hooded men. He eyed Alyson. "The fastest way is through the cloister, but—"

"The archbishop has given me the authority to go where I please, Brother," said Crispin. "As for Mistress de Guernsey, she is my agent and must accompany me. I know it is usually not permitted for laymen, especially women, to enter the cloister, but in this instance we may all go with impunity."

They seemed less than satisfied with Crispin's pronouncement but could not argue with him. They lifted the Prioress's sheet-clad form, and carried her out the cloister door and down the dark walk.

They made a turn and entered the cellar. The cold air smelled of must. The monks placed the bier on a long table and stepped back. One said to Alyson, "We will bring you sponges and basins of water. We have rose water, if that will do. Also a shroud."

"That would content me, Brothers," she said with a bow of her head.

She waited stone-faced for the monks to return and placed the basin and sponges beside the body. The monks bowed and quickly left. Alyson removed her cloak, rolled up her sleeves, and looked over her shoulder. She tucked her linen veil behind her ears. "Are you staying?" she asked.

"No. But"—he rubbed his chin—"I need to see the wounds. When you are done, if you will . . . will turn her over—"

She nodded. "Wait outside and I will call you."

Crispin paced outside the cellar. Without wishing to, his ears picked up the sounds of Alyson's work; the thump of the body as clothing was removed; a rag being rung into a basin. He imagined the water blooming with swirls of red. There were long moments of near silence before Alyson sighed and muttered a prayer.

Surely the dawn would soon break and he could view the murder scene in lighter surroundings. Leaving the sounds of Alyson's preparations behind, he followed the cloister walk and slipped into the church, adjusting his eyes to the dark. Ahead of him lay Saint Benet's chapel. Already monks were scrubbing away all traces of blood and death. They turned to look at him but did not stop in their task. He walked past them to the north aisle and sidestepped the scaffolds. Again, the silence struck him. Except for his boots striding up the aisle and the swish of the monks with their rags, there was not a sound. He climbed the steps to the Chapel of Saint Thomas and headed straight for Saint Thomas's shrine. The canopy was replaced, and for all the public knew, Becket's bones were still within. Crispin took a candle from one of the four candlesticks surrounding the shrine and walked around the stone plinth, looking carefully along the edges. He hadn't the slightest idea what he might be looking for, but he hoped some clue to the scoundrel's identity might turn up.

The candle glow swept over the floor several times before it caught a faint highlight between Becket's shrine and Edward's tomb. Crispin bent to look. At first, it had no significance for him. Just a tiny bit of stone wedged into a crevice between the stone tiles. Probably kicked up from all the work of the stone masons. But when Crispin picked it up, he knew instantly that it wasn't a piece of stone at all.

With a rush of excitement, he examined the tiny triangular object lying in his palm. The candlelight gave it shadows, depth, texture, though it was white and bleached. He turned it. No doubt about it. A finger bone. The tip. "Saint Thomas," he whispered.

Crispin had viewed many saint's relics in his day. They had all been ensconced in great shrines such as Saint Thomas's, sometimes touched, sometimes only seen through cloudy glass.

But to hold Saint Thomas, to touch the past, nearly took his breath away. Crispin stared down at the small bone in his palm for a long time and then finally raised his head and looked around somewhat sheepishly. Gawking like a schoolboy! He shook his head at himself and carefully placed the bone in his money pouch, sorry he did not have a cloth in which to wrap it.

He continued his search along the floor for more remains. Before he had been struck, he remembered hearing a door bang, but the nature of the cathedral made the placement of sounds nearly impossible to fathom. Where was the nearest door?

The transept doors were far away. The closest to the shrine was behind him: the stairs to the roof of the Corona tower. Crispin hurried to the door and pulled. Locked. But it might not have been locked before. After all, the killer certainly had his own set of keys. Perhaps the murderer waited behind the door for the church to empty before he slipped from his lair to dispatch the Prioress and plunder the bones. But he hadn't counted on Crispin being there. Had the killer crept past him while he slept? Could the killer have counted on Crispin's sleeping? Or was he prepared to dispatch Crispin as well? *But if so, why am I still alive?*

He held the candle high and searched every recess and dim corner. A dark patch appeared at the foot of the doorpost. Crispin bent to look. Stuck between the door and the jamb was a small square of cloth. Grasping it, he pulled it free. Someone had caught their gown or cloak in the door and tore this bit, leaving it behind. Scarlet material. Most likely a gown. He examined it a moment longer before he tucked that within his pouch, too, and gave one last look around the quiet chapel before descending beneath the church to the cellar door once more.

Alyson was waiting for him. "Ready," she said.

He gave a quick nod and stepped into the room. The Prioress lay covered with a sheet. "I will dress her with a shroud when you are done," said Alyson solemnly.

Beside the body sat a basin, water clouded with red. It looked like a bowl of blood.

Alyson grasped the edge of the sheet and slowly peeled it down to the small of the Prioress's naked back.

Crispin bent over the thin white body. He felt a tinge of shame peering at so chaste a woman.

The scent of rose water wafted from the newly bathed skin. With wounds cleansed he could plainly see how each blow cut and how deeply.

"The assailant used the sword to chop at her vertically, with little side to side movement," said Crispin mostly to himself. He pointed to the wounds from the neck down. "See how this chop goes this way, then this one the other way, thus." He demonstrated the chopping motions with an invisible sword. "A sword is easier to use this way. I might make a guess that this stroke to the shoulder was first. It is a timid stroke. After blood is spilled, bloodlust takes over. She was kneeling, I think, and this last stroke at her shoulder blade was taken when she was completely prone. They came in quick succession." He pictured it in his mind. Of course he'd been in many a battle himself. A sword was not an elegant weapon. Not like a dagger. A dagger was for stabbing or slashing. But a sword could be employed as a chopping weapon with slightly more finesse than a battle-ax, perhaps, but used with the same accuracy.

He glanced at Alyson to confirm his hypothesis. Her face had gone white. He cursed himself, pulled the sheet over the body again, and took Alyson's hand. "Forgive me. Fatigue must be to blame for my thoughtlessness."

She squeezed his hand once before releasing it. "I am only a woman and not used to violence."

"My words may seem casual, Mistress Alyson, but I am far from used to this." He turned to look at the cloth-covered Prioress.

A pause. "I will finish quickly, Master Crispin. And then I hope to go back to the inn."

"Of course. I thank you, mistress, for your kind service." He bowed and left the room again.

He stood, hands behind his back, and stared blankly at the carved arch of the cloister walk. Few sights troubled him more than that of a dead woman. *Heinous, heinous.* Murder of any kind was unacceptable, but this murder of a holy woman . . . He ran his hand over his eyes. *Jesu, but I am weary!* Getting back to the inn sounded like a good idea. He'd drop into his bed and wouldn't mind if he didn't wake till next Sunday.

At the sound of steps he looked up. The young monk, Brother Wilfrid, approached, and by the look on his face he was as agitated as his step. He greeted Crispin and then looked back over his shoulder.

"Brother Wilfrid. Is there something—"

"Master Guest, I—"

Alyson emerged from the door and shook her mantle over her shoulders.

Wilfrid turned to Crispin. "I will speak to you later," he said in a husky whisper. "I must go to Vigils before I am missed." He turned abruptly and scurried back down the cloister, casting a furtive glance back.

"Fitful things, aren't they?" said Alyson, gesturing with her head toward the retreating monk.

"He is naturally nervous at these events. Are you ready to go?"

"Bless me. What a night it's been."

He escorted her back to the inn in silence.

Jack snored, sitting alone at a corner table lit by a gentle flicker from the smoky fire. Crispin bid his good nights to Alyson, walked over to the boy, and nudged him. "Where's our room?"

Jack licked his lips and looked up sleepily until he recognized Crispin and became fully awake. "I'll take you, Master. You must be weary to the bone." Jack hurried up the stairs while Crispin trudged after him. They walked along the gallery and Jack directed him to a shadowed corner. He took a key from his pouch and unlocked the door. Jack then tried to hand the key to him but Crispin was uninterested in taking it. Instead, he drew off his hood and mantle and let them drop. Jack scooped them up before they hit the floor.

Tucker stirred the embers in the hearth. Since it was a small room, the evening fire had kept it warm, warmer than Crispin was used to.

Crispin sat heavily on the bed to take off his boots and Jack hurried to do it for him. He quickly surveyed the room over Jack's ministrations. A cot sat in the far corner. *Looks like Jack will have a bed at last.* There was also a table, two chairs, and a coffer. Not unlike his lodgings back in London. Except for the wrapped sword propped in the corner.

Once his belt was off and his boots hit the floor, Crispin fell back on the bed. He closed his eyes and started to unbutton his cotehardie when Jack drew the blanket over him. He didn't see any reason to divest himself further when he was warm and comfortable.

He dozed, drifting. He dreamed of bones forming into skeletal monks. They danced to the tune of a bagpipe played by the Miller. Chaucer was there, smiling and clapping to the bagpipe's rhythm, but his hands were covered by what looked like leather pouches. Some of the other pilgrims lingered in the background, but he couldn't seem to remember their names. The dream changed again, and one of the skeleton monks pointed a finger at him, and then it became only a boney hand floating in a dark space. He drew closer to it, but the ground became mushy like a bog, so thick that he had a hard time pulling each leg from the mire. Panic set in when he began to sink, but then a loud bang stopped the action and then the knock sounded on the door a second time and he realized he was awake.

He groaned and drew the pillow over his head. Jack whispered in the doorway, arguing with the caller. The whispering sounded too much like snakes hissing and Crispin couldn't stand it anymore. "Who is it, for God sake?" he growled from under the pillow.

"Master, I hate to bother you. But it is Mistress Alyson. She said the nun has awakened at last and begs to speak with you."

6

ALYSON STOOD IN THE dark gallery, holding a candle. Her eyes glittered from the small flame, and his sleepiness fled. He followed her with Jack on his heels.

When they arrived at the nun's room, Alyson knocked lightly on the door and entered without waiting for a reply.

Dame Marguerite sat propped up in the single bed she had shared with the Prioress. Her brown veil had been removed and her wet wimple hung by the fire, sending up a veil of steam. It had been splattered with blood, and Alyson had no doubt done her a kindness by washing all traces of the horror from it. The nun's hair was shorn and stood out from her head in brown thatches. Her pale pink face looked like alabaster.

She barely acknowledged Crispin's bow. Alyson scurried to the bed and leaned toward her. "You asked for Master Guest, my lamb. Here he is."

"Please, madam," said the nun in a small voice. "Please fetch Father Gelfridus."

"Of course, lamb." Alyson looked up with a solemn set to her mouth before scurrying out the door.

Dame Marguerite's eyes roved around the dark room. Her lashes flickered, seemingly aware of him but not looking in his direction.

Crispin leaned over and whispered to Jack, who hurriedly left.

"Dame Marguerite," Crispin said softly.

Her brown eyes lit on him. They were round and glossy and exuded a sadness he could almost feel. Her voice was small but remarkably steady. "Is it true that you make your trade in seeking out those who do evil? Are you very good at it?"

He kept eye contact though he wanted to look away from that raw expression. "Reasonably."

Her small face with its incongruously short hair and large eyes conveyed a sense of vulnerability. Her lips were dry. "I shall try to answer your questions. If I am able."

Crispin swallowed. Jack wasn't the only one defenseless under the eyes of a beautiful face. He moved closer. He almost sat on the bed. Instead, he lowered to one knee beside it and leaned forward. "Tell me what you saw."

Her brows crumpled, and she fumbled at her bedclothes. Crispin noticed she clutched at a rosary. Her fingers ticked over the beads.

He glanced at a jug sitting on the sill, hoping it contained wine in case she fainted.

"My Lady Prioress was praying and I was trying to follow the words," she said in a breathy voice. "We were in such a holy place; I did not think it mattered if I could not keep up with her. I followed when I could, but mostly, I closed my eyes and made my own prayers."

Crispin remembered hearing both of their voices together, but sometimes just the Prioress alone. The echoes often made it sound as if two were chanting. He remembered hearing as much . . . before he fell asleep.

He edged closer. "Did you see the assailant?"

She gazed past Crispin into the dim corner of the room. "I don't know. There was a dark figure. A cassock—no, a cloak. Maybe both."

"Did you see his face?"

"He did not turn to me. He . . . he just . . . just—" A fit of trembling overtook her and she hugged herself and dropped her head.

"Dame Marguerite. Can you be certain? *Was* it a cassock you saw?"

The door opened again, and they both turned. Jack stood in the doorway with an elongated bundle wrapped in linen. Crispin stood and joined him at the door. Jack handed the bundle over without looking at Crispin and moved to the head of the bed. The lad's voice was gentle and his manner more refined than his usual. "Can I bring you water, Dame? Anything?"

She looked at the boy with little recognition. Crispin took Jack gently by the shoulders and pulled him out of the way. Then he clutched the bundle and knelt again. "Dame Marguerite. You are doing very well. If you can just tell me. What did he look like?"

She shook her head and pulled the covers up to her chin. "I don't know."

"Tell me the rest."

"I do not remember much. It's . . . all foggy in my mind. I know he killed her."

"But you were standing right there. Did he try to . . . to . . ."

"That's right," she said, her voice sinking into the blankets. "He did turn to me. He . . . said something, but I do not know what it was."

"Another language?"

"Yes. Yes. Latin, I think."

"But you speak Latin—"

"Only enough to understand the Divine Office. Nothing more. Yes. It must have been Latin."

"Do you know what it was?"

"No," she said vaguely. "Perhaps—" She screwed her face and stared at her rosary. "*Fortis et Patientia?*"

Crispin stored this information for later and unwrapped only the pommel of the sword. He gingerly presented it to Dame Marguerite. "Do you recognize these arms?"

The pommel with the red enamel and the bear head glinted in the candlelight. He expected that she might pull back in horror, but she barely glanced at the sword's pommel and shook her head. "I never saw it before."

"Do you know any reason why someone would wish to harm the Prioress?" *And not you* were his unspoken thoughts.

The door opened again and in bundled Alyson with a sleepy-eyed Gelfridus. Crispin threw the wrappings over the sword hilt again and rose. "Father Gelfridus is here. I will take my leave."

She reached out a white hand toward Crispin. The thin fingers stretched wide apart like twigs, the skin spreading taut over her hand. He was too far for her to reach but the gesture stopped him nonetheless. "You must do your best, Master Guest."

He stood stiffly a moment, merely staring at her outstretched hand. "I will." He bowed.

The wooden floor creaked under his heavy steps. He took Alyson aside while the priest bent over the girl in the bed.

"So much sadness in so young a life," she said, shaking her head again. Crispin warmed to her sincerity. "She told me of her life in the priory," she said softly. "How her mother became with child and was forced into the life of a scullion."

He looked at her anew. "She said her mother was a servant. But it is unusual for the daughter of a servant to become a holy sister."

"Ah, but you see, her mother wasn't always a servant." Alyson sidled closer and settled in. "Now mind you, I do not believe I am taking liberties when I tell you, for she freely told me her tale in that flat, odd way she has." Crispin nodded, reassuring her with his attentive expression. "Now then. She told me her mother got with child . . . with her . . . and was forced to find a place to call home. She said her mother was not of lowly origin and she spoke well, not like the other servants. She could read and write. The Prioress took pity on her and took her in. But because of her obvious sinful state she did not make life easy for Marguerite's mother. She said she was beaten, and rightly so, to strike the Devil out of her. Imagine throwing away your birthright for a moment's rutting. Foolish, foolish girl. Living like a bond slave in a nunnery, not even becoming a sister herself but a servant, and a scullion at that! I would have beaten her myself!"

He couldn't disagree. Though it was a harsh man indeed who would toss out his own daughter, even a wealthy man or lord, Crispin doubted he could have been as ruthless. Even so, a man's honor was a precious thing. It would take a man of great integrity to persevere amid the whispers and rumors.

But one's own daughter . . .

"And now this," said Alyson. "So much sorrow. How will she endure it?"

"Her faith will no doubt sustain her."

"Indeed. God's great mercy will offer her sanctuary as He has done for so many."

He reached into his pouch and withdrew the many loose beads, cradling them in his hand. "I found these in the cathedral."

"I put the Prioress's rosary into her closed hands myself. This must be Marguerite's." She cupped her hands to accept them. "I will string them for her."

Crispin nodded to her and left the room quietly amid the soft voices of priest and nun.

Back in his room he tossed the sword on the cot and closed the door. The nun spoke of someone who perhaps wore a cassock, and this troubled him. He, too, saw a vague cloaked figure who struck at him, but it happened so quickly he couldn't tell if it was a cassock or not. Could the archbishop be right about one of his monks? What was it that Brother Wilfrid wanted to say to him?

He lay on the bed, still in his clothes, and closed his eyes. But Dame Marguerite's words kept playing in his head. *Fortis et Patientia:* Strong and Enduring. The little scrap of red cloth. Becket's finger bone. Sleep seemed a useless exercise.

CRISPIN GROANED, SNAPPED AWAKE, and sat up. He glared perplexedly at the open window and the sunlight splashing on the floor.

Jack's writing things were spread across the table. A broken quill and scraps of parchment made up his small retinue. There were no Latin texts to copy, only those parchments with Crispin's careful penmanship to guide the boy in his practice. At least Jack had taken some time for his studies, though his haphazard script looked nothing like Crispin's.

The boy was no longer at the table but by the fire, singing a ribald tune he'd no doubt learned at the inn. He looked up from over the steaming pot on the hearth.

Crispin eased his legs over the bed and scratched the sleep from his head.

"I've made hot water for your shave, Master," said Jack.

Dressed, shaved, and reasonably clean, Crispin trod downstairs to the inn's hall. The pilgrims were talking together, but when they noticed him they fell silent. He called for wine and food and sat on a bench by the fire, doing his best to take no notice of them. He drank his bowl slowly and ate his fill, perhaps not with relish, but with dignity.

The Franklin's shadow fell over him. "The great Tracker. Is that all you're going to do? Just sit and eat while we are trapped in this accursed inn?"

He glanced up at their faces. "Some of your fellow travelers do not feel, as you say, 'trapped.' They are not here, in fact. Where are Master Chaunticleer and Master Maufesour? Or Chaucer?" They looked at one another. Crispin shook his head. "Truly, Sir Philip, if my orders to remain at the inn cannot be obeyed, then there is little hope of my succeeding."

"So they are orders now?"

The young merchant waved a shaky finger in the air. In a clear but broken voice, he said, "Master Guest made that very admonishment last night. I heard him quite d-distinctly."

Bonefey glared at the youth.

Crispin smiled. "So says our merchant."

"Er . . . Thomas Clarke, master. Manciple."

"Ah. Forgive me. Why debate the point, Sir Philip?"

"I am an important man," said Bonefey, chest puffed. "I cannot wile away my time in Canterbury indefinitely. I want to know and I want to know now. Do you suspect us of these crimes?"

Crispin dabbed at his lips with the linen tablecloth and brushed bread crumbs from his coat. He rose, adjusted his belt and dagger, and shimmied his cloak over his shoulders. "If you are not guilty, what is there to fear?"

Sir Philip huffed through his cheeks and spun on his heel.

Alyson pointed a finger at Bonefey and quoted Scripture. Clarke stuttered some point of law while the Miller quaffed cup after cup of ale alongside Harry Bailey. They all stopped abruptly at the creak of the stair.

Dame Marguerite, shaky and white, took wilted steps down the stairs, leaning heavily on Father Gelfridus on one side and Jack on the other. Alyson moved first, and then the others met the nun at the bottom step.

"My dear Marguerite," cooed Alyson. The lady from Bath had been awake almost as long as Crispin. Her cheeks were not as rosy as they were yesterday and her eyes were rimmed with red. Even her coif was slightly askew revealing shiny brown hair. "You should not be out of bed."

The nun, her cleaned brown veil affixed to her stained wimple again, shook her head. "Father Gelfridus thought it best I do. And in all obedience . . ." She stepped away from his grasp as if to prove the truth of it. Jack edged forward, his face pale, hands open to catch her.

Bonefey threw up his arms. "Christ wounds, Gelfridus! Can't you see the wench has had a shock?"

Marguerite waved him off. "There is nothing as wastrel as lying about in bed. I have learned this lesson well from my Lady Prioress." She crossed herself unsteadily. "*Requiescat in pace.*" She made her way to the bench and melted into it. Jack knelt beside her and whispered something. The nun raised her eyes to him and seemed to see him for the first time.

Crispin watched the exchange with concern. "Come along, Jack. We must see the archbishop. Go up to our room and get the . . . the object."

Jack glared at him. It was a new face for Tucker. The boy seemed to be blossoming into a man before his eyes, but at a most inopportune moment with an equally inopportune object of affection.

"Jack," he repeated gently.

Tucker snapped out of his mood and his eyes were shaded with embarrassment. He took a moment to gather himself and loped up the stairs, returning only a moment later with the wrapped sword. He scampered ahead of Crispin to open the door for him but the way was blocked.

"Good morrow, Cris," said Chaucer, standing in the doorway. He was as loud as usual but his voice struck Crispin as a little over-enthusiastic for the hour.

He narrowed his eyes at Chaucer's ankle-length red gown. "Geoffrey. Where have you been? I wanted to talk to you." He took the poet by the arm in a firm grip and steered him back outside.

Standing on the stone threshold, Chaucer shook him off. "What do you think you are doing?"

"I said I want to talk to you."

"That's a rather accusatory tone, Cris." He straightened his houppelande. His thin brows lowered over his eyes. "What vexes you?"

"Have you not heard?"

"By God's toes, heard what?"

"Last night. The Prioress was murdered."

Chaucer recoiled. "Madam Eglantine? Are you jesting?"

"No jest. Last night. In Saint Benet's chapel."

"God's wounds!"

Crispin strode quickly up the avenue. Chaucer did his best to keep up. "And more. Becket's bones were stolen." Chaucer stopped. Crispin turned to face him. "And so I ask again. Where were you?"

Chaucer stared for several heartbeats before an uncertain smile slackened his taut face. "By Christ! You're not accusing *me*? Say you are not."

"No. But I need to know—"

"Are you sheriff now? Or coroner?"

"Neither. I am commissioned by the archbishop—"

"Oh, I see! It all falls into place." He laughed without mirth. "The Tracker! You feel the need to 'track.' And you have tracked . . . *me*?"

Crispin crooked his eye at the very public street. "Don't be a damned fool!" He took Chaucer's arm again and pulled but the man refused to budge.

"I'm not one of your chessmen, Guest. You think you can manipulate me?" He ran a finger around the collar of his houppelande. "I don't need you to make a mockery of me. I can do the job quite adequately on my own."

"You are damnable, Geoffrey!"

"Yes, I know." He glared a moment more before he offered a brief smile. "I was in town. On business."

"All night?"

"Yes, all night."

"I thought you were here for the pilgrimage."

"Among other things."

If Chaucer wished to keep silent on a subject, Crispin was no match to drag it out of him. He gave a conciliatory nod and Geoffrey's face drew on a flat expression, though he also had that sharp look in his eye that Crispin remembered from long ago, a look that proved he meant to get something out of Crispin.

Chaucer suddenly whirled on Jack, who had run to catch up, the linen-shrouded bundle tight in his arms again. Jack dug his heels in the road. "I'm sure Young Jack here can go on ahead to whatever mischief you had in mind."

Jack eyed Chaucer and then looked to Crispin for confirmation. "I'll . . . go on ahead, shall I?"

Crispin nodded and Jack bowed to both before skirting his way around them and trotting toward the cathedral gate.

When they were alone, Chaucer turned to his friend. "He's a fine lad, is your Jack. He reminds me a little of you at that age."

"I was never that age."

Chaucer frowned. "This is damnable business, Cris. How was she killed?"

"By the sword."

"God's blood and bones!" Geoffrey muttered. "Who did it?"

"I do not know. Yet."

Chaucer fell silent. Only the noise of their feet sucking in the muddy avenue accompanied the morning sounds of commerce. "Then . . . this is truly what you do now? Inquire about crimes?" Chaucer's voice sounded hollow and surprised.

"What did you expect?"

Chaucer shook his head. "I don't know. I suppose . . . I just thought being this Tracker . . . I thought it might be a metaphor."

He snorted. "Metaphor. Only *you* would think such."

They walked several more silent paces until Geoffrey took a deep, sighing breath. "I also thought you would clap me in your arms like an old friend, Cris. And yet you continue cold as ice."

He felt the hot blood creep up his neck. "You know why," he said huskily.

"Afraid treason would rub off on me?"

The silent shopfronts and the gold-tinged street gave no respite to the look on Geoffrey's face. "*You* knew I was still in London. Yet not one word from you."

"True. Contact with you was, shall we say, discouraged. Especially by my wife. I think she did fear treason was somehow transferable."

"For my part, I took the king's words as Gospel. He said that those who gave me succor would suffer my same fate. I felt it best I have no contact with former friends." He stopped and threw his head back, staring up at the misty morning sky. "Dammit, Geoffrey. I wanted no harm to come to you."

"And no harm has."

"You are still Lancaster's man."

"Yes. And you?"

Crispin furrowed his brow, toed the mud. "Not as much these days."

"Oh? Is the well poisoned?"

"It's just that . . . his grace and I . . . Lancaster . . . he . . . he . . ."

"Good Christ. If you'd rather not say—"

Crispin unclenched his hands and nodded stiffly. "I'd rather not."

"So that subject is closed. But what of us? Too many nights we spent drinking together." They both smiled and then quiet fell between them. The smell of mud and horse dung grew stronger in the rising light. A long time passed before Chaucer whispered, "I'm glad you're alive and free. Those were the best tidings . . . and most unexpected, under the circumstances."

"Yes," he muttered. "I am alive."

Chaucer toyed with the buttons on his gown. "So. *Tracker*, they call you. Tell me about this unusual title. *Not* a metaphor."

He shrugged. "I find things. Documents. Jewelry. Even murderers on occasion."

"That sounds like the sheriff's job."

"Have you *met* the sheriffs of London?"

His friend chuckled. "Indeed."

"These are the tasks my clients would rather not trouble the sheriffs with, if you understand my meaning. Consider me a *private* sheriff, if you will."

Geoffrey leaned into Crispin's shoulder. "This murder was unexpected, but you said you came here on assignment for the archbishop of Canterbury. Are you in his permanent employ, then?"

"No. The assignment is temporary. And that's how I would have it."

"You always were your own man. You didn't like following orders."

"Do you?"

"I've grown accustomed to it."

"That's not the Geoff Chaucer I knew."

"The Geoff Chaucer you knew is eight years older, with a wife and children."

Crispin lowered his eyes. "How fares your good wife?"

"Well. And the children. We are happy in London." A pause. "And . . . where in London do you reside these days?"

Crispin was used to saying it, but it somehow stung today voicing it. "I live on the Shambles above a tinker's shop."

His friend fell silent. Geoffrey's hand slid toward his money pouch. It rested there a long time before he allowed his hand to fall away. "Can you . . . will you tell me your tale?"

"What tale should I be telling you?" Silence. Crispin looked sidelong at his friend, who seemed to be deciding what to ask.

Shopkeepers were just opening their doors, sweeping away the dew. Young apprentices and servants brought forth the wares and set them on tables. "Tell me a tale of long ago, Cris. Eight years ago, to be precise."

Crispin watched Tucker's back as the boy made his way toward the cathedral, legs working, arms swinging. "I know that you sometimes serve as the king's spy. Don't you know all my tales already?"

A sly smile curled the poet's mustache. "By the saints! How did you ever discover that?"

Crispin snorted. "I'm the Tracker. Remember?"

"Well." Chaucer looked behind him. Crispin followed suit. No one of any consequence there on Mercy Lane but the usual merchants and shoppers, from lowly to upper class. "When I do spy for the king," said Geoffrey quietly, "it is hardly ever on these shores. Only abroad."

"Indeed." Crispin kept his eye on Jack far ahead. He offered an enigmatic smile. "You've already told me you are aware of the plot that felled me. The plot devised to depose King Richard and put Lancaster on the throne."

"Yes," Chaucer said steadily, quietly.

"Then what is your question?"

The poet kept his voice unnaturally low. "Since you were accused of high treason, if you were truly guilty, why did Richard let you live?"

"Oh, I *was* guilty."

Chaucer stopped and grabbed Crispin's arm, pulling him into the shadow of an overhanging eave. All trace of amusement left his face. "I do not understand."

"I was guilty, but there was no plot. The plot was a sham to catch the enemies of the throne. I was only one of many fish caught in the net. Lancaster begged the king for my life and the king granted it. With . . . provisions."

"That your barony, lands, and knighthood be stripped from you."

He looked at Geoffrey's solemn expression. "Were I a Franciscan I would have been utterly ecstatic."

"What did you do?"

"I took to the streets. And then I starved." He nodded to himself, remembering. "I became good at that. You see, I couldn't quite believe my predicament at first. It wasn't until I was on my last legs that I begged food at the alms doors of many of London's churches."

Chaucer kicked at a stone and they both watched it bounce along the avenue. "Why did you not take to the highways and become an outlaw? You would not have starved."

"Some men are made for that. Not me. I preferred to earn my keep honestly. And I did so. My first job was as a gong farmer." Chaucer grimaced in sympathy. Crispin said it with relish, almost enjoying the slap of the pronouncement. "Mucking a privy isn't so bad. It's mucking hundreds that makes it unbearable."

Chaucer checked behind him again. "But what of your other skills? Could you not have gained employment as a scribe?"

"I did. Eventually. And an accounting clerk. But I did so for merchants. Court was closed to me."

"Then how did you fall into . . . into . . ."

"My present occupation? It began as a simple challenge and then evolved. And now it is my sole means of employment. It does not pay well, but I find it intellectually stimulating. And I am my own man." He glanced up at the cathedral. "Most of the time."

Chaucer smiled and stroked his beard. "This is a finer tale than I could ever weave even from my fertile imagination."

"Just keep me out of your writings." He stopped and looked up at the church ahead. "I have my work to do. Have I satisfied your curiosity?"

"Satisfied? You've only piqued it." He grinned, his old self again. "May I go with you? I've never watched a murder inquiry before."

Crispin shut his eyes. He didn't see how he could divert Chaucer. Besides, a small part of him wanted his old friend in his company.

They walked in silence up the long pathway to the cathedral where Jack stood at the foot of the stair to the archbishop's lodge and waited for them.

7

BEHIND THE QUIET JACK Tucker, Chaucer followed at his heels, an annoying smile on his face. They were led to Courtenay's apartments and when Courtenay saw all of them, his face darkened.

"Master Guest," he said. The tone in his voice asked many questions. Crispin tried to answer some of them.

"Master Geoffrey Chaucer, my lord," he said by way of introduction.

Chaucer bowed, stepped forward, and kissed the ring on Courtenay's hand. "Your Excellency."

Courtenay's hand hung limply for a moment as if the archbishop were wondering what to do with such an honor. Courtenay's heavy red cloak hung about his shoulders, making his larger-than-life figure that much larger. He angled his shoulder, dismissing the presence of Chaucer. "Have you anything to report to me, Master Guest?"

"Yes, Excellency."

Chaucer looked amused. It irked.

Crispin reached into the pouch at his belt and drew out the

bone. "I have recovered only a small portion of Saint Thomas." He dropped the bone into Courtenay's open hand just as Chaucer gasped. "I found this by the tomb," Crispin went on. "Obviously left by hasty thieves."

"God blind me!" whispered Jack before he slapped his hand to his mouth.

Courtenay did not move but stared into his palm. A fire crackled in the hearth, but no other noise disturbed the archbishop's reverie. He muttered something. A prayer? A curse? Finally the archbishop closed his hand into a fist, capturing the bone. "I thank you for this at least, Master Guest."

Crispin bowed. "Your Excellency." He wondered whether to bring up the red scrap of cloth, his only real clue besides the sword. He couldn't be certain, of course, if the cloth had been left behind earlier and thus had no relation to the murder and theft, but it was all he had. He reached into his pouch and his fingers eased over one leftover rosary bead before they closed on the scrap. He lifted it just as Courtenay turned, his cloak sweeping across the wooden floor. And there, near the hem, a jagged tear.

Crispin paused and withdrew an empty hand from his pouch. "Excellency, your cloak appears to be torn."

Courtenay looked down. He dismissed it with a careless brush of his hand. "I am always getting it caught in doorways. Thank you for bringing it to my attention." He sat and curled one hand around the chair's arm. The other holding the bone remained tightly closed. His eyes flicked to Jack and Chaucer. "Have you come to any conclusions about the horrific murder of the Prioress?"

"No." Crispin edged toward the fire and stared into it. His mind ran ahead, working independently of his mouth. "Only that if the Lollards are behind the murder and theft, their peaceful methods have changed." He looked at Jack clutching the wrapped sword.

Tucker's face turned toward the window and the burgeoning sunlight. "You did not by any chance personally know the Prioress, my lord, did you?"

The archbishop blinked slowly. "As it happens, I *was* acquainted with Madam Eglantine."

"Indeed. And may I know the nature of this acquaintance?"

Courtenay's eyes were a remarkable shade of blue and they fixed on Crispin like gems. He'd seen the like before on necklaces and crowns, but those gems had no more animation than did the archbishop's suddenly cold glare. "A year ago," he said stiffly. "I presided over a judgment. The priory's lands encroached on the land of a Franklin."

"And that was when you met her?"

Courtenay said nothing. His hand tightened on the chair arm.

"Did you exchange words with her, my lord? Then, or more recently?"

Courtenay's countenance grew stonier. His mouth curved into a frown.

Chaucer moved hastily in front of Crispin. "I must apologize for my friend," he said jovially, looking back over his shoulder. "So long from court, he is unused to civilized conversation. Come to think of it, even at court he never proved himself all that well versed in polite discourse."

What the hell was Geoffrey doing? Crispin had the urge to throw him aside, but he knew the man well enough to recognize the cautionary note in Chaucer's voice.

"And you are master of polite conversation, are you, Sir Geoffrey?" said Courtenay. "I remember you, too, good sir. Poet to the king. Lapdog of Lancaster."

Chaucer drew his cloak about him and shivered melodramatically. "Fie! It's chilly here of a sudden. The mere mention of Lancaster has blown an ill wind through the hall. Pray, your Excellency, why so cold when the discussion turns to talk of my master? He is the king's uncle, his most trusted counselor, a patron of the arts—"

"You neglected to mention advocate of the Church, Master Chaucer. With good reason. For he is not. I have little trust for his grace's intentions. Or that of his servants."

"Oh dear." Chaucer released his cloak with a flourish. "Is it because my master supported John Wycliffe—"

"The heretical Lollard," Courtenay injected.

Chaucer raised his hands in a shrug. "I am not a theologian, Excellency. Only a poet. Everything is grist for my mill. Heretics, kings . . . clerics."

"Much like a jester does, eh Master Chaucer?"

Geoffrey smiled and bowed in such a way that Crispin could well imagine him in motley. "As you will, Excellency."

Crispin sidestepped Chaucer and motioned for Jack to come forward. He took the sword from the boy's hands and unwrapped the pommel. "My lord, have you seen these arms before?"

Courtenay leaned forward. "Is that the weapon that committed this most foul deed?"

"Yes, my lord."

His spine seemed to conform to the straight back of his chair and his voice fell to a deadly tone. "And you bring it here?"

"My lord, the arms—"

"Have you no delicacy at all, Master Guest? Faith! I should have known better than to go to London's streets for help and contented myself with the king's sheriff. Look what has happened under your watch, Guest. A horrible murder. A great theft; a theft *you* were supposed to prevent!" He snapped from the chair. "This is outrageous. Take your foul weapon from my chamber and never bring it again!"

Trembling, Crispin wrapped the bundle and tossed it across the room to Tucker. The boy barely caught it. "Do you free me from my obligation, then?" Crispin asked tightly.

"Free you? Out of the question. I want you to find those bones!" He thrust his hand forward and displayed the tiny finger bone lying on his reddened palm. "Do you think this will satisfy? I want Becket back! *All* of him. And I want that murderer to hang. Consider Canterbury your new home."

"Then I will need the keys to the church."

The archbishop's face reddened with new outrage. "What?"

"I want the keys. I must have free rein to explore the cathedral grounds. Has a locksmith been called to change the locks as I instructed? I spoke of this to Dom Thomas Chillenden yestereve."

"I do not know. You will have to discuss it with him. Go to the church and I will have him sent to you. And Master Guest." He grasped the edge of his cloak. "Have you made any progress on the . . . other matter?"

Crispin racked his brain and then remembered. The archbishop was certain one of his monks was a Lollard. This was still within the realm of possibility and it would have to be dealt with soon, but the murder quite drove it out of Crispin's mind. "No, Excellency. But you can be assured—"

"So far, Master Guest, you have assured me of very little."

"Excellency, 'It is possible to fail in many ways, while to succeed is possible only in one way.'"

"Then in future, Master Guest, see that your successes exceed your failures. We've had quite enough of those." He raised a shaky hand and signed a hasty benediction over them, though Crispin thought the man would rather be waving a sword.

Crispin bowed low, mostly to shield from view the angry trembling of his hands. He spun on his heel and took long, swift strides to the exit. Not waiting for Chaucer or Jack, Crispin took the stairs two at a time and made his way into the church.

Hard steps conveyed Crispin almost all the way up the north aisle before Jack, out of breath, caught up to him. He held the sword over his shoulder like a shepherds crook. "Master. Please. Master Chaucer is coming, too—"

"Well, where is he, then?" he growled.

"Here!" said Chaucer. He trotted forward and stopped next to Jack. He, too, was short of breath. "Good Christ, Guest. Is that how you conduct an inquiry? It's a wonder you do not get yourself arrested. Or excommunicated."

"Aren't you bored yet, Geoffrey?" he snarled.

Chaucer postured. "Is the mummery over?"

Crispin mumbled a curse and glanced at Saint Benet's chapel. All trace of the Prioress's blood had been washed away. No one would ever know that two murders had been committed on the same spot divided by the span of two hundred years. A pang of guilt warmed his chest, but he pressed on before he decided he didn't know where he was going. He'd have to wait for Dom Thomas to arrive and there was little he could do but wander through the nave, looking like a lost pilgrim.

"Crispin." Chaucer was suddenly at his side. "What have Lollards to do with the bones of Saint Thomas?"

"Leave it, Geoffrey," he snapped.

Masons were perched on the scaffolding again. Their interminable hammering echoed throughout the church and stone dust showered in rhythm to their strokes. "Oi!" cried one mason to another on a far scaffold. "Have you spoken to the treasurer, Master?"

The stout man on the far scaffold lowered his hammer and moved to the edge of the platform. "I'm waiting for him," he said, gesturing with his chisel. "It's time for another talk."

The man—a journeyman, most likely—nodded knowingly and went back to his business.

Crispin watched them at their tasks for a span, watched the artists paint the stone, and then pounded a fist impatiently into his palm, pacing. He hated waiting.

Chaucer and Jack stood nearby. Jack hugged the sword, trying not to look at Chaucer. Geoffrey leaned against a pillar but Crispin felt their eyes on him and scowled deeper. *Stare, then, if you must.* He hadn't actually accused the archbishop, though he'd seen enough guilty noblemen to know that crimes were committed by the lowest to the highest member of society. Not that he could possibly accuse Courtenay. And if the young nun did see him commit the crime, was she truly at liberty to say so? Her archbishop? It might as well be the pope. It could be that the scrap in his pouch was from the archbishop's cloak, and it also could be that it was an entirely innocent accident. But in this business, accidents were seldom innocent and coincidences almost unheard of. It would certainly be impossible for him to get the archbishop's cloak and test it.

He glanced at his young thief, Jack, with a smirk. Well, almost impossible.

A figure hurried through the church from the south aisle but slowed when spotting Chaucer and Tucker. Chaucer smiled and bowed to the man and Tucker belatedly bent his head.

"Master Guest," said Dom Thomas, his face skewed as if he smelled something unpleasant. "The locksmiths are here. It will take the better part of the day for them to change the locks."

"Fine. I will collect my key when they are done."

"Your key?"

"And I will need an old key now. I need to examine the environs."

Dom Thomas's jowled face paled. "I do not know that I can give you any keys—"

"Come, come, man. The archbishop already gave me permission. You're wasting *his* time now, not mine." He held out his hand, wiggling his fingers.

The monk stared at Crispin's outstretched hand for a long moment. He reached for the key ring on his cincture and pulled a long silver key from its brothers on the ring. "I give you the means to all places public and private, Master Guest. Have a care with it."

He took it solemnly and placed it in his money pouch. "You can trust me, Dom. I am fully aware of my responsibility."

Chillenden glared from one face to another before looking back over his shoulder toward the shrine with its long line of pilgrims. "The archbishop has given me no instructions as concerns the shrine. I do not know if I am permitted to allow the pilgrims to come forth. I understand that the news that the bones were taken was not made public."

"Indeed not. Then I suppose you may permit pilgrims to enter."

"But . . . there will be nothing there to pray to."

"Alas, Brother. Yet if the pilgrims are ignorant of that, do you truly think God will mind?"

"But the fees?"

Crispin's scowl darkened. "Perhaps the fees can be waived."

"Waive the fees?"

Bless me, but I think I might be siding with these Lollards. "Do what you will, Dom. It is not my affair." He brushed past the monk and up the aisle before slowing to a stop. "Isn't the church to be closed?" Dom Thomas stood mutely. He fumbled with his keys. Crispin swiveled toward him. "Well?"

"I have had no instructions on this," said the monk carefully.

Crispin drew back as if slapped. "Not close the church! But surely it needs to be reconsecrated after a murder—"

Dom Thomas clenched his hands and thrust them into his scapular. "There has been no instructions from the archbishop. I suggest you keep out of it, Master Guest."

He stared hard at the monk whose apparent frustration colored his face in blotchy red. "I see. This murder is then to be kept very secret." He tried to inhale a cleansing breath but instead took in stale incense and dust. "Brother Wilfrid needed to speak to me," he said. "Send him to the Chapel of Saint Thomas."

Chillenden did not acknowledge this when he spun on his heel, but his progress was halted by the mason yelling down to him. "Oi! Brother monk! Wait a bit." The large muscled man grabbed a rope and descended the side of the scaffold. It shook with his weight and dusted the floor with particles of stone.

"I ask again, Good Brother, when I and my men may receive their payment. You are overdue."

The monk glanced hastily at Crispin and set his chin high. "The archbishop must approve all payments from the treasury, Master, and I am sorry to say, he has not yet done so."

"We have been delayed too long, Brother. If you do not wish to pay—"

"Payment will come to you anon. I suggest you and your men practice patience."

"We may practice more than that. On the morrow, we may find it difficult indeed to locate the church."

"Do you threaten me? I can get any number of masons here to do this work."

"They'd have to traffic with the guild . . . and get past us to do it," he said, laying his considerable hammer over his shoulder.

Dom Thomas pressed his lips tightly together and gave one

more look toward Crispin. "I'll see what I can do," he muttered and hurried away.

The mason watched the monk leave and offered Crispin a curt bow and a smirk before he hoisted himself up the scaffold again.

Over his shoulder, Crispin watched the man climb while his feet took him to the shrine to await Wilfrid. Though he made no motion to Jack or Chaucer, they followed him anyway, silent as shadows, to Saint Thomas's chapel. Thousands of pairs of feet had passed this same way for two hundred years, hollowing each worn step, all to venerate a saint, an archbishop of Canterbury.

"You'll find those bones, won't you, Master?" said Jack at Crispin's elbow.

He nodded. "I want them back almost as badly as the archbishop does." He glanced at Geoffrey who remained mercifully silent. "Saint Thomas was martyred because he would not allow crimes against the clergy to be tried in any other than an ecclesiastical court. To King Henry's mind, this meant treason." Jack nodded. This much he knew. *Treason,* thought Crispin. *How easy it is to commit. How hard to endure the consequences.*

"'Will no one free me of this troublesome priest?' was King Henry's cry," Crispin went on. "And four barons took their king at his word."

"And then the king humbled himself at the martyr's tomb," said Jack. "A humbled king. I would like to have seen that."

"As would I." He walked up to the shrine. "Such grandeur. Yet with all its gold, jewels, and magnificence of the craftsmen's art, the tomb lies empty."

"What will they do now, Master Crispin?" Jack's voice was quiet. "Do?"

"What if . . . what if you never find them bones?"

He squared his jaw. "I will find them."

He heard Chaucer's step along the chapel's perimeter. "But they are only the bones of a man, after all," Geoffrey said, his voice echoing hollowly.

"A holy man, sir," corrected Jack. "A holy saint."

"A stubborn archbishop who would not accede to the demands of his king."

Crispin slowly pivoted. "Do you suggest a bishop of the Church should accede to the wishes of his king over the pope?"

"The king is his sovereign lord."

"And the pope?"

"A foreign prince."

"Why Geoffrey. You sound like a Lollard."

The poet made a half smile. "Perhaps I am more parrot than Lollard. I repeat what I hear my master say."

"Say it too often and you may be summoned by the Church to repeat it. I do not know you can plead that your master says and thus so say you. Torture is not pleasant."

Geoffrey's smile faded and he looked at Crispin with a renewal of something he had not wished to elicit: pity.

Crispin turned away and stared up at the many miracle windows instead. The light shone through them and their glorious colors glowed brightly. He stood thus for a long time until he heard, amid the hammers and shouts of masons and artists, the hurried steps of an approaching monk.

Brother Wilfrid, his shiny-tonsured head bobbing over his rumpled cowl, trotted forward, lifting the hem of his cassock to trundle up the stairs. His face opened when he saw Crispin. It wasn't exactly relief, but something akin to it. "Master Crispin! Praise God. I must tell you—"

Geoffrey stepped out of the shadows and Wilfrid turned at the sound. His eyes rounded and he took a step back. When his eyes turned back to Crispin there was a veil of fear over them. "I thought we were alone," he said breathlessly.

Crispin looked toward Chaucer. "I think the mummery is over." He did not mean to have such a sneer of finality to his voice, but this time Geoffrey was visibly taken aback. He flicked his gaze toward the monk and then to Crispin. He merely bowed and turned away. His heavy steps echoed and he soon disappeared down the stairs.

Wilfrid didn't seem satisfied and trotted to the top of the stair to see where he'd gone. He waited, listening, until there was no more sign of Chaucer. The monk looked at Jack but he seemed unruffled by the boy's presence. Wilfrid, his back to Crispin, gave a great sigh. At last, he returned and gathered his hands under his scapular. His face was pale and tight. "I could not talk in front of him. You see, I saw him here last night."

"With the pilgrims?"

"No, Master. Last *night*. I made my rounds with the keys and locked the doors. And when I was leaving Saint Benet's chapel, I saw a shadow. One gets used to the shadows here at night, Master Crispin. The faint of heart might take scaffolding and pillars for people or demons. After years in this place, I know the difference, I can assure you. And when I turned I saw the shadow of a *man*. I called out. I told him the church was to be closed and locked. But he did not answer, perhaps thinking I had deceived myself. But I was not deceived. I said again, louder, 'You must leave now. I see you there. Behind the pillar.' It was only then that he came out. The church was dark but I recognized it to be that gentleman."

"Do you know who that gentleman is?"

"He is Sir Geoffrey Chaucer."

"And how do you know this?"

"He was here a fortnight ago and someone pointed him out to me."

He looked back the way Geoffrey had gone, but he saw only the scaffolds and arches. "Was he?"

"Yes."

"What was he doing here two weeks ago?"

"He came as a pilgrim to the shrine. I remember him."

"Why do you remember him in particular? Did he speak to you?"

"No, sir. But I do remember his red gown. Such a striking red, sir. Much like the archbishop's cloak. A color difficult to forget."

A strange and uncomfortable feeling rumbled in Crispin's belly. "I see. Did he do anything else here then, that fortnight ago?"

"No, sir. He came with the pilgrims, as I said. He kept his hood up, but I did remember him."

"He did not meet with the archbishop, for instance?"

"No. At least, I do not think so."

"And last night?"

"He came out of the shadows and chuckled. He said to me, 'But is not God's house open to all?' 'Indeed, sir,' I answered him. 'But the chapel of Saint Benet is open for that. Surely you must understand that the shrine must be kept safe at night.' But he would not move. 'You must come with me,' I told him more insistently. But still he did not move. I told him I would go and get the chaplain. I did so. When I returned he was gone."

"Are you certain of that?"

"Yes, Master. I searched in all the usual places. You see, I know of certain thieves in this town and I have learned some things. All the doors were locked. But no one was here. Until the Prioress and her chaplain came in. And then you, sir."

"Well . . ." Crispin looked back the way Chaucer had gone. "Master Chaucer is a . . . he is the king's poet and is often—" He shrugged. "Imaginative men. Who can understand their ways?"

"Lurking in the shadows of a church? At night? What is imaginative in that?" He shook his head. "No, Master Crispin. I do not think him up to any good."

"Here, now," said Jack pressing forward. He gestured with the wrapped sword. "Master Chaucer is Master Crispin's friend."

The monk was startled and his eyes widened. "Oh. Oh . . . I . . ." He backed away. "I meant no offense, Master Guest."

"I am not offended. You had a tale to tell me and I thank you for doing so."

"You mustn't—" Wilfrid was shaking his head and backing away. "You must forget I said aught, Master Guest. Please. Disregard my words. Surely . . . surely . . ."

"Wilfrid, it is well. You did nothing wrong."

"You mustn't tell the archbishop I told you. It is nothing, after all. I knew I shouldn't have come to you. My brother monks told me not to. They warned me to leave it alone. But I don't think it fair. But it's only about Master Chaucer that I told you. I'll say nothing about—" He clamped his lips shut. His rounded eyes ticked from Crispin to Jack before he simply fled. The morning shadows swallowed him and soon his footsteps, too, vanished.

"What do you suppose that was all about?" asked Jack.

"Secrets, Jack. I don't like them. I never have. I will deal with Wilfrid anon. But for now . . ." He made for the steps and trotted down. Walking up the aisle, he didn't see Chaucer at all until he found him on the steps outside in the courtyard. Geoffrey turned and hooked his thumbs in his belt. "And so. What did your little clerical friend have to say?"

Crispin tried to hold at bay the uncomfortable feeling in his gut. He knew Geoffrey acted as a spy—he admitted as much. He spied for the king and, no doubt, Lancaster, who had ultimately betrayed Crispin.

If foster fathers could do such, then why not friends?

"He told me that he saw you lurking in the church last night."

Chaucer laughed. "'Lurking,' was it? Now why would I have cause to do that?"

"And so, too, did I wonder."

The poet's laughter subsided. "This has gone far enough. I am your oldest friend, Cris. You can't honestly believe—"

"Nor have I received a satisfactory answer from you."

Geoffrey's face darkened. "Very well. I *was* in the church. But I certainly wasn't 'lurking.' I was praying. Isn't a man allowed his time with God?"

"The church was closed—"

"Isn't that the best time? When all is silent and dark? His holy presence is most notably felt at such times. Certainly even you can appreciate that, Master Guest."

"Noted. But why did you not mention being in Canterbury a fortnight ago?"

Chaucer's face, bright with triumph, suddenly fell. He tried to hide it by turning toward the sky and adjusting the liripipe tail trailing from his hat to his shoulder. "Is that what he said? I was here a fortnight ago?"

"Yes. He remembered you well. You wore a scarlet houppelande, much like the one you are wearing now. I wonder if I may examine it."

Geoffrey slowly pivoted. "Why?"

"Does it matter?"

"It damn well does!" Chaucer tossed his cloak aside and strode briskly back and forth before the immense west door.

That pang in Crispin's heart struck again, the feeling of distance between those he loved and the reality of their betrayal. Would these wounds ever heal? Where was honor? Where loyalty? He ran his hand over his brow. "Harken to me, Geoffrey. We must be frank with each other. I know you deal in secrets. It is not my intention to make them known. But I must venture into all avenues to solve this heinous crime. Surely you can see that."

Chaucer raised his head but did not look at Crispin. "I might as well tell you now, for it will surely come out eventually. I, too, knew Madam Eglantine prior to this pilgrimage. In fact, I was also at the trial mentioned by the archbishop."

Crispin's hand dug deeper into his brow. "And why were you at this trial?"

"Because . . . I was a witness for the petitioner . . . Sir Philip Bonefey."

8

CRISPIN TOOK A BREATH and raised his eyes to his friend Chaucer. "So then you knew the Prioress. Did you speak to her at the trial?"

"Oh yes. We exchanged words, to be sure. Very heated ones. She is—*was*—a formidable woman. Bonefey was furious and still is. The archbishop did not help matters. At first he sided with Bonefey. In the end he and the judges ruled for Madam Eglantine, but no one in that chamber was satisfied." Crispin watched his face change. "Do you suppose I was so angry at her words that I bided my time, followed her to Canterbury, and took a sword to her? For something that happened a year ago?"

The wind gusted through the courtyard, winging blossoms into the air. Crispin buttoned his cloak over his chest. "Well, I concede that you don't seem to have had a vested interest in it."

"No. But Bonefey does. I defended Bonefey because I was asked to. And because it was another instance of the Church treading where it should not go."

"Spoken like a Lollard."

"And what if I am? I follow the dictates of my liege lord who is also a Lollard."

"Lancaster." He scowled.

"For a man whose life was purportedly saved by him, your opinion of Lancaster seems unnaturally low."

He bared his teeth. "Saved my life. And would that life have needed saving if he had not schemed and plotted?"

"I don't understand you. He raised you. He knighted you. He made you—"

"What I am today? Indeed, yes." Chaucer, in all his finery, stood with his fist at his waist, a courtly posture. It annoyed Crispin. "Our liege lord, the man to whom we both swore oaths of allegiance, the man for whom I would have gladly laid down my life . . . this man betrayed me! I was used. To discover his enemies *he* engineered the treasonous plot. And I, the loyal servant that I was, fell into the web."

Chaucer's face blanched. "No! It is a lie!"

"I heard it from his own lips."

Geoffrey paced in stunned silence. He looked once at Jack huddled on the stone steps clutching the wrapped sword to his bosom. "Are you telling me that my Lord of Gaunt *tricked* you into committing treason? Do you actually have the temerity to say that?"

"Temerity? I not only say it, I avow it. It happened. Jack is my witness."

Chaucer looked at Jack again who suddenly shrunk under their scrutiny. "*This* is your witness?" he cried, raising his arm and pointing toward Jack. "This . . . this *beggar*? This pathetic excuse for a *protégé*?" He laughed unpleasantly. "You may very well blame Lancaster for your misfortunes. God knows the great Crispin Guest would never blame himself!"

"I *have* blamed myself. Over and over in my mind. Don't you think I do? Don't you think I would rather have died for Lancaster than smear his name? If he had but told me before it all happened, explained it! But no." Geoffrey's expression infuriated him. "Fie! It's wasted breath on you. I'll never make you see that I have paid my penance. But has he?"

"You speak of payment and penance as if they are owed you."

"They *are* owed me! Look at me, Geoffrey. Look at me! Do you have any idea what my stinking lodgings on the Shambles are like?"

"You chose your lot, Guest. You chose to throw in with traitors. You swore your life to Lancaster, and suddenly you forget that he may do as he wishes with it. Even throw it away. He owes you nothing." Geoffrey straightened his gown and climbed the steps, skirting Crispin and Jack. "I have business within. Go back to your inquiries. Find your murderer and your bones. That's where it seems to suit you best. Amongst the dead."

Chaucer's footsteps receded.

Crispin lowered his head and panted. What was the matter with him? Why was he suddenly fighting with Geoffrey?

All this for one scrap of cloth that may not be a clue at all. He dug into his pouch and pulled out the bit of fabric, rubbing it between his calloused fingers.

"He won't stay angry," said Jack quietly. He had crept up beside Crispin without notice. "You haven't seen each other in years. There are bound to be misunderstandings."

"You don't have to mollify me," he grumbled, but he was grateful that Jack tried.

"What's that, Master Crispin?" He switched the sword to the crook of his arm and took the cloth scrap out of Crispin's hand.

"A clue. I found it stuck in the door of the Corona tower last night."

Dawn broke on Jack's face. "Is that why you asked about the archbishop's robe? Master Crispin! You don't think—"

"I don't know what to think. His robe might have been used as a disguise by any monk here. Remember, the archbishop suspects one of his own."

"But he ain't the only one with a scarlet robe."

"My friend Chaucer."

"Aye. But I was thinking of Sir Philip Bonefey."

Crispin stared at Jack. "So he does."

"And Rafe Maufesour the Summoner, for good measure."

Crispin chuffed a breath. "Perhaps we had best make a list of those who do *not* have a scarlet gown. It's a smaller roll."

"Now Master, it's not so difficult. We will examine their robes one by one to see how this scrap may fit. That will eliminate the innocent."

Crispin smiled in spite of himself. "That is very orderly thinking, Jack."

"Well, I was taught by the best, now wasn't I?" His pale cheeks flushed. "Now then. You've got this key, do you? Shouldn't we use it?"

"Let's begin with that tower stair." He took the cloth scrap from Jack's fingers and led the way back into the church. Pilgrims had already gathered with other faithful who came into the disorderly dust and work of the church to pray. Crispin shook his head and mouthed a few choice words describing the archbishop. Why had he not closed the church? A murder certainly required reconsecration. But the archbishop flouted canon law. Why? Greed? How much did they take in from the martyr's shrine? He guessed it was a goodly sum, possibly half of their income for the year. If that coin flow should be cut off for a year or more . . . ? He glanced up at the masons hammering, mortaring, pulling up stones by ropes and pulleys. The master mason said their payments were overdue. Was there a possibility of a shortfall in the cathedral books? If that were the case then the treasurer had some answering to do. Crispin wondered vaguely if Dom Thomas had a scarlet cloak as well.

A monk was giving a tour to the pilgrims on their slow progression toward the shrine. Crispin avoided them by taking the south aisle and climbing the steps opposite, near Prince Edward's shrine.

"It was here, Jack, that I found the scrap of cloth. Let us see what lies beyond this door."

He pulled the key from his pouch, fit it in the lock, and turned it twice. The door pushed open and Crispin stepped in. He expected a narrow spiraling stair and found it much wider, enough for two men side by side. It did spiral upward and was made of stone with carved niches along the curved walls. He looked down at the door and found only a few red threads.

"No blood," he said.

Jack nodded. "So he didn't come here *after* the murder but before."

"Very good, Jack. Hiding and waiting for the moment. Except—" Crispin looked up the tower. Slit windows slanted golden light down the tower and revealed another door near the top. "If he hid in here he would first have encountered me by the shrine. Why wasn't *I* attacked, then? Why go directly to the Prioress?"

"Well, he might have seen you and thought to create a distraction— No, that sounds poor even to me."

"*If* Madam Eglantine was the intended target."

"Meaning?"

"Meaning that perhaps the bones were merely a distraction."

"So he stole the bones as an *afterthought*?" He stared hard. Crispin was making his way up the stairs. "That's cruel work getting that canopy off the casket. And more work to move the lid."

"Not as an afterthought," Crispin confirmed.

"No, eh?" He followed up the stairs. "I'm stumped, then. If he did not mean to kill you and take the bones first, but he meant to kill the Prioress, then I do not understand his intentions."

"Perhaps the *murder* was a distraction to keep our eyes away from the bones."

"Blind me! That's . . . that's . . . horrible!"

Crispin nodded, climbed, and made it to the door at the top. It had no lock, so he grasped the ring and pulled the door open and stepped out onto the wide, round tower. The wind whipped at his hair, sending it stinging into his eyes. He looked out past the battlements across plowed fields to the east bordered by dark hedges and more meadows. Sheep grazed, looking like little white pods far below. Moving along the edge and peering between the merlons, Crispin gazed southwest toward Canterbury and its many red-tiled roofs. Smoke lingered above the rooftops, embracing chimneys and spires. Jack stood beside him, drew up his fretted hood, and fell silent. His cloak flapped against his flanks as he, too, assessed the church and abbey grounds.

Jack's head came to Crispin's shoulder. The boy was gaining height and a broadening of his chest. He hadn't noticed before how big Jack was getting. He seemed to have shot up like a bean sprout. His body didn't swim in his tunic any longer and his arms were overreaching their sleeves. He still thought of the lad as a child. Though Jack's voice had begun to change, he still sported the soft, rounded cheeks of childhood. At nearly thirteen, Jack walked the fine line between his formative years and adolescence.

Crispin turned his attention from Jack to the tower floor, looking for anything that might yield something useful to his investigation.

"Master Crispin." Jack stood at the tower's edge, the sword he grasped in his hand now hanging by his thigh. His gaze was fixed somewhere in the distance but his voice was strong against the wind. "I heard what Master Chaucer said . . . said about me. You ain't—*aren't*—ashamed to have me as your protégé, are you? If you were, I'd understand if you weren't to call me that no more—*any*more."

Crispin rose and clapped the dust from his knees and hands. "Who said I was ashamed of you?"

"It ain't—*isn't* what was said. It was the way he said it. He's an important man, isn't he? You meet other important men all the time for your work, sir. It's hard to impress them. There is only your reputation as the Tracker. We both ain't got fine clothes, like you was used to." He clenched his eyes in frustration. "*Were* used to. And here I am. A beggar. I told him so m'self, didn't I? And that's what I am. And that's what I look like. Maybe you'd be better off without me in the way. I'd still want to be your servant, mind. But . . . I'd stay out of the way. So's they wouldn't know."

Crispin sighed and measured the broad horizon that disappeared in a misty gray fringe of trees. "That was a fine speech. Worthy . . . But I think you're a fool."

Jack whipped his head toward Crispin. His hood flung back and his red hair flared in the wind like flames. "A fool?"

"You must not allow men like Geoffrey to intimidate you. It is their chief weapon. For the last time, I am not ashamed of you. You *are* my protégé. I am proud to call you so and I don't want to hear anything more about it again, either to gain sympathy or a raise in your wages."

Jack raised his hood against the wind. His face broke into an uncertain smile before he grinned wide, freckles and all.

Crispin wrapped his cloak about him. "I'm cold and there is nothing here. Let's go back down."

He trotted down the steps with Jack at his heels. They reached the bottom, stepped through the door, and Crispin locked it again. "I believe he hid there waiting for the appropriate time to strike. And the cloth must be from that night. Someone would have noticed it before then. Some monk scrubbing the floors. See how clean they keep the stairs? Let me see that sword again." Jack handed it to him and he unwrapped the pommel. A muzzled bear's head on a red field. Crispin ran memories of his jousting days through his head but he could not recall ever seeing this blazon before. "*Fortis et Patientia*," he muttered.

"Latin, right, Master? *Fortis*. Strong. *Patientia*. Patience?"

"Enduring. Do you suppose it is the motto to this blazon?"

Jack snapped his fingers. "Course it is. Isn't that something like your motto, sir?"

Crispin eyed Jack. "And how would you know what my family motto is?"

Jack's face slackened. Caught. "Well . . . I came across them rings you got hidden, sir. Came across them last year."

"Indeed." A blend of emotions crossed his heart. Was he angry? Jack was prone to find secret places in their lodgings. He had his own cache of hidden goods, so he supposed it was not unlikely Jack could find Crispin's meager treasure. Two family rings with the Guest blazon on them. His father's ring and his own. It was all that was left of the Guests. All the memory allowed him. Their family banners had been struck from the Great Hall in Westminster Palace. His surcote of colors long gone.

Crispin lowered his brows. "Are those rings still there?" Even as he asked it he knew the answer.

Jack looked aggrieved. "Master Crispin! What do you take me for? I would never touch your family rings, sir. I know what they are."

A corner of Crispin's mouth drew up. "Anyway, my motto is *Suus Pessimus Hostilis.*"

"'His Own Worst Enemy,'" Jack recited. "What does that mean, sir?"

"As I understand it, the arms were first granted to my ancestor by King Henry Fitzempress."

"Saint Thomas Becket's King Henry?"

"The very same. My ancestor was Welsh but fought for England, thus becoming his own enemy. Or so the story goes."

"How come you don't wear your ring no more—*any*more, sir?"

"You know why, Jack."

"But I don't, sir. You've still a right to it. No one else's name is Guest. It's yours and will always be so. It's your family, sir. And you weren't no bastard. The king can't do that to you, now can he?"

Crispin sighed. "'Dignity consists not in possessing honors, but in the consciousness that we deserve them.'" He stared at his feet. "My name is my name, true, and he cannot take that away. But what good is a blazon without a proper dynasty? No, they are better kept safe in their not-so-secret hiding place."

He handed Jack the sword and straightened his coat. He raised his head to take in the chapel and the nave beyond it. "I wonder what business Geoffrey had in the cathedral." He did not see the poet and when he moved past the pilgrims poised in rapt attention around the shrine, he did not see him in the south aisle either. But something in the aisle did catch his attention. His careful steps toward it soon became a trotting run.

He heard Jack's footfalls behind him and then the muffled clang of the sword dropping on the tiled floor. Crispin bent over the dark lump of clothes that wasn't a lump of clothes at all. A monk lay on the floor and an all-too-familiar dark pool grew around him. He turned the body and saw the young white face of Brother Wilfrid, quite dead.

9

"IT'S BROTHER WILFRID!" WHISPERED Jack. His fingers dug into Crispin's shoulder as he leaned over to stare at the dead monk. "God help us." He crossed himself.

Crispin pulled the dagger free and a small amount of blood oozed from the wound in the monk's throat. He stared at the knife and its bejeweled pommel, unwilling to believe what he was seeing. It was a very familiar dagger. A dagger he'd given as a gift to one of his very dear friends some fifteen years ago. He raised his face and was suddenly aware of people running and then a woman screamed.

He drew back, barely aware that he was pushed aside by many hands, all reaching for the monk. Soon a crowd clustered around the becassocked form and Crispin was vaguely aware of Jack pulling him completely out of the way and under the shelter of a shadowing alcove. "Master Crispin," he whispered. "Come, sir. Snap out of it." The sword's pommel smacked Crispin on the side of the head and he glared at Jack. Tucker retracted the sword and nodded. "Thought that would bring you round."

"It's impossible."

Jack raised the sword again and Crispin blocked it with his hand. "There's no need for that. It's just . . . I know this knife."

"It's Chaucer's, ain't it?" Jack's rasping voice dropped to a deadly tenor. All of Crispin's muddled emotions were mirrored on Jack's face: betrayal, rage, vengeance. Jack whirled toward the pilgrims, his bottled energy thrown outward. He waved the sword at them, moving them back. He ordered a monk to get the archbishop, and he patrolled the body like a Centurion, letting no one near it.

The archbishop arrived with Dom Thomas Chillenden and Brother Martin. Courtenay stood over the monk and murmured a prayer before he raised his eyes to Crispin. There was no Christian charity within them. "The church will be closed," he announced, but his eyes were still fixed on Crispin. "A despicable crime has occurred on this most holy ground. We will need to reconsecrate. Send the pilgrims away." Dom Thomas nodded and moved to comply. More monks came running, one carrying a bier.

"Master Guest," said the archbishop. "You are to come with me."

He followed Courtenay like a condemned man walking to the gallows. Jack followed close behind, handling the sword like a club. Was this death his fault, too? Was his old friend guilty? Even when Brother Wilfrid told him the facts, he hadn't believed it had any bearing on this case. How could it? But there was no question that Wilfrid had been frightened of Geoffrey.

Courtenay pushed open the door to his chamber and slammed the table with his hand. The candlestick wobbled. "Blessed Mother of God!" He whirled. His reddened face scowled. "What have you brought to my church? Death and more death follows in your wake, Guest."

He fisted the dagger and pressed it tight to his thigh. "I am not the cause of these deaths, your Excellency. Indeed, I am trying to discover the culprit—"

Jack pitched forward out of the shadows. "But you *know* who killed Wilfrid!" he cried.

Crispin whipped around to glare at the trembling boy. Jack's pale face reddened with anger.

Courtenay postured. "So! A conspiracy, is it?"

"No conspiracy," growled Crispin. "The evidence is conditional. I do not believe—"

"It matters very little to me, Guest, what you believe." He looked at the dagger in Crispin's hand for the first time. "This killed Wilfrid?"

"Yes, but—"

"Curse you, Guest! Do I throw *you* into gaol?"

He lowered his head, took a breath, then another. His hand whitened on the knife's grip. Damn Jack! He'd given him no time to think. Slowly he raised the weapon and showed it to Courtenay. "This is the dagger." He placed it on Courtenay's table. "It belongs to . . . to Geoffrey Chaucer."

Courtenay threw his shoulders back and Crispin scowled to see a small smile crack the archbishop's lips. "Indeed. Master Chaucer, eh? Well, well. Yes. I think it time to call in the sheriff."

"My lord, I cannot imagine an instance when Master Chaucer would resort to murder of a monk. It is impossible!"

"Clearly not, Master Guest, for the evidence is before us. Our very dear brother has been foully murdered in the church. It is likely he also killed the Prioress."

"It isn't *likely* at all! My lord, you must listen—"

"I remember well the trial, Master Guest," Courtenay trumpeted. "Master Chaucer was most eloquent when he testified. He made a very convincing case on behalf of that scoundrel Bonefey. Even I was tempted to be persuaded toward the Franklin's cause. But Chaucer was so infested with Lollard platitudes that I was

swayed from his startling rhetoric and supported Madam Eglantine's view instead. How full of ire he was at the trial's end. I witnessed for myself how he stalked up to her and without remorse
for his inelegant actions, tore into her reserve with a string of foul
invectives."

"I cannot believe—"

"Believe it! I was there." His eyes shone with a bitterness that
took Crispin aback. "Oh he was charming and light, oozing his
eloquence, but he used his tongue like a knife to cut her down.
And only a year later . . . well. It was an actual sword he used in
the end."

Crispin's mind paused. For the tiniest fraction, he considered
the archbishop's words. This was a side of Geoffrey he knew well.
He could, indeed, cut a man or woman down to size with words,
all the while saying it with a smile. Sometimes the target of his
attack was not even aware of the infliction of wounds until it was
too late, so clever was he. And it had been a full eight years since
he had set eyes on Chaucer. It came as a great shock when he discovered Geoffrey served as a spy for the king. He knew that Geoffrey was a man reaching to better himself and skilled at finding
his opportunities. When his sister-in-law became Lancaster's mistress, he exploited that relationship to his advantage, and when he
lived in Lancaster's household with Crispin he sought every opportunity. Yes, Crispin remembered well how Chaucer elevated
himself with dealings he thought at the time clever. But looking
back, they had the smell of cunning with an undercurrent of
deceit.

Courtenay was still talking and Crispin raised his head to
catch the last. ". . . Come, Guest. Even your own man here will
not defend Chaucer. Don't get yourself mixed up in it. You've had
enough troubles."

"His Excellency is right," said Jack.

Crispin's rage ballooned and he took three steps, reached for Jack, and dragged him forward. "You don't know what you are talking about. You are to keep silent, curse you!"

Jack's eyes enlarged with fear but he raised his chin as much as he could with Crispin's hand fisting his shirt. "I can't keep silent when I see you on the wrong side of the law, sir," he said, voice unsteady. "Maybe I have no right to speak, Master, but you are always telling me of justice and weighing consequences. You live by this rule, sir. How could you go on if you threw it away?"

He glared at Jack so hard his eyes watered.

"If Master Chaucer is innocent," said Jack softly, "then let him prove it. Let him answer the charges. That is justice, sir. Or does it only concern those who are not your friends?"

"You found his dagger in our poor Wilfrid," said Courtenay from a distance. Crispin suddenly remembered the archbishop was there. "You will arrest him and bring him to the sheriff. You will do your best to find him. Is that clear?"

Crispin clenched his eyes shut. It must be done. Geoffrey *had* to answer for these charges. "Yes, Excellency," he said between gritted teeth. He opened his eyes and glanced at Jack. Slowly, he lowered him and released his shirt. Jack straightened his tunic and stepped back, red-faced.

Weary. Crispin felt it in his bones. Too many betrayals, too many lies. Lancaster was one thing. He was almost a king himself, so far above him now that he might as well be a beggar. But Chaucer! Chaucer was below him in status—*was* below. No longer. But he had been his dearest friend. How could Geoffrey have lied so cavalierly to him?

He wanted dearly to be home or at least at the inn, smothered under the blankets. But he made no move to leave. He stared instead at the stained-glass window and its depiction of Thomas à Becket with his monks. They clustered around him, their hands uplifted, their faces blank but adoring.

"Brother Wilfrid spoke of a disagreement with his fellow brothers," said Crispin hoarsely.

"Did he?" Courtenay sat and leaned his head back against the carved wood.

"Yes. He said they told him not to come to me, that it was something they wanted to keep quiet. Do you know what that might be?"

"If you will recall, Master Guest, this was the reason I called for you in the first place: I believe one of my monks is a secret Lollard."

"Yes. Or more than one. I need to speak with them."

"But if Master Chaucer is your culprit—"

"I explore *all* avenues, Excellency, not merely the easy ones. I presume *that* is why you called for me. *I* get results."

Courtenay's smile was wry. "Then what do you propose? They will tell you nothing if you question them."

"I don't know." He pressed a hand to his throbbing head. His jaw still hurt where he was struck and Jack's insolence and Chaucer's lies were giving him a supreme headache. "Perhaps disguise myself as a monk and blend with them, interrogate by listening."

Courtenay shook his head. "They've already seen you. They know what you look like and who you are."

Crispin nodded. "Yes. Curse it. But it's still a good idea. What I need is someone they have not yet seen." He walked to the far wall, wishing the monks hadn't seen his face. There were so many questions he wanted to ask. He paced, wondering just how he was going to interrogate them when the idea hit him square in the forehead. He stopped and slowly pivoted toward Jack.

Courtenay turned his eyes to Jack, too, and Jack looked from Crispin to Courtenay, suddenly nervous. He pulled at his collar and asked a meek "What?" with a wince as if he already knew the answer.

10

"YOUR LATIN IS GOOD. Good enough for a young man in a monastery." Crispin ushered Jack hurriedly through the street, but Jack resisted each step.

"I won't do it, Master Crispin. Why won't you listen to me?"

"I'm serving justice, remember?"

Jack crossed himself. Crispin shoved him forward. "Curse them words for ever leaving me mouth."

"'*Those* words for ever leaving *my* mouth,'" he corrected.

"What difference does it make? No one will ever believe that I am a m-monk."

"People will believe anything you tell them as long as it is dressed in the proper form. A beggar can be a king . . . and vice versa. That's why we seek a tailor. Ah!"

A wooden sign painted with a golden scissors wobbled in the breeze under a thatched eave. He tried to push Jack forward but the boy dug in his heels.

"Master Crispin! Wait! Now have a care. I'll foul it up, you know I will. I haven't got the sense you've got. Someone will find me out and then all will be lost. Don't force me to it, sir, I beg you!"

Crispin rested an arm on the shop's doorframe and leaned over Jack. "You are the one who spoke of justice."

"Aye, I know it. But justice for you!"

"Justice is justice—for me, for you. For those poor souls who lost their lives in the cathedral. They must have it. I personally do not believe Geoffrey is guilty, but . . . My good sense in these matters of former friends and lords . . ." He sighed. "I must admit to a certain lapse in judgment of late. I need this information if only to eliminate the wrong path. I know you can do it. Don't you remember telling me only last year you could never learn to read or write? How many languages can you read now?"

"Three, sir. Almost four."

"True, your Greek is rusty, but you will improve. You've a head for it. Faith, Jack, with your learning you may be the most highly educated monk there."

Jack considered, his mouth drawn down in a frown. "Do you truly think so?"

"Only one way to find out."

Jack glanced at the tailor's sign, then at the ground. "You are my master. Do I have a choice?"

"Yes."

The freckles nearly disappeared as Jack's eyes widened and his brows leaped upward. "I do?" he whispered.

"You've always had a choice. I have no bond with you. You owe me no fealty. We have sworn no oaths to each other. You are free to leave me at any time."

Jack swallowed hard. His ginger brows knitted. "I never said I wanted to leave you, sir."

"And I've never asked you to stay. Well"—he fit his thumb in his belt—"now I am."

"Oh for Christ's bones! So now you would!"

"I don't know how much clearer I have to be. Didn't I declare my intentions on the Corona tower?"

"You want this that bad?"

"No. But it is clear you must know exactly where you stand with me." Crispin pushed back from the wall and took a step into the muddy street, the air filled with the smells of wet thatch, stone, and horse droppings. "It grieves me to see that most of my former life has been a lie. Lancaster, Geoffrey. I didn't realize the level of deceit. Perhaps they are merely the symptom of a greater disease. A disease I was never aware of, foolish, naïve man that I am." He gazed at Jack fondly. "But I will not have that with us. There are to be no lies, no secrets. My 'yes' means 'yes' and my 'no' means 'no.' And thus it will always be between you and me." He thrust out his open hand but Jack only stared at it.

"Master Crispin, you shouldn't aught to do so much. I'm . . . I'm no one."

"And so am I." He smiled. "What say you, Jack Tucker? Shall you be in league with the scoundrel and traitor Crispin Guest once and for all, forsaking your soul and your peace of mind?"

"I done that already," he muttered. He eyed Crispin's hand as if it were a snake. "You want me to do this, don't you? I don't think you truly know what you are asking."

"But I do." He cracked a lopsided grin. "Must I *foster* you to show you my sincerity?"

"No, Master! I . . . I believe you. Very well, then." He reached a trembling hand forward and grasped Crispin's, guardedly at first then stronger as Crispin shook it once and released him.

"Good. Now, can we please go inside?"

"Aye, master." He grabbed the door handle and stopped. "But I ain't calling you by your Christian name. That I will not do!"

"Of course not. I am your master. That would be improper." He gestured for Jack to pull open the door.

Inside, the cold of April succumbed to the golden tones of the warm room. It smelled of a toasty fire, cloth and pungent wool, acrid dyes, and habitation. A man scuttled down the ladder of a loft and turned his head once to spy the customers. "Bless my soul! It's Crispin Guest!"

"Greetings, Master Turpin."

"My, my," said Turpin, reaching the ground level and turning round. His frame was similar to Crispin's, though his hair was sandy and thin, unlike Crispin's own thick, dark locks. "It *has* been a long time, hasn't it?"

"Indeed."

"As I've told you before, any favor I can render, any at all. I am your man."

Jack eyed Crispin and muttered, "Is there no one that don't owe you a favor?"

He ignored him. "This is something of an urgent nature, master." He stood behind Jack and dropped his hands on the boy's shoulders. Quietly, he said, "I need to style this young lad as a Franciscan friar."

Turpin's eyes enlarged but he never asked. "I may have something that will suit. I'd merely need to hem the bottom and the sleeves. I take it you need it right away."

"If we can wait for it?"

"That urgently? Of course, Master Guest. When was 'leisure' ever part of your lexis."

"Once, Master Turpin, a long time ago."

"Very well, then. Young man," he said to Jack. "Please remove your cloak and tunic."

Crispin took the wrapped sword from Jack's hands and set it aside.

Jack looked from one to the other and slowly peeled his chaperon hood off his head and shoulders. He made as if to drop it on the floor but Turpin took it tenderly between his fingers. Except that Jack would not let it go. "What will you do with that, sir?"

"I'm merely putting it aside."

"Tell him, Master Crispin. Tell him that's all I got in the world."

"He knows it, Jack. Do as Master Turpin tells you."

Reluctantly, Jack released the hood and unbuttoned his cloak, which Turpin also took. He unbuckled his belt with a reddened face. He unlaced his tunic and pulled it over his head, leaving him in his stockings and shirt.

"Dear me," muttered Turpin, examining Jack's threadbare clothes. He folded them into a neat pile without further comment and placed them on a shelf. "If you will excuse me." He disappeared through a curtained doorway.

Jack rubbed his arm self-consciously. "I feel like a sheep being sheared," he muttered.

"Nonsense. A sheep looks happier."

Turpin returned, a brown gown draped over his arm. "This will do, I think. I can sew on a hood and provide a belt. Er—"

Crispin stepped forward. "I can pay you, Master Turpin." His pouch bulged with the archbishop's reluctant generosity.

"Oh no, think nothing of it. I owe you after all, Master Guest. But—"

"We will return it when we are finished. Will that suffice?"

Turpin's pointed face did its impression of a grin. "Oh indeed! Indeed!" Crispin flashed Jack a quick, reassuring smile. "Now, young man, if you will . . . will . . ." He urged the gown on Jack. Jack took it in both hands and meekly lifted it over his head. "Other way, other way," chirped Turpin. He grabbed the material wrapped around Jack's head and twisted. Jack released a muffled curse and his head finally popped through. Turpin pulled it down over his torso and lifted Jack's arms into the sleeves. Jack stared at him as if he were mad. He took Jack's shoulders and turned him around pulling up the collar of the robe and measuring across his shoulders with a string. He turned Jack around again to face him and ticked his head at the hem. "The hem seems fine but the sleeves are a bit long."

"That's fine the way it is," said Crispin. "But it needs the cowl."

"Yes, I have something. Very well, young man. Off with it."

Jack gave a pleading look before Turpin whisked it up his body, obscuring his face.

The tailor disappeared once more and left Jack standing in his shirt and stockings again. His sorrowful expression caused Crispin to chuckle. At least it made him forget the circumstances for an instant or two. But then he thought again about Chaucer's dagger back in Courtenay's lodgings and the mysterious and secretive monks of Christchurch Priory. What was it they wanted to hide? *Did* Dame Marguerite see a cassock on the assailant as she thought? Though by her own admission she wasn't certain. If not the archbishop—and it truly seemed an outlandish supposition—then perhaps one of the monks. Any one of them could have used the archbishop's cloak to hide themselves. But what was the reason for killing the Prioress? Was it merely a distraction to hide the theft of the bones? And what did Chaucer's dagger have to do with it? No, something was amiss. The only certainty was the missing bones. He only hoped they hadn't been destroyed.

Turpin returned and showed his handiwork. Crispin smiled

and nodded appropriately and Turpin proceeded to entangle Jack in the cassock again. He tied the laces at the yoke of his neck, adjusted the belt, threw the hood up over his head and opened his hands. "And there. One young Franciscan, Master Crispin."

"Excellent, Master Turpin. I thank you for your time. And one more thing." Crispin whispered in his ear and Turpin withdrew from him with a wide smile. "I would be most pleased, Master Guest."

"Good. Take your time. Fare you well."

"God protect you, Master Guest. And you, too, young man."

"And you, sir," mumbled Jack. He walked out of the shop and stood in the street, head down. "I feel like the proper fool."

"But you look most convincing." He handed Jack the wrapped sword again as they walked back to the cathedral.

Jack pulled uncomfortably at the gown, loosening the leather belt. "I can't do it, master."

"Yes, you can. You disguised yourself so once before to steal into court."

"But that was different! I didn't have to talk to nobody!"

"Stop sniveling and listen. When you greet someone you say, '*Benedicte.*' And they say '*Deo gratias.*' Got it?"

"Aye. *Benedicte. Deo gratias.* Christ's toes."

"And no oaths. You don't want them to flog you, do you?"

"What!"

Crispin hid his smile by glancing ahead. "At meals there are considerably more prayers before you may eat. Never touch your food until the prior touches his, and don't eat as if you will never get another scrap."

"I don't eat like that."

"Yes, you do. A slower pace, Jack, remember."

"What if they ask me to say a prayer?"

"Then say one."

"I don't know no prayers."

"You don't know *any* prayers. And yes, you do. *Pater Noster, Ave Maria, Gloria Patri*—"

"Very well! I know them. But the chanting. I don't know that."

"Feign it."

He glared. "*Feign* it? That's your great advice? *Feign it?*"

"You'd be surprised how often that advice works . . . in all circumstances."

"How can I feign—"

"Then feign a cold."

Jack blinked. "Oh aye. I can do that."

He shook his head. "For a boy who made his living stealing men's purses you seem to have an awfully weak stomach."

"I knew what I was doing there, didn't I? I was quick."

"And you'll be quick at this. Don't do much talking. Listen. Discover if you can why they needed to keep secrets from Dom Thomas and if they know anything about Becket's bones. I've told you the Lollard philosophy. Listen for any signs of that. And don't make yourself obvious. Blend in."

"If I'm to blend in, then why am I dressed as a *Franciscan* in a *Benedictine* priory?"

"Because a monk visiting a monastery who comes from a traveling order like the Franciscans is more easily explained. We must keep our lies to a minimum in order to keep your story straight."

"One lie at a time, eh?"

He patted Jack's shoulder. "That's right, Jack. One lie at a time. Now you are gaining understanding."

Crispin continued his tuition, telling Jack what he could expect as a monk. When the shadow of the cathedral draped across their path, Crispin stopped. "Here's where I leave you, Jack."

"What? I thought you would go to the priory with me." His eyes were bright.

"No, Jack. They mustn't see you with me." He took the wrapped sword out of Jack's hands once more. "Only a few monks might have caught a glimpse of you in the church, but it was dark and your hood was up. So keep your eyes down. You are Brother John now. Answer to nothing else."

"I'm Brother John. Holy Christ Jesus' toes." He took a step and then stopped. "Oh wait! How will I know when I'm done inquiring?"

"When you find out something. Good luck, Jack."

"*Pax vobiscum*," he answered, making the sign of the cross over Crispin that quickly turned to a rude forking of his fingers.

CRISPIN DRAGGED HIMSELF BACK to the inn. What if Geoffrey was there? There had to be a reasonable explanation why Geoffrey's dagger was used to kill Wilfrid. He racked his brain, but he could not recall if Geoffrey was wearing the dagger when they went to the cathedral or not. If he had left it behind or lost it, anyone could have retrieved it and used it. But why? Who would have cause to kill Wilfrid? The monk was a puzzle, but the Prioress's death less so. He needed to talk to Bonefey. Of all the pilgrims, he was the one with the biggest grudge against the Prioress. He was anxious to corner him and maybe have a look at his red gown.

He turned the street corner and spied Maufesour and Chaunticleer creeping back to the inn. Maufesour looked over his shoulder and gripped the door when he spied Crispin. He ducked hurriedly inside and Crispin mouthed a few choice oaths.

He reached the door and yanked it open and merely stood in

the doorway surveying the subdued company. Even Harry Bailey's usual cheerful exterior was showing signs of wear. Crispin cut his glance to Maufesour and grinned maliciously at him before he greeted the Miller, who stumped forward, bagpipe in one hand, beaker in the other. "Master Guest, what is the word? We have since heard terrible tidings at the cathedral. It seems the devil has come to roost in Canterbury."

"Indeed. You may be right, Master Miller."

"It is Edwin Gough, good sir. At your service. Anything that you need, I will aid you."

"Thank you, Master Gough." He shouldered his way through the others and sat heavily on a bench, laying the sword across his thighs. "But what I need is Master Chaucer's whereabouts."

"We haven't seen him," said Clarke, the Manciple. He sat almost apologetically next to Crispin and rested his long pale fingers on the table before him. He made a sharp glance over his shoulder at the Summoner and Pardoner. "But his whereabouts aren't the only mystery of late."

"I see I have been disobeyed again."

"There is nothing you can do with those two, Master Guest."

"Call me Crispin."

"And you may call me Thomas." The Manciple edged closer and spoke quietly. "While it is true that my occupation only involves ordering provisions for the law students under my care, I have come to view the law with fascination. I sit in on the trials, you see. A Manciple I may be, but a man can show his worth by acquiring a wider sphere of knowledge." Crispin nodded approvingly. "A particular law student makes me aware of unusual cases. For his trouble, I make certain he receives an extra measure of ale. Would it surprise you to know that I am aware of the trial of

Madame Eglantine and Sir Bonefey?" Crispin was taken aback but tried not to show it. "I myself was not at that trial," he went on, "but I studied the transcripts." He answered Crispin's quizzical expression. "The trial was curious and contentious."

"Had the Prioress a legitimate claim?"

Clarke made loops on the table with his fingertips as if scribing his parchments. "I read the notes thoroughly, Master Crispin. I am no lawyer. But I have immersed myself in enough law to be a fine apprentice of it, I can tell you. Better than some of the students I have encountered." He flushed from his own presumption. "But from what I could make of it, Sir Bonefey should have been the clear winner."

"Then why wasn't he, I wonder?"

Clarke opened his mouth and then closed it again. He made his imaginary scribing on the table and eyed Father Gelfridus talking quietly to Harry Bailey. "He challenged the Church," he whispered.

"I understand Master Chaucer testified on behalf of Sir Philip."

Clarke's nervous fingers twitched on the wood. It began to irritate. "That is what I read, Master Crispin. I know he is a friend of yours, but—"

An icy hand clutched his heart. He knew he didn't want to hear what the Manciple had to say, but hear it he must. "Master Clarke. Thomas. I should like to know."

"Well, he . . . he spoke on behalf of what he called the common man faced with the . . . the . . ." His voice fell to a whisper again. "The *tyranny* of the Church."

Crispin sat back. He could easily see how that would not sit well with the archbishop. He could imagine the rest. Did Geoffrey have to paint "Lollard" on his forehead?

"Thank you, Master Clarke. Is Sir Philip here?"

"I thought he was in his room."

"And Dame Marguerite? Is she better?"

"She has been out walking in the garden."

He nodded and inquired which room was Bonefey's. He rose and then leaned down close to Clarke. "Do me the favor of keeping an eye skinned on these two," and he gestured toward Maufesour and Chaunticleer. "I'd hate for them to nip off again without my having a talk with them."

Crispin climbed the stairs. When he reached the landing he went to his chamber to discard the sword and quickly left before the call of the soft bed became too great to bear. He walked along the gallery to the last door and knocked.

He heard shuffling. A chair skidded across the floor. Then, "Who is there?"

"It is Crispin Guest, Sir Philip. May I enter?"

A pause. "If you must." The bolt grated and the door flung open. "Well then?" Bonefey planted himself in the doorway. "Do you have good news to report?"

"I would rather not stand in the gallery, Sir Philip. If I may?" He advanced and Bonefey was forced to retreat. Making a cursory inspection of the room Crispin turned to his host. "There has been another murder."

"God preserve us! Who?"

"A monk. Another innocent. In the church."

"Absolutely monstrous. What has become of this town?"

"Gough the Miller says the devil has come to roost."

"I think he is right. Do you insist we continue to stay?"

"I do."

"To what end? It must be clear to you by now that we have nothing to do with these murders."

Crispin glanced out Bonefey's open window. It overlooked the courtyard and the stables. A lone stableman pitched hay into a stall and a shaggy horse bent its head to nuzzle the golden fodder. "I wonder about your disagreement with the Prioress."

Silence. Crispin turned, making certain Bonefey was still in the room.

"Why?"

"Because she's dead. And because you were the only one to have a motive to kill her."

Bonefey drew his sword. His reddened features twisted with rage. "How *dare* you!"

He merely looked at the naked blade gleaming in the firelight. "You like your sword, do you?"

"You insult me, sir! You accuse me of a most foul deed!"

"And you have drawn your blade on a man who owns no sword. Yes, you are brave indeed, Sir Philip. And what weapon do I use to defend myself? My fist?"

Bonefey's sword wavered. His murderous eyes never flinched from Crispin's, but his face lost its initial dark hue. Finally he lowered the sword but did not sheath it. "That is a foul charge."

"Merely an observation." He studied Bonefey's sword. "By the way, what are your family arms?"

"What?"

"Your blazon, sir. What manner is it?"

"It's a black shield with five feathers. Why?"

The hearth belched a spiral of black smoke and Crispin looked, eyes suddenly widening. Three steps took him to the fire and the gown smoldering in its midst. He grabbed the poker and yanked the garment from the coals, but the red gown was too burned to make much of it. He threw the poker down and glared at Bonefey. "An unusual laundering method."

Sir Philip still held his sword at the ready. "It was an old gown. It was of no further use to me."

"No further use, eh? Did it by any chance have a rip in its hem? Or was it covered in too much blood?"

Crispin felt the sword whistling toward him. He grabbed the chair and met the blade with it. The sword clattered against the wooden legs and with a twist, he sent the weapon flying free from the Franklin's hands. Lunging forward he pinned Bonefey to the wall with the chair. "Come at me with a sword, will you?" he hissed between clenched teeth. "I'll have your head, Bonefey. I'll see it hewn off."

"You're mad! Get off me!"

"You are as guilty as they come. And I'll not rest until I see justice for the innocent you slaughtered."

"I did not kill the Prioress. And you are making the biggest mistake of your life. If you do not unhand me now, I'll see *you* on a gibbet!"

It was a stand-off. Crispin snapped back and tossed the chair across the floor. The sword lay on the other side of the room. He sneered at the Franklin when he reached the door. "My eye is on you, Bonefey. Don't try to leave this inn or you'll spend the rest of your time in a Canterbury prison."

He slammed the door and stomped across the gallery. Should he get the sheriff now? Crispin swore. He needed far more proof before he could accuse such a wealthy man. The sheriff would never take his word over a Franklin's. Besides, he couldn't call in the sheriff without mentioning Chaucer. God's blood! He was too pent up now to go to his room, and wine sounded like a better option.

He trotted down the steps. Alyson sat near the fire, a cup in her hand and a full jug in front of her. When she looked up, she motioned to him to join her.

"Your brow is furrowed for one so young," she said and poured more wine into her cup and handed it to him.

His fingers brushed hers as he took it and tossed back the cup. She chuckled and poured another. "I'm not so young," he said.

"You're fifteen years my junior, I'll warrant." She eyed him up and down before raising her chin. "I'm five and two score and proud of it."

He nodded. "You are a good judge. I am one and thirty." He took another long swallow.

"I know my men," she said. He handed the cup back to her and she sipped at it. But by the color rising in her cheeks and nose, he suspected she had the lead of him. When she handed back a full cup, he did his best to catch up.

"I heard about the other murder," she said, leaning back. She ticked her head. "This pilgrimage has turned to a right nightmare. Ever since Cain brought murder to Mankind, there has been no peace."

"How fares Dame Marguerite?"

Alyson sighed. "Poor lamb. She tries to bear up. Father Gelfridus is with her often and his presence gives her strength. But I do not know. Such a shock for one so young and innocent. But she will survive because of her faith." She swirled the jug and smiled. "I strung her rosary for her. She was pleased to have it, but there was a bead missing."

Crispin reached into his pouch and felt the lost bead at his fingertips. "Alas," he said.

"It is no matter. She will work it out."

He shook his head and brought the bowl's rim to his lips. He drank and set the bowl on his thigh. "I came here to do a simple job. But it has turned to murder. And more." He tilted his cup again and wiped the spilled wine from the side of his mouth.

"You have a haunted look about you. What more troubles you?"

"I do not wish to burden you."

She elbowed him and smiled. Her face brightened with it and she leaned toward him, her ample bosom pressing against his arm. He inhaled her earthy scent. He could easily see how she acquired so many husbands. "Burden me. If not me, then whom? 'When he cries out to me, I will hear him, for I am compassionate.'" Her smile turned to a sad one. "And I am just as involved. It was I, after all, who dressed Madam Eglantine for her final reward."

He sighed. The wine warmed his belly and added a soothing buzz to his head. He took another long swallow and allowed Alyson to fill the cup again. "I am weary of deceit. All of my life seems to be woven with it."

She studied him over the rim of her cup. "I do not see your friend Chaucer here. You don't mean him, do you?"

He set his mouth. He'd spoken too much already. "I implore you, madam . . ."

"Now, now. I'm growing quite fond of you. Can't you see your way to using my Christian name?"

He smiled, weakly at first, then more boldly as she greeted him with her brash grin. "Alyson. And you must call me Crispin."

"I shall. You were telling me?"

His smile faded. "You must be cautious of Sir Philip," he said quietly. "He is a very dangerous man."

She leaned in. "Is he the murderer?" Her words slurred but she didn't seem to notice.

"He's a scoundrel," he said, or at least tried to, but the word "scoundrel" caught on his tongue. He stared at Alyson. "I beg your pardon, but I seem to be getting drunk."

"There's no need to beg my pardon, Crispin. I seem to be a bit drunk myself." Her hand fell to his thigh and stayed there.

He looked down at it. When he glanced up again she had edged closer, so close, in fact, that her soft hip pressed warmly against his. He decided he liked the feel of it. "Alyson, are you trying to seduce me?"

"Bless me," she said with a sultry chuckle, "if I were better at it you wouldn't have to ask."

11

JACK TUCKER WALKED THE longest mile of his life to the door of the Benedictine priory of Christchurch. The ancient door was tall, of dark oak, hewn and carved centuries before. Even its black iron hinges seemed impenetrable. Hanging just to the side was a bell rope and, with a trembling hand, he grasped it. With a murmured prayer to the Almighty and a curse to Crispin, he pulled.

He waited. One moment. Two. He listened to his heartbeat, surely loud enough for anyone to hear. Finally he heard feet approaching. He clenched his hands into fists, forced them down to his sides, and caught his breath just as a smaller door within the larger swung open.

"*Benedicte*," said the monk in the doorway, eyeing Jack carefully.

"*Deo gratias*," Jack gasped. He ducked his head in a curt bow but never let his eyes leave the monk. In a rush he said, "My name is Brother John and I come from the south to see the martyr's shrine."

The monk looked as if he would burst into tears. His mouth trembled and his eyes were already rimmed with red. "Of course you may enter, Brother John, but I fear you have come a long way for nought."

He stepped aside, and Jack passed into the cloister. He jumped when the door slammed behind him and the monk locked it. He swallowed, but the hard lump in his throat wouldn't seem to leave him. *I should never have let Master Crispin talk me into this. I'll foul it up.* Aloud he said, "Why do you say that, Brother?"

"A great evil has come to Canterbury Cathedral, Brother John. A great evil. Death, heretics. You would do well to leave this place immediately. I fear God is raining His justice upon us."

Jack didn't know what he should say to that and was reprieved from a hasty comment when another monk rushed around the corner. He stopped short when he spied Jack.

"Brother Arthur, you are wanted. Who is this?"

"Father Cyril, this is Brother John. I tried to tell him he has come at a wretched time—"

Cyril grabbed Arthur's arm and pulled him aside. "What have you told him?" he hissed.

"Only that evil dwells here now," he sighed miserably.

Cyril frowned and pushed him forward. "Fool. Keep silent." He stared at Jack while Arthur shuffled away. "Some of our brothers here know no discretion. I hope you are better schooled."

Jack bowed, not knowing what to add. It seemed to be the right response. Cyril's lids were drawn low over his eyes, and his aristocratic nose arched over a small pursed mouth. He gestured for him to follow. "I will take you to the prior. Of course we will give you hospitality, Brother, but if you have come to see the shrine . . . well. I'll let the prior attend you."

Jack allowed himself to be led. The cool shadows of the cloister walk enclosed him. In the little square surrounded by the gray stone of the cloister ambulatory, the sun shone brightly. The recently mown green grass and the budding flowers breathed their fresh fragrance into the air. But they offered no comfort to him moving behind the silent monk under the cold stone arches. His eyes darted from carved granite to the peaceful garden and back again. Already he missed the freedom of the sunshine as they ducked through an arch and entered the cooler precincts of the priory.

He followed Cyril up some stone steps, down another corridor, and up to an oaken door. Cyril knocked, heard a reply, and entered, waiting for Jack to pass before he closed the door behind him. An old man, balding, with fluffs of white hair spraying over his ears, looked up from his chair by the fire. "Forgive me, my Lord Prior. But this is Brother John come from far away and wishes the hospitality of Canterbury."

The prior turned rheumy eyes toward Jack but only fleetingly. "You are welcome, Brother John." He made a cursory cross in the air in Jack's general direction. "But alas, you've made a futile journey. My heart is heavy on it. Please, Dom, you tell him."

Jack turned to another monk in the room and met the eyes of Dom Thomas Chillenden. The monk's eyes fixed on Jack's for a long moment before they enlarged to round disks. Jack's grew almost as large, pleading for the monk to say nothing. "Er . . . yes, my Lord Prior. I will . . . I will show this fine brother the precincts and explain it all to him."

He took Jack's arm roughly and steered him out the door. Two monks had gathered to talk furtively to Father Cyril, and Dom Thomas ushered Jack in the other direction until the monks were only distant shadows. "By all that is holy what are *you* doing here?" he hissed in Jack's ear. "And dressed like that!"

Jack peeled the monk's hands from him and stepped back, adjusting his collar. "There's no need for that. My master sent me here on the word of the archbishop."

"You were sent to *spy* on us!"

"Well, just a little."

"Just a *little*? God preserve us!"

"Do you not want to know who killed the Prioress and Brother Wilfrid? Or where the bones of the sainted martyr are?"

Dom Thomas's face sobered. He wrung his hands. "Poor Brother Wilfrid. He did not deserve that. I shall do much penance for what I have wished upon his killer!"

"And so. Master Crispin thought this the best way to find out the doings, seeing that the monks most like would not talk to him."

Dom Thomas swept his disdainful gaze over Jack. "So he made you a monk, damning your soul to this sham, this blasphemy."

"He didn't damn me to nought. It ain't a sin to pose as a monk." But then a grain of uncertainty crept in. "Is it?"

"Why didn't the archbishop tell me himself?"

"Does he have to make all his decisions through you?"

He raised a brow. "Insolent. You had best watch yourself, Master Tucker."

"It's Brother John, if you don't mind. Why don't you help me if you're so keen to see me leave? The sooner I find out something the sooner I can go. Are there any monks that you think might be suspicious?"

"It's absurd. Of course not. All our brothers are trusted without question—" But as he spoke, a faraway expression intruded on his blushed countenance. He fell silent.

Jack placed his hands on his hips impatiently. "Looks like you ain't all that trusting."

Dom Thomas glared. "Find out what you will. I will not interfere." And he turned on his heel.

"But you'll not help?" Jack called after him.

The monk stopped and pivoted long enough to say, "You seem

to have all well in hand . . . *Brother John,*" and left him alone on the cloister walk.

Jack mumbled a very unclerical curse, and looked around. He didn't know where anything was, where his room might be, even the privies, and he was feeling the need for the latter. He'd have to look about for himself and hope he didn't get into trouble. If he was caught, he'd be able to tell them in all truth that he was lost. One lie at a time, indeed.

Jack made his way through the cloister and came to another door. He slowly pulled it open and saw that it led to another smaller courtyard with a set of huts, trees, grass, and foliage. An old man was hoeing his own little garden, the dark earth turning with his blade. Tall sticks were propped together into a cone shape in anticipation of the young bean tendrils to come.

Taking a swift glance, Jack didn't notice any privies and turned to go when the man looked up. He smiled under a white beard and mustache and lifted an arm with a wave.

Jack turned back and approached. He reckoned the man was a caretaker. Perhaps he might know something.

"Good day to you, young friar," the man said, and rested his hands on his hoe when Jack neared. He did not sound like a caretaker. He sounded more like a man in the manner of Crispin.

"Good day to you, sir." Jack stood with his hands behind his back and surveyed the patch of cultivated ground. "You've been very diligent."

The old man's cheeks flushed. "Why yes. It is now a passion of mine. Such passions are allowed within a monastery." He chuckled.

"Are you— Do you work here? You do not appear to be a monk."

"No, I am no monk. This is my retirement. I live under the care of the good brothers here. I have given up my worldly goods, my estate, to pay to be cared for here under the wings of God."

"I see," said Jack. He looked at the old man with admiration.

"Would you like refreshment?" He leaned the hoe against the side of his rustic cottage wall and ducked as he entered under the low lintel. "Come in," he called from the shadows.

Jack scanned the courtyard for other faces, saw none, and entered after the old man. The cottage was small, only one room, a little larger than Crispin's lodgings in London. The air seemed to sparkle with motes of dust and hay. Shafts of sunlight angled toward the wooden floor, and though it was mean lodgings, it was clean. Shelves and tables lined one wall and Jack was surprised to see them filled with layer upon layer of scrolls and even a few books. He glanced casually at them, noting a few colorful drawings of shields and animals on one open scroll.

"This is far less than I was used to, I assure you," said the old man, pouring ale from a chipped jug into a wooden beaker. "But I can equally assure you, I am content with what I now have."

Jack took the offered beaker and drank hastily. He hadn't realized how dry his throat was.

The old man poured a beaker for himself and drank thoughtfully, eyeing him. Jack lowered his cup. "Forgive me," he bowed. "I am Brother John. I have come to visit Canterbury from the south. But—" He tried on a dramatic expression. "The monks all appear to be anxious about something. I've only just arrived and no one will say."

"Oh." The old man sat on the one chair and offered a stool for Jack. "Yes, great tragedy is here in Canterbury. The monks try to hide it but I see much." He leaned toward Jack and said solemnly, "I do not wish to alarm you, but there have been two murders in the church within the span of two days."

Jack did his best impression of horror. "No! God preserve us!" He crossed himself. "Who?"

The old man shook his head and ran his hand over his white beard. "A prioress, visiting as a pilgrim. And one of our very own monks. He was a young man. About your age." His sincere expression of sorrow brought a lump to Jack's throat.

"How can such a thing happen?"

The man sighed deeply and lifted his yellowed eyes to Jack. "Murder is a terrible thing. But there is something else. The monks have been acting like agitated bees in a skep. Though in truth, much of it began happening before the murders, if I am not mistaken. As an old man, I sometimes confuse recent events with older ones." His eyes traveled and landed on Jack again. He smiled. "I don't know why I am telling you." He sat back and held his cup to his chest. "Perhaps because you remind me of Brother Wilfrid, who was kind to me. Or perhaps because, as a visitor, you have a right to be warned. There is something about the martyr's relics. I am not certain exactly the circumstances, but I know that this mischief concerns them. The strange thing is, there seemed to be a flutter about the martyr's remains well before these deaths. Or perhaps my mind is playing tricks on me."

Jack leaned forward. "What kind of 'flutter'?"

He shook his head and shrugged. "Talk of nothing but. And much whispering when others drew near. I gathered there had been rumors and threats against them."

Jack nodded. "Who do you suppose did it? The murders, I mean."

"Who can say? But I can tell you this; a rumor amongst the brothers owes these deaths to the curse of Becket's bones."

Jack's eyes rounded. "C-curse? I never heard of no curse."

"Becket was killed by four knights. Reginald Fitz-Urse, Hugh de Morville, William de Tracy, and Richard le Breton. Their families were torn apart by their betrayal and foul deed. The men were banished from England, doomed to wander the earth in penance for their sin. Many of their descendants changed their names to avoid association. Even two hundred years later, the stain of their sin remains."

"So . . . what is the curse?"

"No less than calamity to the families of the murderers. And so it happens, that the Prioress, Madam Eglantine was a descendant of Hugh de Morville."

"No! You don't say."

"Indeed. And our own Brother Wilfrid who met with the same fate, his surname was de Tracy."

Jack gasped. His hands trembled when he lifted the beaker to his lips. He drank gratefully, the ale warming his cold chest. "Two of the four. You think this place is cursed, then?"

"Not the monastery or church, no. But the circumstances seem to give truth to events now well out of our control." He sipped the ale, staring into his thoughts until his eyes focused again on Jack. "I told you this only to inform you as to why your fellow monks act as they do. You must forgive them." He smiled, lightening the dark mood threatening the little cottage. "Of course you *can* and *must* forgive. But forgiveness is more difficult in the old." He rubbed his mud-spotted knees. "But you seem very young to be a monk. How old are you, Brother?"

Jack's thoughts furiously spun on the old man's talk of a curse when he suddenly looked up at his open face. Perhaps it was the man's gentle way and soft voice, but Jack didn't want to lie to him more than he already had. "I am . . . thirteen, sir."

"Thirteen! Bless me! It seems they become younger every year."

"Aye, sir."

"You have a way of speaking not unknown to me. From where do you hail?"

"From London, sir."

"Oh yes. But not in its finer halls."

Jack reddened and lowered his face. *Curse my lowly tongue.* "No, sir."

"You must have had a master, then, eh?"

He looked up brightly. The truth came so much easier. He vowed never to lie again. "Aye, sir. A very fine master. He taught me everything. How to read and write Latin, French, and English and even a bit of Greek, though I falter there."

The white brows rose. "Indeed. This is quite the master." He smiled. "You loved him. I can see that in your eyes."

Jack's throat thickened. "Aye, sir."

"So was it he who pushed you into the Church?"

Jack's mouth curled ironically. "That he did, sir. Most strenuously."

"Then he must be proud of you." His eyes glazed again and he tapped a boney finger on the cup. "I loved my master as well. He taught me all I know." Taking a deep breath, he lowered his eyes. "He's been long dead now these two score years. So much time has past. So much we did together. He was like a father to me, for I did not know mine. My sire died when I was quite young and I came to my master a mere whelp of a boy. Was it so with you?"

"Aye, sir. My master took me in . . . when no one else would."

"Then he saw something special in you and cultivated it. It is a rare man who can see beyond the face of things. What is his name?"

Jack stiffened. For once in his life he couldn't think of a plausible lie. His mind simply blanked. The man was staring at him. He couldn't very well stall too long. "You wouldn't know him," he said feebly.

"It isn't likely, is it? Still, I should like to remember him in my prayers."

"Crispin Guest," he gasped aloud, but the moment it left his mouth he thought of Gilbert Langton, the tavernkeeper of Crispin's favorite haunt the Boar's Tusk. Why didn't he use that name?

"Crispin Guest. Crispin Guest. No, it isn't a name that comes immediately to mind."

Jack blew out the breath he was holding.

"My master was William Baldwin. I married his daughter and we had a good life together, though there were no children. She died three years ago." His eyes flicked to a jug of dried flowers. Jack's heart stabbed with the thought of this lonely man cultivating flowers to keep in memory of his dead wife. "I was happy to follow in my master's footsteps, become the man he made. I hope that he smiles down on me from heaven, for surely he is there."

"I am certain that is so," said Jack quietly. Looking at this old man, he couldn't help but feel as if he was peering into his own future. He swallowed more ale before he said, "But sir, you were telling me about the martyr's bones. What is it I should know about them?"

"Alas. I have no proof, but I have every reason to believe they are no longer in the shrine."

Jack blinked. "And why would you say that, sir? What might you have heard or seen that would lead you to reckon it?"

His eyes focused suddenly and sharpened on Jack. "These are personal matters amongst the brothers here. I do not wish to commit the sin of gossipmongering. None of it may have any foundation in fact. And I am a man who lives by such." He rose. It was Jack's cue as well. "I hope you will come back to visit me. You bring to mind very pleasant memories."

"I shall. And I thank you, good sir, for your hospitality." He put the cup on the table and looked up with a pinched expression. "Might I ask one thing more?"

"Of course."

"Do you by any chance know where the privies are?"

ONCE JACK RELIEVED HIMSELF he straightened his cassock and blinked at the shadowed arches that seemed to march away in an infinite redundancy of perfectly designed architecture. "Now where, by Christ, am I?" He scanned the buildings rising above him, but they all looked the same with their buttresses and reticulated windows. Startled at the sound of the bells suddenly tolling, he looked up though he couldn't see the bell tower from where he stood. Bells meant something. They called the monks to prayer and to everything else. It was past noon, so it wasn't the Angelus, but it might just mean dinner.

He lifted his head and tried to follow his nose, but the constant breeze whisking throughout the cloister grounds made finding the kitchens impossible. He shrugged to himself and just started walking. How far could the great hall be? He turned a corner, and as luck would have it, he found several monks heading in the same direction. His belly growled. He hoped they were heading toward the hall. It seemed a long time ago since breakfast.

Some monks greeted him cordially but without speaking, while others eyed him with wide stares and pursed lips. Jack made a mental tally of those faces.

As a herd—or, he supposed, flock—the monks meandered down the long walkways and left the cloister precincts. Jack began to wonder just where they were going when they all entered a large hall and the smell of food touched his senses. A long table at the front of the hall was probably set for the prior. There were many tables and benches perpendicular to the head table. Jack moved slowly forward, uncertain where he was to go when he noticed Father Cyril motioning to him. Gratefully, he picked up his cassock and trotted forward, then slowed when he realized everyone else took on a slower pace.

Cyril motioned for him to stand before an empty wooden plank and Jack turned to watch the rest of the monks file in. There were more than he realized and his heart sank. How was he to question all of these? He'd be stuck here till Doomsday!

Finally, three entered and strode right up to the head table: the prior, another monk that Jack took to be the sub prior, and Dom Thomas. They sat in their places and the prior began by intoning a string of Latin prayers. The assembly crossed themselves, responded, and then all, with the loud scraping of benches on the wooden floor, took their seats. Jack watched the head table as the prior leaned in toward the sub prior and spoke to him. Dom Thomas's glare directed toward Jack. Jack made a dismissing gesture, and looked at his plate and that of his fellow diners. No one spoke a word, and if they needed anything, they made a series of hand gestures to get across their meaning. All over the room was a fluttering of hands and moving cassocks like small dark waves. One monk stepped up onto a raised platform and sat before a lectern. A large book lay open there, and with his finger the monk traced over the page, cleared his throat, and began to read the Latin in a loud, clear voice.

Platters on the table were filled with dried fish, cooked leaks, and hunks of cheese. A small wooden bowl of pottage and a round loaf of barley bread just for him sat before his place. A leather beaker and a jug of ale also stood at the head of his place setting. At least these monks ate well, he thought, and took out his eating knife to stab a fish. He scooped up a handful of leeks and placed it on his plate and took them up in his fingers to chew them down like a rabbit.

He glanced sidelong at Cyril, wishing he could ask a question or two, but plainly, speaking was forbidden during meals. While he ate, he looked at the other diners. Dom Thomas had turned his attention to the prior and sub prior, but when Jack swept his gaze across the hall, a monk sitting close to the head table seemed to be staring at him. Brother Martin. He scrutinized Jack with narrowed eyes, and Jack worried the monk might recognize him. The monk squinted at him a bit longer, and then turned to his meal.

Jack concentrated on eating slowly. He wished the monk would stop reading. His low drone was annoying, like the buzz of an insect. He tried to ignore it, and when he did, surrounded by all these silent diners in their cassocks, his mind unbidden lit on the young nun, Dame Marguerite.

Never had he met a more refined and gentle lady. And so beautiful. Her hands were delicate and her face had the look of a stone saint. He reckoned she was his age or a few years older. When she talked to him, she used a soft voice with demure eyes always aimed downward. He wished she would look up more often because those eyes were very dark and sympathetic. Crispin didn't like his talking to her, but he didn't care. Didn't Master Crispin say Jack had a choice to obey him or not? Though probably not in all things. Still, the saying of it was easier than the doing of it. He still felt obligated to the man who rescued him from Newgate Prison and gave him a decent life.

He sighed, thinking of Dame Marguerite. *Marguerite.* When he got out of this monastery, he vowed to speak to her, tell her how he felt. Perhaps she really didn't want to be a nun anymore. His brow wrinkled. Was a body allowed to stop being a nun? He wasn't certain. He could make her forget the horror of the murder, take her back to London, and then . . . Then what? Crispin paid him a wage but it wasn't very much. He sipped his beer and rested his arm on the table. Wasn't he getting ahead of himself? First things first. He'd have to talk to her.

Benches scraped back and Jack looked up alarmed. The meal was over and the monks were standing for their benediction. Jack scrambled to his feet and bowed his head, looking up through his fringe at the others. The monks filed out and Jack followed, staying close to Cyril. He stood outside the hall and Brother Martin skirted past him, eyeing Jack the whole time.

Cyril, too, watched Martin go. "Oaf," murmured Cyril under his breath. Jack whipped his head around to stare at the man, who shrugged. "So he is."

The monk moved on back to the cloister and Jack followed. "I thought fellow monks always spoke well of each other."

Cyril exhaled a snorting laugh. "We live in close proximity for all the years of our lives. There's only so much forgiveness to share. As Benedictines we are not allowed to traipse all over the countryside as you and your Franciscan brothers do." He looked at Jack's expression and patted his shoulder. "Don't vex yourself, Little Friar. We live in relative harmony. It's just that some of us are more harmonious than others."

The monks seemed to mill about and Jack guessed this was the time of day for leisure, since the rest of the monk's day was devoted to prayer and work. "Father Cyril," Jack ventured. "I have heard the rumors—"

"Bless me, but I brace myself."

"Well, that there is something amiss with the martyr's bones."

Cyril stopped and suddenly grabbed Jack and dragged him into the shadows. "Best not to say these rumors too loud, Friar."

"Brother John," muttered Jack.

The monk nodded disinterestedly. "As you will."

"But I heard that they may no longer be in the shrine. Is this true?"

Cyril sighed and kept an eye peeled for anyone who might overhear them. "I fear it is."

"How can we find them?"

"His Excellency has hired a man from London. A sour-looking fellow named Crispin Guest. Though I do not know why the archbishop should put his trust in a traitor."

Jack clenched his fists and kept them at his sides. "Traitor, Brother?"

"That's what I hear. I do not know much about him. The other monks do not trust him."

"Because he is a traitor?" Jack sputtered on the word.

"No, because he used to be the duke of Lancaster's man. The duke is said to be a Lollard sympathizer. For the most part, my fellow brothers would have great objections to helping such a man. But there may be one or two . . . well. Perhaps I have spoken too much already. I think the ale has gone to my head. I should go to the privy."

"I will go with you." Jack walked alongside him, occasionally passing other monks along the way. "If the monks do not trust this man Guest, why did the archbishop hire him?"

Cyril gave another snorting laugh. "Why indeed!"

"I do not get your meaning, Brother."

"Well, it's just a curiosity, isn't it, that he hired this fellow to guard the bones and the moment he arrived they disappeared. And then the murders."

"Do you think it the curse?"

They reached the privy stalls and Cyril hitched up his cassock. Jack did likewise beside him. "Oh ho! You've been talking to Edward Harper."

"Who?"

"Our pensioner."

"Oh. Is that his name?"

"He holds great store by family curses. I fear certain monks have given him notions." He finished his business and washed his hands in a nearby bucket, shaking them out.

"Who was the monk who was killed?"

Cyril took a deep breath and his face fell to a solemn configuration. "Young Wilfrid. The horror of it." He crossed himself. "He was the treasurer's assistant. You might have met the treasurer in the prior's lodge."

"Aye, we've met."

He gauged Jack's expression. "Yes, I see you have. Wilfrid was Dom Thomas's assistant. They had many secrets, those two. But I do not think poor Wilfrid was up to the task. Perhaps in time and with more experience. But alas."

"Not up to what task, Brother?"

Cyril smiled and continued through the cloister. "You are a very curious fellow. It does not do well to ask too many questions here. My brothers keep a closed lip."

Jack put on a merrier face. "I am a traveling friar, Father Cyril. I am more used to a loosened tongue, I fear. You must pardon me if I seem to ask too much."

He patted Jack's shoulder again. "I do not fear your questions. It is good to talk to someone new."

"I wonder, Brother, if you can direct me to my quarters. Dom Thomas neglected to tell me where they are."

"I'll show you." He took Jack through a door and down a long, dark corridor lined with many cell doors. He went to the last one and opened the door. Jack peered in at the dismal surroundings, not much better than a cell in Newgate. A bare cot, a fireplace, a tiny window, a shelf, a table with a stool, and a crucifix on the wall.

Jack brought up a smile. "It's wonderful," he said weakly.

Cyril's drooping lids rose only momentarily. "Is it? You must come from a very poor place indeed."

"Father Cyril—"

"Sorry, Friar, but I must return to my work now. Sit next to me at the Divine Office at None. That place is empty now. It belonged to Brother Wilfrid."

He bowed to Jack, stuffed his hands within his scapular, and trudged away. Jack turned to the cold little room and shuffled to the stool. He sat and stared into the dead hearth. So far, he'd found out a few things. One: No one there trusted Crispin, and in fact, all wondered why he was even called to Canterbury. Two: There was still some hidden secret among the brothers. And three: Brother Martin might prove to be a problem. Tricky business, this tracking.

12

CRISPIN AWAKENED IN A strange bed, his face buried in long strands of brown hair. Hand resting on a plump, pink hip, he paused, thinking about it for a moment before he remembered. He snaked his hand around her thick waist and nuzzled the back of her neck. A female moan emerged from the cloud of hair, and she turned over to look him in the eye. She smiled and sighed lustily, stretching her arms up around his neck. "Crispin Guest," she purred.

"Ah, so you remember me."

"Very well indeed."

"And you are Alyson, as I recall."

"Mmm."

"The both of us had a bit to drink last night."

"We managed quite well anyway. Several times."

He smiled. "So we did."

"That's why I prefer a younger man. More stamina! 'Rejoice O young man, in thy youth!' I shall never marry a man my age again. Only younger men."

"'Men'?"

"Five times a widow now, Crispin. I expect there will be more than one husband hence."

He rolled to his back and pillowed his head in his intertwined fingers. "Perhaps you wear them out."

She laughed. Her ample breasts shook and he watched them. "Perhaps I do." She drew the blankets to cover her chest and propped herself against the wall. "But at least it takes our mind off our troubles, if only for a while."

"Yes." He shifted upward and leaned against the wall beside her.

Her gaze was sympathetic. "Is this the normal course of things during an inquiry? This waiting. Searching. Worrying."

He breathed deeply. "Yes. Especially when murder is involved. The culprit rarely confesses. And I must use all means and cunning to ferret him out."

She crossed her arms over her chest. "Do you truly think the culprit is Sir Philip?"

He laid his head back against the wall and stared up at the beams. "I know he has something to do with it. Blood is on his hands, I am certain. As for the rest, I am puzzled."

"The rest?"

Crispin nearly spoke of the missing relics but caught himself. He said nothing instead and let his lids fall closed.

"And what of your friend Chaucer?"

He snapped open his eyes. "Geoffrey," he breathed. "I . . . I must arrest him when he shows himself again."

"Arrest him? Lancaster's poet? Whatever for?"

"Murder," he growled.

Alyson shifted upward. "Murder?"

"Geoffrey's dagger was found in the neck of Brother Wilfrid. He must face the sheriff and explain it."

She leaned toward him. He felt her radiating warmth and all

he wanted to do was sink down into the mattress again and wrap his limbs around her. The smell of their coupling was strong within the bestirred sheets. His eyes roved longingly over her bare, white shoulders and décolletage. "Do you believe he did it?" she asked softly.

"No. I can't imagine it. But it *was* his knife. And he had the opportunity. And he *is* hiding something." He stared at the blankets for a moment before he threw them off and stood up. He retrieved his stockings, still tied to his braies, and slipped them on one at a time, drawing them up. He shrugged into his shirt and searched for his coat.

"I'm sorry you have to leave," she said, still clutching the sheets to her bosom.

He grabbed his coat from under the bed, dug an arm into a sleeve, and glanced back at her. He offered a crooked smile. "I'll be back. Will I be welcome?"

"Most heartily," she said. She smiled broadly, revealing her gat-toothed grin.

Buttoning his coat, he leaned over the bed and kissed her, tasting her generous mouth. It was soft and moist. "Bath must be a very accommodating city. I must visit it sometime."

"You would be welcome there, too."

He made his farewells and left, standing outside Alyson's room a long time. Finally, he stared down the gallery toward Bonefey's room and decided to pay him another visit, despite the early hour. Raising his fist, he pounded on the door. He heard grumbling and shuffling and then the bolt was thrown. Bonefey's squinting face appeared when the door opened a slit and then his eye widened when he saw who it was. Crispin stuck his foot in before Bonefey could slam the door. He pushed the door open and backed the man to his bed where he stumbled and fell onto it. "Where's your sword now?"

Bonefey's eyes darted to the chair where his clothes and scabbard lay.

Crispin smiled. "Mind if I look at your dagger?" He went to the pile of clothes and pulled forth the dagger, examining the blade. Good condition. Very sharp. He was tempted to toss it in the coals on the fire but resisted and instead sheathed it again and tossed the belt aside.

Bonefey trembled with fury. "Your insolence, knave, will cost you."

He spared him only a glance. "I doubt that."

Grasping the chair with Bonefey's sword and clothes, he tipped it, dumping its contents to the floor. Setting it upright, he sat and studied Bonefey. "Tell me your exact whereabouts the night the Prioress was slain."

"I will do no such thing."

Staring for a moment at Bonefey's hairy, bandy legs below his long chemise, he drew a breath, then pulled his dagger free from its sheath and looked the Franklin in the eye. "I don't believe in wasted time, Sir Philip. I mean to get my information. By any means necessary."

Bonefey's eyes grew to great white-edged disks. "What do you mean to do with that?"

"Whatever I need to. Now, I suggest you start talking."

Bonefey never took his eyes from Crispin's sharp blade. "I . . . I was here. At the inn. The whole time."

"Witnesses?"

"Everyone! They all saw me. I never left."

Crispin frowned. "Surely a moment to go to the privy?"

"Perhaps, but not for more than a few moments."

"That's all it would take."

Bonefey's hands began to tremble.

"What about last night?" he asked.

Bonefey stared at the blade. "I won't say anymore. You are mad."

He rose. "I won't ask a second time."

Bonefey rolled off the bed to the other side. "Help! Help! Murder! He's murdering me!"

"Oh be still, you coward!"

But it worked. Soon fists pounded on the door and men rushed into the room. Crispin slammed his blade into its sheath and turned to face Harry Bailey and Edwin Gough, the Miller. "Master Crispin!" cried Bailey. "What goes on here?"

"I am merely interrogating this man."

"Interrogating?" Bailey and Gough both looked to the disheveled and underdressed Bonefey and to Crispin, his hand resting on his knife hilt.

"A murder inquiry is a serious undertaking, Master Bailey. I will get little out of him now. But see to it that he doesn't leave his room. I'll have more to say to him later."

"You can't keep me a prisoner here, Guest. And Bailey and Gough had better not threaten me. I shall take you to the courts. I shall own the Tabard Inn when I am through with you, Bailey."

Bailey looked worried.

"Empty threats," said Crispin, but he could tell Bonefey's intimidation was working. Damn the man to the lowest level of hell! "Do what you can," he muttered to Bailey and pushed past him out the door.

He stopped in the gallery and stared down the stairs. The innkeeper stood at the bottom looking up, a pitchfork in his hands. "A false alarm," Crispin called down to the man. "All is well."

The innkeeper sighed and lowered the fork. The man went back to his room but Crispin stood as he was, thinking. *All is not well.* He looked back at Bonefey's closed door, heard him argue in a loud voice with Bailey and a drunken Gough, and shook his head. Chaucer's room was the next door down. He pulled his jacket to straighten it, strode up to the door, and knocked.

Nothing.

It was almost a relief. He knocked again just to be certain and he was greeted by silence. He tested the door and was surprised to find it unlocked. Carefully he pushed it all the way open and quickly glanced around. No Geoffrey.

He stepped in. The room was neat. Geoffrey's fire was covered with fine ashes and his toiletries were laid in a line. Parchment and quills were set in perfect order on the table: used parchment in an exact pile on one side, unused on another. He remembered Geoffrey being meticulous but he seemed to have become even more so over the years.

He drew close to the chest and exhaled a long breath before he knelt and opened the lid. Inside, his extra coats and gowns all folded; braies rolled alongside rolled stockings. And an extra pair of long-toed poulaines lay atop them all, their exaggerated tips curled up against the wall of the chest. Crispin dug down and found a red, ankle-length gown. His heart burned with a wash of heat when he saw the color. It was close. Very close. He dragged it from the chest and laid it on the bed. His breathing quickened as he carefully folded over each pleat of the hem, going slowly over every inch of it. And then—

His breath caught. A tear. A square hole torn from the fabric. His hands trembled as he reached into his pouch and withdrew the scrap of cloth. He knew it long before he ever laid it over the tear. It fit perfectly.

"What by all the devils are you doing!"

Crispin whirled. Geoffrey stood in the doorway clutching the doorposts. His eyes were dark with menace.

Crispin rose to his full height and faced Geoffrey. He felt as if a leaden ball sat in his stomach while a knife pierced his heart. "Geoffrey Chaucer. You must accompany me to the Lord Sheriff. You are charged with the murder of the monk Wilfrid."

13

JACK AWOKE EARLY THE next morning with a start and leapt up from his bed. Bells. Constant bells. It was unnerving. He looked at the small window but saw that it was still dark. What the hell?

He went to the bucket and washed his face with the icy water and wiped his nose and cheeks on his sleeve. He remembered now. Monks rose before the sun to pray the Divine Office. He shook himself fully awake and opened the heavy door with a creak. He poked his head out and saw the sleepy monks meander toward the quire.

He joined them, using the same sleepy stride they used. *Bunch of sarding sheep.* He followed them into the dark church. The only light came from candles set on either end of the quire stalls, where the monks followed their chantry in their books. Jack made his way to Wilfrid's old chair, feeling a bit guilty for using it thus, and looked up curtly at Cyril who seemed to be dozing. They all stood when the prior took his place at the head and then the chanting began. Jack cringed at it. It echoed all around him. He did not think it possible to fill the space within the hulking cathedral, but it did. Unearthly. Magical. He listened, forgetting he was supposed to be participating, yet he could not have if he tried. The notes followed their own pattern, like a path through a forest, meandering this way and that, finding alternating sunshine and shadow, cool and warm. The beauty of it struck him deeply in his heart. He did not know such feelings were within him. He was glad they were. He felt God's presence in the music and the words and he understood then, for at least that moment, why a man would wish to become a monk.

By the time the Office was complete, it was time for their meal. Jack wanted to ask more questions of Cyril but he took his cue from the others and did not talk unless they talked first. And now they were going to another silent meal. Frustrated, Jack ate and drank down his beer as if by his hurrying he could hurry along the others. Finally, the silent time was over and they shuffled outside the hall to their separate tasks. Jack got separated from Cyril and tried to spy him among all the identical cassocks. *Like a needle in a haystack.* He stretched up on his toes to look above the cowled heads when an arm tugged him against the wall.

Jack looked up into the pointed face of Brother Martin. "Don't I know you?" asked the monk.

Jack shook his head vigorously. "Oh no, Brother. I don't see how."

His eyes roved over Jack's face thoughtfully. "What monastery are you from?"

"Oh . . . er . . . do you know Saint Michael's in Suffolk?"

"Why yes, I do."

"Well I'm not from there," he said quickly. "I'm from a very small friary south of there. You wouldn't know it."

"Still, you have a familiar look about you."

He smiled. "I have that kind of face."

Martin sneered. "I do not know why you stay. Hasn't anyone told you? If you've come to see the martyr's relics, they are gone." His expression was far from one Jack expected. He seemed almost . . . glad.

Jack decided to play his hand. "So I heard. Truth to tell, is it not better for the common folk if such things were not here to tempt them to spend their hard-earned wage?"

Martin raised his chin. A few hairs bristled there where his razor missed. "You have a shrewd head, Friar. But I would not mouth such sentiments"—he looked over his shoulder—"so freely."

He shrugged. "I am not learned in such things, so maybe I am in error. For it does seem to give them comfort—"

"They should find their comfort in God. His only Son sacrificed Himself for us to offer the comfort of Heaven. Should that not be enough?"

"But so, too, did Thomas à Becket sacrifice himself for the love of the Church, Brother. Is that not a good example? Is that not why we venerate the saints?"

"We venerate, yes. But a saint is not God. And some would place their precious saints before the worship of the Almighty. I have seen it too many times, Brother. It sickens me. And this monastery is the worst of the lot. Thomas à Becket has become little better than a slab of meat hanging in a butcher's stall. The best cut goes to the richest and therefore the least deserving. I rue the day I chose this place and not some humbler institution. But youth," he said, eyes glaring at Jack, "is flawed."

That was an earful if ever Jack heard one. "Er, well . . ." He didn't quite know how to respond but he didn't need to. Martin narrowed his eyes at Jack and released him.

"I have my work to do." He offered one more backward glance and scurried away, boots slapping the stone.

"And *I* have found my Lollard," Jack whispered. He allowed Martin to get ahead of him and shadowed his steps.

Martin hurried forward. Jack held back, unseen by his quarry but keeping him within sight. The monk moved with purpose and it soon became very apparent that the man was headed into the church. Jack hid behind a column. Martin entered the church door and it closed after him. Jack scuttled forward. He waited another beat before he grasped the handle and pulled the heavy door open. He allowed his eyes to adjust to the dim surroundings but used his ears and turned his head to the left. He heard Martin's frantic footfalls and pursued, careful to keep his own steps quiet and to stay to the shadows or behind pillars.

The church was otherwise quiet. The artists painting the stone runners and ceilings had not yet arrived. Nor was the furious pounding from the masons shattering the still of the cold interior. Just Martin's footsteps . . . except . . .

Jack slowed and Martin's steps, too, faltered.

Whispering. Two men were talking somewhere in the cathedral. The sounds—their sibilants hissing into the canopy of stone above—rushed here and there. It could have been coming from the quire as much as the sanctuary. But no. It was down there in the nave, Jack was certain of it. But where was Martin?

He heard the soft slip of a shoe on the floor. Yes. There he was. Crispin was fond of telling Jack that whispers never boded well.

He slipped back behind the gates of the quire and made his way past it. He cocked an eye back and saw Martin several pillars down, listening. Jack hurried as quietly as he could, catching an occasional glance at Martin through the pillars and tall seats of the quire as he shot past. Finally, the whispers were closer and he slid his way forward. He crouched down behind a thick stone column abutting scaffolding.

Dom Thomas Chillenden was there and his exasperated whispers were directed to a burly man Jack recognized as one of the stone masons. Jack leaned against the column, trying to sift the echoes from the hushed voices.

Dom Thomas raised a small sack in his hand and reached in. He pulled out several gold pieces that made Jack nearly salivate, and the monk thrust them into the mason's hands. "There!" said Chillenden with a sneer. "Is this not what you asked for?"

The mason looked at the gold in his hand and considered. "Aye. It is a goodly sum."

"Is it enough for your silence? I have had enough of your innuendos."

The mason closed his large hand over the coins and rocked his fist as if weighing them. "My silence, Brother? But of course." There was more amusement in his voice than commitment.

"Master Nigel." He moved closer to the man and looked as large and as threatening as he could, though he stood several inches shorter than the broad-shouldered mason. "I will make no more payments. I had your word that this was the final sum. The archbishop will become suspicious."

The mason chuckled and tucked the gold into the money pouch hanging from his thick leather belt. "I gave you my word, sir, and it is my bond."

"Your bond!" the monk sniffed. "Extortion comes with honor, does it?"

"I gave you my word," the mason said loudly. The monk looked around worriedly. "But I'd like to know who's the more dishonest, *Brother*: the man who committed the crime"—and he pointed a stubby finger at the monk's chest—"or the man who witnessed it," and he thumbed his own. "Fear not. I will not reveal your sins, for you have paid right well for my silence. You have only God to contend with you now." He straightened his leather tunic, gave the monk a derisive snort, and turned his back on him.

Dom Thomas stood frozen and watched him leave before he seemed to snap out of his torpor and spun on his heel. His quick steps soon disappeared.

Jack slumped against the cold stone and slapped his hand over his mouth, for surely he'd blaspheme himself in the church if he allowed himself to speak. What had he just heard? Dom Thomas was guilty of something. Was it murder? "Jesus preserve us," he whispered. A monk. Guilty of murder. Of Brother Wilfrid's? It was almost too much to bear. How could he face him again? He had to get out of the monastery and soon!

He forgot all about Brother Martin as he left the church. He needed to get out and tell Crispin all he had heard. Preoccupied with his thoughts he never noticed Edward Harper until he smacked into him.

"Oh! Master Harper!"

Harper steadied Jack with a smile. But Jack's thoughts were still of murder and he looked back anxiously over his shoulder toward the church. "You're up early, Master Harper."

"There is no reason not to rise with the sun. And sloth in a monastery is not to be borne."

"But you are a pensioner." He tried a smile in answer to Harper's raised brows. "I talked to Father Cyril. It was he who told me your name."

But Harper must have noticed Jack's demeanor for he moved forward and touched his shoulder. "Brother John? You look ill. Come. Some refreshment may revive you."

"I would be pleased," he said distractedly. Reluctantly, Jack followed the man back to his mean lodgings and entered the little hut. Harper searched for a cup and Jack leaned against the table, fidgeting with the curled parchments and books. His eyes glanced lists of names, charts, long descriptions in French going on about something he didn't quite understand, like a code. He snapped up his head when Harper brought him a cup.

"Now tell me," said Harper. "What troubles you?"

Jack paused. *Well, I think one of the monks here is a murderer.* No, that would never do. He realized he would have to lie again. Harper was like Crispin. Maybe he could help Jack better understand the circumstances. "I have traveled far and wide, to many a monastery," said Jack carefully. "But I have never been to a cloister where its monks had, well, heretical leanings."

"Never? I find that hard to believe."

"Well, some not so obvious. But here, well. To put it another way," he whispered, "I think there is a fox in the henhouse."

Harper pulled an indulgent smile and sat with his cup. "Indeed. And what heresy does this fox bark?"

He could think of a number of things, but the only one he could speak aloud he did. "I think he's a Lollard."

Harper's smile froze and gradually faded. "Truly? What makes you say so?"

"Well then. He didn't seem to think that the missing relics were all that bad a thing."

He nodded and drank, measuring Jack over the rim of the cup. "Why do you suppose he said that to you?"

"Well, I don't know. Perhaps because it is easier saying such to a stranger."

"Perhaps. Still, I think I know of whom you speak."

"You do?"

"Was this Brother Martin, by any chance?"

Jack rose in his seat. "Aye! You've heard him, then?"

"He is most indiscreet. I do not blame a man for a conscience, but a man who takes vows should show more loyalty."

Jack nodded and wiped the beer froth from his lips with his sleeve. "To me, loyalty is a sacred thing."

"Indeed? Then I wonder . . ." Harper glanced at his parchments and looked back at Jack. He seemed to be deciding something. "Never mind. I must be getting back to my garden, as you must be getting back to your prayers."

Jack put down his empty cup and headed for the door before he slowed down. "Master. What would make a man . . . commit murder?"

Harper studied Jack a moment. "Surely it is the Devil that puts a man to such treachery. Ever since Cain slew Abel, Mankind has been so cursed. Who but God is ever certain what lies in a man's heart."

Jack remembered a similar discussion with Crispin. Slowly, he said, "But did not Cain kill Abel because of his heart's sadness? Because the Almighty was not as pleased by his gifts as he was with Abel's? A man's heart, then, seems to be a fragile thing, not necessarily a thing of sin."

Harper laid his hand on Jack's shoulder. "That is a very compassionate assessment. Perhaps you should consider the priesthood, young man."

Jack backed away. "Oh no! Not for me! I ain't worthy of that!"

"Certainly men of less worth have taken vows."

Jack scanned the planes of Harper's face, the crags of wrinkles and lines, the ruddy windswept complexion, and considered that this man would have done well as a priest, too, except for all his dabbling in his books and strange parchments. Jack turned toward the colorful drawings and all the lines connecting them. He even raised his hand and ran a finger along the leaf of a book lying open. "Master Harper, I wonder if you can tell me again the names of Becket's murderers."

Harper raised his white brows. "Of course. Hugh de Morville, Reginald Fitz-Urse, William de Tracy, and Richard le Breton."

Jack shook his head. "There's something about them names. It's all familiar to me."

"Surely you have heard them many times before. Who does not know the story of the sainted martyr?"

"Aye. But the names. You've got me vexed about this curse, sure enough, master. It's got me to thinking."

"Well, don't let it distract you too much from your duties. Wilfrid was also fond of spending time with me, much to the consternation of Dom Thomas. I would not see you in similar straights."

"Never fear for me, master. I owe no allegiance to Dom Thomas."

He nodded. "Will I see you tomorrow, Little Friar?"

"No, good sir. I think this will be our farewell. I hope to leave this afternoon."

"So soon?"

"Well, with no relics to see it is hardly worth the stay. You see, I am no Lollard."

"Nor am I. I have seen for myself the power of relics."

"As have I. If only my former master were as convinced."

"He is not a Lollard sympathizer by any chance?"

"Oh no, sir. But he has had his fair share of relics and they are sore trying to him. Er . . ." Jack realized too late that he'd spoken too much yet again. "Well, I must take my leave. God be with you, master."

"And with you."

Jack made his way back to the main cloister and saw Cyril across the greensward. He hurried to him with a greeting.

"Brother John."

"Father Cyril. Where might I find Dom Thomas?"

DOM THOMAS CHILLENDEN REFUSED to look up from his books, taking his time carefully scrawling numbers into columns. Jack rocked on his feet, staring at the monk's bushy brows, his fringe of hair, his gnarled fingers curled around the goose quill. The treasurer had him standing there a long time. Jack wondered how much longer. He didn't feel it his place to confront the monk, and indeed, if he were a murderer, he'd rather Crispin do the honors. But he must complete his duty so that he could report back to his master. "There are important matters I would discuss with you, Dom Thomas," he said tightly.

The monk's eyes looked up. Slowly, he laid his quill aside, folded his hands before him, and raised his chin. "Very well, then. Go on."

Flustered suddenly at the attention, Jack adjusted his cincture and pulled at the yoke of his cassock. "First of all, I think I have discovered the identity of your Lollard."

The brows rose. "Have you? That was quick work, *Brother John*."

"There's no need for that," said Jack with a scowl. "We know who I am. I'd 'a thought you'd be interested to know who the heretic was amongst you. Makes me think that maybe he ain't the only one."

Dom Thomas snapped to his feet. Jack cringed back. "You insolent cur! If you did not have the protection of the archbishop I should strike you down!"

"Now that ain't very Christian, is it?" Jack strained to get his breath under control and pasted on a confident sneer. "What makes you so angry?"

Thomas pushed at his books so violently they skidded across the table. He tramped forward and came to rest a foot from Jack, his nostrils flaring, fists tight to his sides. "Because I have known of these difficulties for quite some time and my pleas for help have gone unanswered. Until now. Now suddenly the archbishop acquiesces to my wishes. Why? I can only speculate and none of it bodes well."

Jack drew back. He expected an outburst, just not one with those sentiments. "So . . . *you* knew there was a Lollard here undermining the shrine?"

"Yes," he hissed. He eyed Jack with a deepening scowl. "And I don't need the lackey of the likes of Crispin Guest telling me my job."

"I ain't—I'm *not* telling you your job. I am merely doing mine. Do you wish to know or not?"

Dom Thomas sighed deeply and lowered his head. "Yes."

Jack moved closer and spoke in a conspiratorial murmur, "It is Brother Martin."

The monk's face blotched with fury. "I know that! Do you think I'm a complete fool?"

Jack's jaw dropped several inches. "If you knew that then why didn't you do anything about it?"

"What could I do? He is a good worker. He makes no trouble. For the most part, he has kept his opinions to himself, though lately I have noticed his becoming more vocal on . . . certain topics."

"Like the martyr's bones, perchance? And his stealing them away? What about murder? Does that warrant your attention?" Jack hoped to provoke a reaction and kept his hand on his dagger just in case.

The fury on the monk's face subsided and in fact drained of

color. His eyes drew on a sunken, forlorn appearance. He collapsed on the edge of his table, arms hanging limply. "No," he whispered. "I refuse to believe he had anything to do with these deaths. Least of all for Brother Wilfrid's." He raked his hand over his eyes.

Again, Dom Thomas did not react as Jack expected. If speaking of murder did not make Dom Thomas wrought with denials, then what was behind that scene in the church?

Jack lowered his hand from his knife and softly offered, "I have learned through these last two years with my master that anyone can be under suspicion. Perhaps something has changed in Brother Martin to force his hand."

Thomas shook his head and then stopped. "There was something last year. He was one of several monks to accompany the archbishop."

"Where?"

"To oversee a trial."

"God blind me!" Jack straightened. "I'll wager my last farthing I know which trial that was!" He ran to the door, grabbed the ring and paused. "Oh! I almost forgot. Why is it the monks here don't trust my master?"

Dom Thomas seemed to have recovered himself and his half-closed lids and customary snarl returned. "Because he is a Lollard sympathizer."

"Where'd you get that fool notion? He isn't. He's just a . . . a thoughtful man. Likes to ponder new ideas. It was the duke that was the Lollard and my master ain't—*isn't* in the duke's retinue no more. But my master *is* a friend of Saint Thomas, of that you can be certain. He came here to root out the evil, not sanction it."

Something flickered in Dom Thomas's eyes and then disappeared again. "That has yet to be proved."

Jack started to make a gesture, but dropped his hand. He

shook his head, trying to keep his anger in check. "You're the fool. *He's* not the one harboring secrets. What was it anyway that got Wilfrid so upset that he wanted to come to my master and tell him?"

The monk lurched forward. "*What?*"

Jack's hand was on his scabbard again. "Before he died, Wilfrid was frightened. Not just of—" He almost said "Geoffrey Chaucer" but decided against it. "He was frightened of something in the monastery. Something Edward Harper said was too much for him to keep secret. What did you have him do?"

"I think it time you leave."

"Answer the question!"

He drew himself up. "I am not required to answer to *you*! Begone, I say."

"Very well. I leave this monastery still suspicious of certain persons," and he screwed his eye and aimed it at the monk.

"Wait! You can't leave in the middle of the day like this. Mass is in an hour. You must stay for the sacrament or it will appear suspicious."

Jack stopped at the doorway. "Mass?"

"Yes." A thought seemed to have occurred to the monk that lightened his mood. Jack was instantly wary. "And to properly receive the communion bread," Thomas continued, "you must be shriven."

Jack blanched. "Sh-shriven?"

Dom Thomas smiled. The bit was in the other's mouth now. "Yes. I suggest you go to Father Cyril since you seem so keen on him."

"Now wait—"

"Will you take the Host with the sin of deception on your heart? Surely damnation is not your preference."

Jack wobbled on the balls of his feet. "I—" It had been a while since he'd received the holy bread. And longer since he went to confession. But with Dom Thomas suddenly looking more authoritative—even for a criminal—Jack did not feel he was at liberty to argue. He shuffled out of the treasurer's office and wandered down the breezy cloister. He asked a monk where he might find Father Cyril and was informed that he was shriving in the sacristy, and after finding out where *that* was, Jack made a reluctant trudge toward the church.

He peered into the dark sacristy lit only by a tall window. "Father Cyril? Father Cyril?"

Cyril poked his head from behind a screen. "Brother John? Have you come to be shriven?"

"Aye. It— Aye." He shuffled forward and took a seat opposite the screen, pulling the scratchy yoke of his cassock away from his throat. He sat a long time in silence, looking up at the dusky vaulted ceiling and waiting for doom to descend. Couldn't he just leave or would it draw too much suspicion on an already jittery monastery?

"Brother?" ventured Cyril after a pause. "Of what sins would you be shriven?"

Jack dug his fingers into his thighs. How could he confess that he was living a lie for the past two days, deceiving everyone he met? But how could he receive the sacrament if he lied in confession? *Hell for certain.* He shook his head and even jerked up from his seat to leave, but stopped and eased back down.

"Well, I have been lying, Father."

"Oh? In what way?"

"In every way. But I can't . . . I can't tell you."

Cyril sighed heavily through the screen. "If you cannot tell me I cannot absolve you."

"I know. That is a problem. But if it is any solace, I am lying for a good reason."

"One cannot sin to do good. It is against God's law."

"It is, is it?" Jack bit his lip. He slid to the edge of his seat and bent over. "If only I could tell you and you couldn't tell no one."

"But of course, Brother John. You of all people must very well know that the sacramental seal binds me. I can never tell a living soul, or suffer great consequences."

"Oh. I . . . forgot." Jack swallowed hard. "Well then, you're certain I can tell you anything and you can't say aught?"

"Yes. Quite certain."

"Not even to the archbishop?"

"Certainly not the archbishop. No one. No matter what you confessed." He peered around the screen again. "Are things done differently in Suffolk?"

"No, Brother. Father." *Hell.* "Right, then." Cyril withdrew again, his shadow bobbing slightly on the wooden screen. "I've . . . I've been lying . . . about who I am. I ain't truly a monk at all. I'm the apprentice of Crispin Guest who's investigating the murders and theft of the saint's bones. He sent me here to spy on the lot of you."

Cyril's head slowly emerged from behind the screen again. His eyes were as wide as they could go. Jack glared at him. "Ain't you supposed to be *behind* the screen?" he whispered.

Cyril ducked back and made some sounds until he finally asked in a hoarse voice. "Are you quite certain?"

"Of course I'm certain! I'm no sarding monk! Beggin' your pardon. I didn't mean to lie but me master begged me do it and it was to discover a murderer and thief and all. I reckon God could forgive that. Can't He?"

Cyril was silent. Jack shifted on his chair and stretched his neck trying to peer over the screen. "Cyril . . . Father?"

"Just wait a moment." Cyril made some more sounds as if he were praying. Finally he intoned, "You . . . you must perform an act of Christian charity, remain on only bread and water for three days, and, er, make a donation to the monastery for your deceit."

"Aye, sir."

Cyril muttered under his breath before he said in something of a flurry, "*Et ego te absolvo a peccatis tuis in nomine Patris, et Filii, et Spiritus Sancti.*"

Jack crossed himself. "Amen."

The monk peered around the screen again. "How long do you plan to stay?"

"Only till after Mass. I *am* sorry for deceiving you, Father Cyril. Truly."

"Hmph! You don't suspect me, do you?" said Cyril

"Oh no! You don't seem guilty of aught to me." He tried to smile.

Cyril made a hasty cross over Jack and ducked away again.

Jack rose and walked uncertainly toward the door. He reached the sacristy's entrance and paused. "Well, farewell, then."

All he saw was Cyril's hand waving from the edge of the screen. "Yes, yes. God be with you. Now go."

"I'm going," he muttered.

When the bells were rung again (*too many sarding bells*) Jack took his place in the chapter house, the church no longer being fit for Mass. He sat next to Cyril's place but the monk was singing the Mass with the old prior, who, with trembling hands, consecrated the Hosts along with the other priest monks. Jack partook with a relatively clear conscience. He slipped a glance at Dom Thomas silently praying in his stall before Cyril returned to his own seat by Jack, eyeing him fitfully.

After Mass he said his good-byes and had almost reached the

door when Dom Thomas, approaching in great rolling strides, stopped him. "Why, Brother John. You must have been long on the road. For shame. You have neglected your tonsure."

"My what?" His hand grabbed for the scalp of his head. The crowns of all the monks' heads were shaved bald, denoting their purity. Jack's was still vigorous with ginger curls.

"But we can help you." He took hold of Jack's arm and grasped it tightly. "How hospitable would we appear if we did not barber you before you depart?"

"Oh, don't trouble yourself, Brother," he said, trying to pull away, but the monk's iron grip of his arm made that impossible. "I'll attend to it as soon as I might."

"No trouble. Brother Matthew here can do the job. Bring a bowl and razor, won't you, Brother Matthew?"

Jack turned a scathing glare on Dom Thomas, but the monk's lips only curled up into a triumphant smile.

14

CRISPIN COULD THINK OF nowhere to take Chaucer but to
the archbishop's lodge where a monk was dispatched to bring the
sheriff. Chaucer scowled and said nothing, but Crispin was grateful his friend had gone with him without protest. He truly didn't
think he knew what he would have done had Chaucer fought the
situation.

The sheriff of county Kent, Thomas Brokhull, happened to be
in Canterbury, and he would arrive in an hour. But the archbishop
urged Crispin to question Chaucer. Refusing, Crispin stared into
the hearth, listening only to the crackling flames, the logs snap,
and the sticks sizzle. How could he even look at Geoffrey! Did he
think his friend was guilty? He didn't know anymore, nauseated
by the whole affair.

Chaucer followed him with his eyes around the room. Crispin
stabbed a look at him and quickly turned away.

Finally, Geoffrey spoke. "I'm to submit to the sheriff without
so much as an explanation?"

Crispin turned. "I'd rather have the sheriff here. A neutral party.
For your sake, it is best."

"For *my* sake? *Now* we are concerned with my affairs?" He faced the archbishop. "If my friend Crispin will say nothing, perhaps his Excellency will indulge me? I take it I am being accused of a murder. Master Guest intimated that Brother Wilfrid was killed."

"If you plead guilty now your soul will have mercy," said Courtenay evenly.

"Right now, I am most concerned with my neck," and he eased his hand across his throat.

"Just keep still, Geoffrey, until the sheriff arrives!" hissed Crispin.

"I'm not particularly anxious to wait," said Chaucer. "I demand leave to send a message to his grace the duke, who will no doubt get a message to the king."

Courtenay eased back in his chair. "In good time."

"Now!"

Courtenay rose and pressed his hands to the table. "Do not threaten me, Master Chaucer. Your life balances on a thread. A good wind might just hack it in half."

Crispin clenched and unclenched his fists. Why couldn't the two of them just keep their mouths shut!

A knock on the door. Crispin sighed with his entire body. It couldn't have come soon enough. He went himself and opened the door and looked into the face of a stocky man with sandy brown hair that wisped over tiny eyes. The man measured Crispin and gave a brief and polite smile. "You must be Crispin Guest. I am Thomas Brokhull."

"Lord Sheriff," said Crispin and stepped aside with a bow.

Brokhull strode into the room and bowed to the archbishop. "Excellency." The archbishop nodded in reply. The sheriff turned to Chaucer. "Why was I summoned?"

"There have been two murders in the cathedral," said Crispin.

"And this man, Geoffrey Chaucer, is being accused of one of them."

"Both," said the archbishop.

Crispin spun and glared at him but restrained from speaking.

Brokhull addressed Chaucer. "You are Geoffrey *Chaucer*? The duke of *Lancaster's* poet?" Chaucer bowed graciously as if he were at court. "By Saint Thomas! What goes on here?"

"Murder," said Crispin.

"Lord Sheriff," said Geoffrey. "I demand to send a message to my Lord of Gaunt. He should be informed that his servant is in peril of his life."

"Surely it isn't that," said Brokhull, noticeably nervous.

Chaucer strolled a circle around Crispin. "Apparently so, Lord Sheriff. My very dear friend here thinks me guilty of murdering one of these monks."

The sheriff looked from Chaucer to Crispin and his expression changed. Crispin knew exactly what he was thinking: Should Brokhull take the word of the court's poet or that of a traitor?

He closed his eyes in consternation. "I have only done what Archbishop Courtenay commanded of me. I have discharged Master Chaucer into the care of the Lord Sheriff. Now, am I free to go so that I may find the *true* killer?"

Brokhull bristled. "True killer? If you do not think Master Chaucer guilty then why must I arrest him?"

Courtenay lifted the dagger from his table. Chaucer saw it for the first time and his face went white. "This was recovered from the throat of our dear Brother Wilfrid," said Courtenay tightly. "Is this your dagger, Master Chaucer?"

Chaucer stiffened. "It . . . is." He darted a desperate look at Crispin. "But I do not know how it was used so foully. It has been missing from my room for days. Someone must have stolen it."

Courtenay gathered the red gown rolled into a bundle, also on his desk where Crispin deposited it. "And this gown with the tear?"

"That . . . is also mine."

"Be so kind as to tell us about the tear, Master Guest," said Courtenay in an inappropriately jovial tenor.

Crispin stood against the far wall in the shadows. "When I examined the locked Corona tower after the first murder—"

Brokhull moved closer. "What first murder?"

"One of the pilgrims. The prioress Madam Eglantine de Mooreville. Two nights ago."

Brokhull stomped toward the archbishop. "I have heard nothing of this crime, Excellency. When were you planning on informing me?"

"It is an ecclesiastical matter. She was a prioress—"

"And the other victim your monk. What is the difference?"

"The difference is Geoffrey Chaucer!" His arm shot up and stabbed a finger at him. "This heretic's knife was found in the throat of my monk. There is a greater conspiracy afoot. More than heresy. More than the Church can root out."

Silently, Brokhull regarded all in the room. "Have you searched this man?" he asked of Crispin. He shook his head. Brokhull strode up to Chaucer and stood toe to toe with him. "Sir, surrender your scrip."

Chaucer took a deep breath and shot another desperate glance at Crispin. He unbuttoned the pouch's straps and handed it to the sheriff. Brokhull dipped his hand in and removed coins, a pouch of more coins, a pilgrim's badge, and a key.

"Wait!" Crispin hurried across the room and pulled his Church key from his own pouch and snatched up the other.

They were identical.

His stomach churned. He turned a deadly glare on Chaucer.

Geoffrey's face paled to a sickly gray. "I would like to confess," he said suddenly, voice strained.

Crispin's heart leapt to his throat. "*What?*"

Courtenay's face lit with triumph. Geoffrey turned to the sheriff. "I would like to confess . . . but only to Crispin Guest."

Brokhull, already up to his ears in confusion, shook his head. "This is all highly irregular."

"I will only give my confession to Crispin Guest. Alone."

Crispin shook his head. "Don't do this, Geoffrey."

"Well, Lord Sheriff?" said Chaucer. "Surely there is a place . . ."

"The Westgate tower is not yet complete. There is another prison across town. But"—he raised his face to the archbishop—"my lord, are there not cells in the monastery? Cells that lock from the outside?"

"Yes, yes." His mouth curved. "And I would be pleased to house such a prisoner here. He deserves our undivided attention."

"No doubt," muttered Chaucer. "Then we may use a cell here. Agreed?" He looked at the sheriff for confirmation.

The sheriff nodded. "If you don't mind, I will accompany you."

The archbishop called for his clerk who escorted the sheriff, Crispin, and Chaucer to the monastery door. They took corridors and stairs to the monks' quarters and found the last cell unoccupied. The sheriff asked the clerk for a key and was given the one on the monk's belt. Brokhull gestured for Chaucer and Crispin to enter, and when they had, he locked them in. "Give a shout when you are finished, Master Guest," said the sheriff.

They heard his steps recede and finally raised their eyes to one another. "What addlepated idea have you hatched, Chaucer?"

At last, Chaucer was visibly shaken. Alone with Crispin, he

could drop his façade. "Lord have mercy. What have I gotten myself into?"

"That's what I'd like to know."

"First of all—" Geoffrey drew back his fist and swung. Crispin's face exploded with pain and he staggered back, holding his chin.

"What the hell was that for!"

"That's for accusing me in the first place. And second"—he nodded—"I can certainly see why you did."

"Then why strike me?" He held his chin, hoping his double vision would soon clear.

"I had to do something." Sitting heavily on the straw cot, Geoffrey rested his cheeks in his hands. "For the love of Christ, what am I to do?"

"You can start by explaining yourself. Why do you have this key?"

He looked up with his hands still cradling his face, mashing his cheeks together. His mustache wept over his fingers. "Well, I suppose that is in order." He breathed raggedly. "You see, his grace the duke was worried about Becket's relics. He knew there was a plot afoot to steal or destroy them, and so . . . so he sent me, well, to fetch them."

"*Fetch* them? Indeed. His new lapdog would do so."

"Don't, Cris. I haven't the wits to match barbs with you now."

"So go on. You arrived a fortnight ago and stole the keys in order to make a copy."

He froze. "How did you know?" Crispin rolled his eyes. "Never mind. You're the Tracker. I concede it."

"Why didn't you steal the bones then and there?"

"No opportunity. And I needed to measure the circumstances. I thought it best to return and travel with another group of pilgrims to mask the deed."

"Very well. You hid in the Corona tower until all were gone and you caught your gown in the door."

"I'd forgotten that until I found you in my room. You are very good at what you do."

"Save it for later, Chaucer. Explain what happened. Did you kill the Prioress?"

"No, damn you! Of course I didn't. Nor did I kill poor little Wilfrid."

"Poor little Wilfrid was frightened of you. Did you threaten him earlier?"

"No."

"This isn't much of a confession."

"I'm getting to that. I had no intentions toward the Prioress. Are we clear on that?"

"So it is merely a coincidence that you knew each other under dubious circumstances."

"Yes, only a coincidence. A horrible and possibly laughable coincidence. I came to steal Becket's bones and only that."

"Oh, well then. I suppose all can be forgiven!" Crispin was so stiff with restraint he was liable to snap. "So where *are* they, Geoffrey?"

"When I snuck out of my hiding place, I heard all sorts of noise. Screams, people running. I suppose that was when the Prioress was murdered. I did my best to stay out of sight. Whatever was happening, I thought it was a fine distraction to do what I needed to do. I did not know that you would return looking for me. Scared me out of my wits. So I'm afraid I . . . I hit you."

"The *first* time you hit me in the jaw," he said resentfully, rubbing his jaw again.

"Sorry, Cris. Couldn't be helped. But I was free to get to the shrine, which I quickly did."

Crispin stood over him. "*So where are the goddamned bones?*"

Chaucer wiped his lips with his hand and exhaled another ragged breath. "Once I had dispatched you, I managed to lift the canopy and push aside the casket lid . . . but the damned bones were already gone!"

15

"MORE LIES, GEOFFREY?" SAID Crispin wearily. "How many more do you have in that pouch of yours?"

"I'm not lying, Cris. The bones were gone."

"And someone just happened to steal your dagger and kill Brother Wilfrid."

"Yes, yes! I don't know when. I don't remember when I had it last."

"How convenient."

Chaucer glared. "This is very pretty. You haven't seen me in eight years and you simply assume now that I am a murderer."

"You've admitted to being a thief and a spy. Can murderer be far behind?"

Chaucer shook his head and rose. "I never would have believed it of you, Cris. That you would have become so hard and immovable. True, you were always a bit stiff but never so hard-hearted."

"Live in my shoes for a day and you might understand."

"Am I to hang for a murder for which I am entirely innocent?"

"Entirely? That is debatable." Chaucer stiffened and curled his hands into fists. Crispin raised his bruised chin. "Are you going to hit me again, Geoffrey?"

"Why bother?" He sat, dropping his face in his hands. Crispin stared at him for a long time and finally spun away, glancing up into the high window, welcoming the watery sunshine on his face.

"Against my better judgment," he said quietly, "I tend to believe in your innocence. At least where the murders are concerned. Doubtlessly, I will come to regret it." He swiveled his head. Geoffrey's face was still buried in his hands. "Exactly why would Lancaster wish to rescue such bones if he has Lollard leanings? I am unclear on this."

Chaucer's voice was muffled by his hands. "He said he admired such a man who stood up against a king for his principles. He said he admired all such men."

Crispin stiffened and clutched his belt with both hands. "He said that?"

"Yes. I found the affair amusing, to tell the truth—"

"The *truth*?"

"Not now, Cris." He heaved a trembling sigh. "I had no idea—how could I? That such events would encircle a simple theft."

"*Simple* theft? Geoffrey! This is Saint Thomas the Martyr! The greatest saint in England. There is nothing simple about it!"

"Yes, well. I know that now, don't I?"

Crispin paced until pacing seemed useless. He dropped heavily into the chair and stared at his old friend. "What am I to do with you, Geoffrey? What can I say?"

Chaucer raised his face. "You could help me escape."

He frowned. "No."

"No? You mean you would let me hang!"

He shook his head slowly. "No. But I cannot help you escape. We must do this logically, legally."

"I haven't a leg to stand on."

"It certainly looks that way. But I am nowhere near done investigating."

Chaucer perked. He threw back his shoulders. "Indeed. Then what—?"

"I can't say right now. Rest assured I will see the real culprit caught and punished."

"I have only one request."

"What's that?"

"Can you do so before they hang me?"

ON THE ONE HAND, Crispin was angry that Geoffrey had gotten himself into this situation, and on the other he was scared. He felt in his bones that Chaucer was innocent of the murders, but he also knew he had been sorely wrong before. He desperately wanted his friend to be innocent, for if he *was* guilty, he wanted nothing to do with it. How could he possibly be responsible for getting his oldest friend hanged?

The sheriff met him again and walked back with him down the cloister and into the dim church. "Do you have any theories, if you do not wish to entertain that Master Chaucer is to blame?" asked Brokhull.

"I have known Master Chaucer for many years, Lord Sheriff. A man can change, but surely not that much. He could not have killed Brother Wilfrid and certainly not the Prioress."

"Then may I ask what it is he confessed to you?"

"Do I have your confidence, my lord?"

The sheriff measured Crispin silently and then nodded. "I know you by your reputation, sir. I have never heard a sour word spoken as concerns London's Tracker."

"Very well. There was a matter of Saint Thomas the Martyr's relics. Did the archbishop tell you . . . ?" The sheriff wore a blank expression. "No. He did not. I feel you should be made aware, that the relics have been stolen."

"Good Christ!" The sheriff glanced instinctively up the nave toward Saint Thomas's chapel.

"Just so. Master Chaucer claimed that he was instructed to . . . to . . . retrieve . . . the bones himself, but that they were stolen before he got to them."

"Do you believe him?"

Crispin paused. "I am not certain of that."

"If you do not blame him for murder, then who do you blame?"

"There is a man at the inn whom I am certain is guilty. He had a grievance against the Prioress. A dire one. He is a man of loose temper and I do not gauge him above murder, though he is a wealthy landowner."

"Indeed. Who?"

"His name is Sir Philip Bonefey.

"I see. Have you restrained him?"

"I have little authority to do so, but I have put him on notice. He may flee."

"Do you want me to arrest him?" Brokhull looked uncertain.

"Not yet. There is little evidence and I would not see you in disfavor from it." Brokhull seemed relieved. "But if you could keep watch of the Martyrs Inn to make certain he stays, I believe I can further the inquiry from there."

"Is there anything else?"

"Yes. The murder weapon. A sword. An old one. There is a blazon on the pommel. I need to find out whose arms those are."

"That may be a long and difficult process. But if I can think of any way to assist you, I shall."

Crispin fell silent, his mouth slightly open. "Forgive me, Lord Sheriff," he began tentatively. "But . . . I am unused to such civility from the authorities. I was momentarily . . . stunned."

"Truly? Surely we must work together for the common good, no? Who has incurred such mistrust in you?"

"I . . . live in London . . ."

"Nick Exton and John Froshe are the sheriffs, are they not? I can see why you are hesitant. Careful fellows, are Exton and Froshe. They are jealous of their power. Perhaps you threaten them in some way."

"Only by being right."

"For them, that is enough."

Crispin scratched his head. "Maybe I should move to Canterbury."

Brokhull chuckled and extended his hand. Crispin took it. "Good luck, Master Guest. I will post a man near the inn as you advise. What does this man look like?"

He described the Franklin and then took his leave of the sheriff, much invigorated that he would get real help this time. And he knew he needed it. Between Chaucer's incarceration and the threats from Bonefey, he was a little unsure of how to proceed. It was as if every bit of this mystery was made of glass: the least amount of pressure one way or the other could shatter it.

He stared at a shadowy statue for a long time before he turned to glance at Saint Thomas's chapel. With a weary heart, he dragged himself up the nave and then around to the pilgrims' stair and entered the rounded chamber. But instead of going to Saint Thomas's shrine, he walked a little further and stood before the latten knight, the image of Prince Edward. He reached out and rested his hand on the cold metal. "Sire," he said softly. "I pray you rest in peace in Heaven where you are, for there is so little of it here below. You left us in great turmoil. I should be angry with you, but alas, I am certain it was not your intention to die so young without a crown. And then your brother Lancaster with a crown snatched from his grasp by your son." He walked beside the tomb, running his hand along the edge of the lid. "Little did we know. Little did we all know." His fingers stopped trailing and he glanced again at the knight in repose, studying the ornate figure with somber eyes.

"Sir, sir! You must come away from there!"

Annoyed, he sneered at a monk gesturing to him and scuttling closer.

"You must come away. You must not disturb the tombs." He faced Crispin, his eyes glittering.

"Worry not, little monk. I will disturb them no more." Gathering his cloak about himself, he strode away down the pilgrims' stair and through the nave. Immersed in his thoughts, he reached the courtyard. But with its merchants and milling townsfolk, he almost didn't hear Jack calling out to him.

"Master Crispin!"

He turned. He was more relieved than he expected to be upon seeing the boy again. "Jack! You're back. You have news?"

Breathless, Jack stopped, leaned over, and rested his hands on his thighs. But when he straightened, he brought up a scowl.

"What's the matter?"

He threw off his hood and Crispin saw. "Oh dear." His mood had been so black that he needed the respite of laughter, and Jack's expression and the gleaming white of his newly shaved tonsure rendered Crispin incapable of suppressing his mirth. But Jack wasn't amused and Crispin tried to recover in order to at least offer Jack some dignity.

"What am I supposed to do about this!"

"Nothing. It will grow back."

"You never said—"

"Jack, I am sorely glad to see you, but aren't there more important things for you to tell me? Why you've left the monastery, for instance?"

Jack cringed and threw the hood back over his bald scalp. "Very well," he grumbled. "I did find out a few things." Crispin urged him back toward the tailor shop as he talked. "For one thing, none of them monks trust you because they think *you* are a Lollard."

"Indeed. Interesting. Who could have told them that, I wonder?"

"My instinct tells me it was the archbishop. They have no cause to connect you to Lancaster unless he told them."

"Quite right, Jack. What else?"

"Well, the Lollard among them appears to be Brother Martin."

"I met him almost the first thing. A sharp-faced fellow. With a dislike for Dom Thomas."

"He ain't the only one," said Jack, scratching his shaved head over the hood. "But Dom Thomas and the others are already aware of him."

"So this big secret that the archbishop would have me discover is not such a secret after all."

"That ain't the *big* secret," said Jack eagerly. "For one, there was some ado about Saint Thomas's bones far before you was called."

"The archbishop *was* anxious about them."

"Not so much that. I think it is something else. Something the monks are keeping to themselves."

He stopped. "The bones were gone ever before I was called."

"That's it!" Jack shook his head, a wide smile spreading on his face. "Aye. That must be it! They were already missing. I'll wager anything—"

"And you'd win. Then why this farce? Why call me all this way to protect something that wasn't even there?" He paled. "Then Chaucer was right."

"Right about what, sir?"

He looked at Jack and took a deep breath. He related the past day's experiences, the clues he'd found, and Chaucer's confession.

Jack's eyes grew wider and wider. "God blind me with a poker! Then it's that Sir Philip what done it!"

"Yes. But then where are the bones?"

"You don't suppose he has them? He is a Lollard, after all."

"I don't know. I have to think about it all. But you said that you had two things to tell me. What was the other?"

Jack sidled closer and said in soft but excited tones, "I seen that Dom Thomas in the church paying extortion money to one of them masons."

"*What?* Are you certain?"

"Aye. I saw them and heard them m'self. The mason said, 'I'd like to know who's the more dishonest: the man who *committed* the crime or the one who witnessed it.'" Jack told Crispin all he had heard and seen.

He listened without interrupting. When Jack finished he said nothing for a long time. "The man in the cassock," he breathed.

"But how does that fit with the red gown, sir?"

"It means that Chaucer did not kill the Prioress or the monk."

"And the bones?"

"Well, that's another question."

"And Sir Philip, sir?"

Crispin gritted his teeth. Sir Philip. If Dom Thomas was a murderer then what part did Sir Philip play in this chess game? Or was it only his desire to see the arrogant Franklin brought low? He cradled his head. His temple was pounding again. Too many twists. Too many guilty parties. And if he made the wrong move it could be him who sent Chaucer to the gallows.

"Let's get to the tailor and then back to the inn as soon as we might."

"Good. I can't wait to get me own clothes back."

The sun was just sinking below the rooftops when he and Jack made it back to Master Turpin's tailor shop. Though the man was about to bar his doors, he opened them for Crispin.

"We have come to return your property, Master Turpin," he said, closing the door behind him. He winked to the tailor.

"Oh yes. Yes, Master. All is ready." He took Jack aside and told him to strip the cassock off. Jack wore a resigned expression and untied his rope belt and yanked the cassock up over his head. When the tailor returned, he had a blue coat slung over his arm. He shook it out and opened it for Jack to slide his arm into, but Jack shrunk back.

"That ain't my tunic, Master Turpin. You've made a mistake."

"No mistake. I made this especially for you, young man."

Jack didn't move, but his eyes did a wild dance scouring the tailor's face, then back to the garment, then to his face again. "Why?"

"Because your master instructed me so to do. And paid me." He smiled.

Jack's jaw dropped several inches. Turpin took advantage of Jack's limp body to pull on his new cotehardie. He yanked on the collar to straighten the shoulders—waggling Jack's loose head—and buttoned it up all the way from the hem to his yoke, twenty-three buttons, just like Crispin's coat.

Crispin folded his arms over his chest and looked Jack up and down, moving all around him. He nodded approvingly. "Perhaps a bit long at the thigh—"

"He will grow, Master Guest. I allowed for that."

"How about the gusset at the armpit? Is that adequate for growth as well?"

"Oh yes. See," and he raised Jack's flaccid arm. "Plenty of room here. Also the waist. His belt should conceal the small amount of extra material."

"Good. Good. I am pleased. And where is mine?"

"Right here, sir."

The tailor scurried to the back room leaving them alone. Jack raised his eyes slowly to Crispin. "You bought me a new coat," he whispered. "You . . . you—"

"That old tunic of yours was an embarrassment. And if you are going to be a Tracker you'd best look the part."

He turned at Turpin's approach but he was thrown nearly to the ground when Jack's arms flung around him. Jack burst into tears, and though he tried to tell him his heartfelt thanks Crispin couldn't understand a word he said. He peeled the boy off of him and held him at arm's length. "Enough!" He stiffened. "The archbishop may be a bastard, but he at least pays me decently."

He unbuttoned his cotehardie and flung it to the ground and gratefully shrugged into the new cotehardie Turpin held out for him. The tailor buttoned it for him while Crispin buckled his belt over it and turned to Jack. "Well?"

Jack sniffed and wiped his eyes with his new sleeve before he assessed Crispin's coat with a perplexed expression. "It . . . looks just like your old coat, sir. It's even the same scarlet color."

Crispin adjusted his old leather chaperon hood over his shoulders. "Of course. I like scarlet."

Jack shrugged and grabbed his own hood, seeming to remember he needed it to cover his shaved head.

With new stockings and new shirts for the both of them slung over Jack's arm, they left the tailor's just as dusk softened the streets of Canterbury. Out of the corner of his eye, Crispin noticed Jack stroking his new coat as if it were a pelt of ermine. He supposed Jack couldn't remember a time when anyone bought him anything. The notion sobered Crispin like none other. He stared straight ahead, doing his best to clear his mind of familial thoughts he'd rather not have.

"I told the sheriff about Bonefey," he said conversationally to the boy.

Jack perked up and nodded like a judge. "Will he arrest him, then?"

"No, I told him not to."

"Why ever not? He sounds like a churl of the worst kind."

"He is. But if he has anything to do with the missing bones, I would prefer to watch him to see if he may lead us to them."

"Is that likely, sir? I mean, it's not as if he'd sell them or even need to. If he had them and was a true Lollard, would he not destroy them?"

Crispin blinked. "Sell them?"

"I said 'destroy them,' sir, not sell them."

"No. But I can think of a pair who might sell them. If they had them."

"That Pardoner and Summoner. Thick as thieves, them two."

"Thick as thieves."

"You don't mean they might have stolen the bones?"

"Since it isn't exactly clear when the bones disappeared, it is difficult to say. I wish I knew when they went missing."

"Perhaps you should call on Master Edward. He's a pensioner in the monastery. He has his theories."

"Perhaps later. My concern is to talk again with Dame Marguerite. I must fix these circumstances in my mind and quickly in order to clear Geoffrey of all charges."

"What will you speak with Dame Marguerite about, sir?"

"To see if she is any clearer on Madam Eglantine's assailant. With some time past she might be more lucid."

"May I . . . may I go with you when you do? So's I can, er, see how you do it."

"I suppose so."

They reached the inn when the shadows had fallen completely and entered into the golden warmth. Harry Bailey greeted Crispin with a salute from his perch by the stairs. Obviously he had taken to heart Crispin's admonition to watch Bonefey. "Master Bailey. Is all well?"

"Indeed, Crispin, it is. Sir Philip expressed an interest in leaving the inn and Canterbury once he knew you were gone. Our friend Gough disabused him of that notion. Rather heartily, I think."

"Oh? Where is Master Gough now?"

"Edwin is sitting on Sir Philip."

"Not literally?"

Bailey's face broke into a wide smile. "Yes. Quite literally."

He beamed. "Well then. There is no fear that he bolted or will any time soon. Is Dame Marguerite about?"

Bailey's face fell. "Poor soul. She wanders in the back garden or stays in her room. I feel quite aggrieved for her."

He measured the time. She was probably in her room. Maybe tomorrow would be better. He looked at Jack and decided. "It has been a long day. I think I will retire."

"What of food?" said Bailey. "Shall I have the innkeeper send victuals to you?"

"Yes. Thank you, Master Harry."

He trudged up the stairs with Jack in tow and entered his room. He realized he had scarce spent any time there in all the days he'd been in Canterbury.

Jack sat hard onto his cot. "I miss our London lodgings."

"I never thought I'd say it, but so do I." He sat on his own bed and wondered if he wanted to bother undressing.

IN THE MORNING, CRISPIN stared at the sword. He had spent the early hours cleaning it with an oiled cloth, taking all the blood and bits of bone from the blade. Still scratched and worn, the sword at least looked more presentable. He studied the pommel, wondering how on earth he was going to find the owner.

Jack was up, making a wide path around the sword and straightening the room and clearing away last night's supper things.

He reluctantly set the blade aside and stood. "Come, Jack. It is time to ask our questions." They left the room and he was about to head toward Dame Marguerite's room when he heard raised voices below. Crispin leaned down over the stair rail to see what the matter was and sprinted down the steps.

16

LIKE DOGS IN AN alley, Maufesour and Chanticleer were at each other's throats, brandishing their knives.

"What goes on here?" bellowed Crispin above their voices.

They turned, but neither lowered their daggers. "He's a thief!" cried Chanticleer, gesturing with his blade at the Summoner.

"Ha!" the Summoner rejoined. "Look who speaks! A master thief if ever there was one."

Chanticleer lunged for him, but Crispin grabbed his arm and spun him about. "Now, now. Is there no honor amongst thieves? Keep it civil."

Even with mouths poised to speak, they both seemed to realize something at the same time and fell silent, eyeing each other.

Crispin smirked. "Will you not speak of your troubles, gentlemen? There was an accusation of thievery. . . ."

But neither would say a word. They shared a look again and even offered artificial smiles. "A, er, minor disagreement over the sharing of funds," said Maufesour. He urged Chanticleer to respond with a waggling of his brows.

Chanticleer got the hint. "Oh yes! A disagreement. To be sure."

Crispin slid his arms over both sets of shoulders. "See how much better it is when two talk it out rather than fight? Sheath your daggers, gentlemen. And sit. I would speak with you two."

"Oh, but we have more business to conduct in the city, Master Guest," sputtered Maufesour. "We must attend to that."

"Oh yes," Chanticleer agreed, trying to edge out from under Crispin's grasp. "You would have no argument to that, certainly."

Crispin strong-armed them to a bench and forced them down. "We'll see. *After* I speak to you."

Both men stared sourly at the table. The other tavern patrons moved guardedly away to their own tables.

Crispin drew his knife and toyed with the sharp blade. "It is interesting that I have repeatedly enjoined the pilgrims to remain at the inn, yet time and time again, you two have flouted my orders."

Maufesour turned a frown on him. "You cannot stop us from doing our duty."

"Indeed," said the other. "We are on the Church's business."

Crispin continued to toy with the blade. "I must tell you a truth about me, gentlemen. I am intolerant of liars. Less so of thieves. Not at all of murderers."

Maufesour sputtered again. "We are not murderers, sir!"

"Thieves, then?"

"No!"

"Liars?"

Maufesour huffed. "It is clear you insist on accusing us of ill deeds. Accuse, then. Say your peace."

He leaned toward them, close enough to smell Maufesour's foul breath and Chanticleer's overly perfumed hair. "You two are as guilty as they come," he said softly. They stiffened at his words. "I am of the mind that you have something to do with the theft in the cathedral." They both tried to rise but he shoved them back down.

"I will give you exactly till sunset to return that item to me or I shall have both your heads on a platter. Have I made myself clear?"

Maufesour tried a "But—"

"Have I made myself clear?"

Slowly, they both nodded their heads. Crispin released them and straightened. "Good. Now. Begone to whatever devilry you had planned." In a flash, they were up and out the door.

He straightened his new coat and looked back toward Jack, waiting by the stairs. Time to speak to Dame Marguerite. But as he approached the stairs Alyson was making her way down. Her face broke into a wide smile on seeing him and she gave a coy lilt to her shoulder. "Crispin," she said. "I missed you last night."

He didn't look at Jack, who was making himself scarce at the other end of the hall. "Alas. I was far too agitated to be of good company, Alyson."

Slowly she descended the stairs until she was at the foot. "But that is when such company can do you the most good."

He smiled. "Sometimes. But murder and the involvement of old friends makes for a troubled mind, which leads to troubles . . . elsewhere."

"Bless me, Crispin! But no man has ever had those troubles in my bed."

He suddenly longed to embrace her, but knew it would not be proper in such a public place. "I do believe you," he said softly. "Unfortunately, I am working at the moment and need to talk to Dame Marguerite. Is she still abed, do you think?"

"Oh no. She is much better these days and has taken to spending time in the inn's back garden amongst the herbs and flowers. I think the fresh air is good for her."

"Can you show me the way?"

She took his hand and led him through the hall to a narrow alley to the kitchens. Jack followed at a discreet distance.

The innkeeper and his staff watched warily as the entourage filed through, and then Alyson opened a back door. At first they encountered a dirt yard with hewn stumps no doubt used for beheading poultry as evidenced by its bloodstains and scattered feathers, but beyond that lay the greening of a garden. "There," she said with a raised arm, pointing. "There is a bench beyond that myrtle. Would you like me to stay?"

He glanced back at Jack, who was pretending to be absorbed by a beetle climbing up a stump. "Thank you, no, Alyson. I prefer to ask my questions without too much of an audience. She might be more at ease with less of us in attendance."

"You know your business best." She turned to leave but leaned back, resting her hand on his cheek. "At your leisure," she whispered.

"As you wish." He watched her backside until his gaze rose and met Jack's. The lad was smiling. "Come along, Jack."

They strode past a short wooden fence and onto a gravel path. The garden showed dark earth with sprigs of green shoots emerging from the tilled rows.

Dame Marguerite sat on a mossy bench and fingered her repaired rosary hanging from her rope belt. Her face was tilted upwards into the spring sun and her brown eyes seemed to be gazing distantly. Encased in her nun's weeds of brown, she blended into the shadows cast by the myrtle and the rear wall of the stable. Crispin and Jack were not necessarily silent as they approached, but she did not acknowledge them.

Finally, he cleared his throat, and she struck her gaze from that faraway place and lowered it to him. She looked him up and down, in fact, and then did the same to Jack. "Master Guest," she said in her same shy way. "And Master Tucker." He did not look at Jack's face, but he noticed the boy throwing back his shoulders in a fulsome manner.

"Dame Marguerite," he said gently with a slight bow. "Forgive me for interrupting your prayers, but have you heard the further tidings from the cathedral?"

"Of the murder of Brother Wilfrid? Yes, it is most distressing."

"Indeed. I came to discover if there was perhaps more you could tell me about the death of your prioress."

She raised her head and cocked it at him. "What more could I say?"

"I hoped you could better identify the assailant. Tell me for certain what he might have been wearing, for instance."

"Whatever I told you before could not have changed."

"But you were in great distress at that time. Now with the passage of days—"

"But why would my words be different? Why would my eyes have witnessed more as time passed?"

He drew silent. Was she being deliberately abstruse? More likely she was just a simple maid who understood little.

"Master Crispin, I wonder when I may be allowed to return to my convent. I must get on with my life in God."

"Your life at your convent is important to you, I know. May I ask how long you have been a nun?"

"It seems all my life, and yet that is not so. I was raised in the convent. My mother worked as a servant, and as I grew and worked with her in the kitchens, I saw the wonder of that life and begged to be a part of it. Madam Eglantine took me as a novice when I was fourteen. I became a nun only last year."

"You speak well for the daughter of a scullion."

She didn't exactly smile, but her face wasn't quite blank either. She offered no more. He shuffled his feet. "Have you given any more thought to what the assailant was wearing? You seemed uncertain whether he was wearing a cassock or not."

"No. No thoughts at all."

"Dame Marguerite, I am trying to ascertain the murderer. Surely you want to help me in this?"

"And should you find him, what would you do to him?"

"I would have him arrested."

"And then what would happen?"

"He would be judged and sentenced to hang."

She lowered her face and studied her belt. "Then I shouldn't truly like to help you if that is the outcome."

"But justice must be served."

"Aye, justice. But does not God ultimately decide justice, no matter what little thing we do on earth to determine it?"

"So says your catechism, but we are mere mortals. We must do what we must to live in a just society, and our society has decided that murderers must die." He stepped closer. "You are not protecting someone, are you? Someone you know?"

She offered him a consoling smile. "And if I were . . . would I tell you?"

No, not a simpleton. He conceded with a bow. "If you have nothing further to offer, then I take my leave." He turned to go but a hand plucked at his sleeve. His eyes fell on Jack.

"May I stay a moment, sir? I would speak with Dame Marguerite."

Crispin looked from the determined face of his protégé to that of the sedate nun and then back again. *What goes on here?* He knew the boy seemed to have an infatuation for the girl. Perhaps Jack might get more information from her than he did. It was a guilty thought, because it meant using the boy, and it also meant eavesdropping. But the flush of guilt was only temporary. There was too much at stake. Geoffrey's innocence for one.

He gave Jack a nod and turned on his heel to walk back up the path. But once Jack turned away from him toward the nun, he made a stealthy journey back behind the hedges to listen, wondering how much of his pride he had to sacrifice for the price of a man's life.

Jack stood uncertainly for a moment, measuring the garden, the sky, anything it seemed but the nun. He checked the knife at his belt, pulled at the hem of his new coat, straightened his hood, and finally dropped his hands to his sides. "Well," he said at last in a halting voice. "I am pleased to see you looking so well, Dame."

She blinked at Jack but said nothing.

Jack shuffled his feet for a bit and raised his eyes again to the spring sky just opening from a lacy cloud cover. "My master is good at what he does, this finding of criminals. Tracker, they call him." He made a halfhearted chuckle. "And though I know you would not see a murderer hang, surely you would see that he is stopped before he can do harm to another."

"Is it always so?" she asked.

"Well, in my experience, the murderer does not stop with one. And poor Wilfrid is the proof of it. Surely you would not see murder done again."

"If it is God's will."

"God's will in murder? That ain't—*isn't*—right, is it?"

Marguerite paused. She shifted on the bench and shook out her veil, raising her face to the bleary sunshine. "I . . . should ask my prioress such a question. But of course . . . I cannot."

Jack edged closer and stealthily found his way to sitting on the bench beside her. He sat quietly for some time.

Crispin clenched his teeth. *That boy has too smooth a way about him.*

"Aye. Well. That is the problem, ain't it—*isn't* it? She was murdered, wasn't she? It's a sore thing to find a murderer. I've been with my master for near two years now and it is never an easy thing. There's danger. Aye, I've seen my share, too, I suppose." He puffed out his chest and squinted an eye toward her, perhaps to see if she noticed.

Crispin put his hand over his mouth to suppress a laugh.

"Aye. My master has me apprenticing to be a Tracker as well. I expect when I come of age I will have learned a goodly amount. He already depends on me. Wouldn't know what the man would do without me."

Crispin smiled and shook his head. *Jesu,* is this what *he* sounded like at that age?

Jack surveyed the garden again and moved marginally closer to her. "If you will not speak of it . . ." And he eyed her but she made no appearance that she would. "Well then. I'll trouble you no more about it." He edged closer. "What will you do now? Will you go back to your priory?"

"Of course. As soon as your master allows it."

"But how can you? After what you've seen?"

She shook her head as if the question were absurd. "What else would I do? I am a nun."

"Well now." Jack rubbed his thighs and looked down at his coat, seeming to remember it was new and how fine he must look in it. He sat straighter. "For a maiden such as you, I would think there were a fair amount of options."

She cocked her head at him much like a dove.

Jack went on. "You're an even-tempered lass. There are many prospects. Er . . . a ladies maid, surely. A chatelaine. Or . . .

maybe . . ." Crispin saw him squirm and swallow. "Maybe even . . . a wife. For the right sort of lad, that is."

Crispin nearly stumbled into the bushes. Good Christ!

But Marguerite seemed none the wiser. She continued to stare uncomprehendingly at Jack, blinking.

Slowly, carefully, as if picking up an injured bird, Jack scooped up her hand and held it in his own. She looked down at her white hand in Jack's and still said nothing. Jack was breathing heavily, his gaze concentrated on her face. "You see, Dame . . . That is, Marguerite. The right sort of lad may be right under your nose. That would be a lad who has learning. And a vocation. Maybe his wage isn't so much, but that will change." He scooted closer until his thigh rested against hers hidden by her brown woolen gown. "A wage, a wife, and maybe a babe or two is all the happiness some lads need. It's . . . all *I'd* need."

She stared at the spectacle of her hand in Jack's but made no attempt to pull it free. "I do not understand you," she said, voice softer. Crispin had the feeling by the look of her eye that she understood him quite well indeed. "Are you saying that *I* should look to another vocation?"

"Well. Mayhap. A maid as young as you are. How can you put yourself away in a monastery? It seems a crime! I mean, you're lovely . . . if I may say so."

For the first time, Marguerite seemed to awaken and she blushed.

This seemed to encourage Jack and he scooted closer, bringing her hand to his chest. "I'm a fool, I know it. But when a lad looks upon such beauty he cannot keep it to himself. He must needs tell the world. Or at least the object of that beauty. And so . . . I am telling you . . . Marguerite!"

Her face turned fully toward him now, and though Crispin thought she should be appalled, she looked far from it. In fact, he was not so certain that she wasn't edging closer to Jack. Jack's attention was on her face alone. The very sky could have collapsed atop him and he would not have noticed. She leaned forward and so did he and suddenly their lips met.

Crispin exploded from his hiding place. "JACK TUCKER!"

17

✠

JACK SNAPPED TO HIS feet, eyes round, face white. He threw Marguerite's hand aside. "Master Crispin!"

Crispin grabbed his arm and hauled him forward, shaking the limb. "You've disgraced yourself! Apologize to Dame Marguerite at once!"

"I . . . I . . ."

Marguerite rose slowly. "Master Crispin. Forgive the boy. I certainly do. It was not his fault. It is the fault of Woman. We are temptresses, no matter our vocation."

"Dame, your charity is exemplary. But it does not excuse his behavior." He glared at Jack. "Come!"

Dragging the boy back through the kitchens, Crispin smoldered. He'd never been so angry at the lad. He said nothing more until he reached the tavern's great hall. He tossed him forward toward the hearth and Jack stumbled before righting himself. He straightened his jacket and faced him, his face composed but fearful.

"I ain't ashamed of what I done. I love her!"

"Tucker, do I have to remind you that she is a holy sister? She has taken vows. Among them is the vow of chastity. What you did was unforgivable."

"I done what I done, and I'd do it again."

Crispin lurched forward, his face mere inches from Jack's. "Harken to me, boy. I am *telling* you that you will not do this again. I am your master and I am *ordering* you—" Crispin stared at Jack's trembling fists, his taut shoulders. Damn the boy! "You will make a confession, do you understand? To Father Gelfridus."

Jack glared back with all his might, his lips pressed tightly together. He made a feral nod of his head and clasped his arms over his chest.

Just as Crispin was about to say more, footsteps lumbered down the stairs. He jerked his head and spied Gelfridus making his way down the steps. "Father Priest!" he called, but Gelfridus seemed distracted and did not notice his hail. The priest walked carefully over the inn's plank floor, kicking the dust with his long-pointed shoes. His hand cradled his jaw, and a finger absently stroked the stubble on his cheek.

"Father Gelfridus," said Crispin again. This time the man raised his head and looked at him, yet his eyes remained unfocused and he could have very well been looking past him. Crispin went to the priest and touched his sleeve. "Father," he said in a softer tone. "What is amiss?"

"Nothing. Nothing at all. What may I do for you, Master Crispin?"

"My apprentice would be shriven, sir."

"Shriven?" he said vaguely, turning his face toward Jack. "Indeed. Everyone seems to wish to be shriven today."

"Oh?"

The look of the priest's face grew stricken and his cheek paler. "Yes."

Crispin glanced up the stairs. "Did Sir Philip make confession, Father?"

"Yes, as I said. Everyone in the inn seems to have done so today." He wiped the sprinkling of sweat from his upper lip.

"And what exactly did he confess?"

Awakened at last, Gelfridus drew himself up. "Sir! I am not at liberty to divulge such matters. It is the sacramental seal. *Sub Rosa*. A priest may *never* reveal what has been confessed to him."

Dame Marguerite entered the room and stopped when she spied the strange tableau of Jack, Crispin, and Gelfridus. She looked from one to the other, bowed to the priest, and trudged carefully up the stairs. Gelfridus watched her go.

"A murderer's confession would expedite matters considerably," urged Crispin, but Gelfridus tried to get away.

"No. Much as I would like to help you . . . no! I cannot. My vows forbid it."

"Father—"

"Master Crispin! You, who have suffered greatly from your sins, must surely be aware that others strive to shield themselves from that same mischief."

He scowled and drew back. "I am reminded daily of my sins, Father. I live with their consequence forevermore."

"There now. You would not wish the same fate to me, hmm? We will discuss it no more." He looked at Jack. "You will be shriven, young man?"

Jack glared. "It would seem so. That's twice today. It'll be bread and water for me again. I'll not see meat for a fortnight!"

"But your soul will be the better for it," said Gelfridus as if by rote. He took Jack's shoulder and steered him to a quiet corner.

Crispin walked to the staircase and looked up into its shadows. That damnable murderer confessed, and he was helpless to do anything about it! If only this priest were a weaker man—but no. Here he was wishing sin on another. Gelfridus was right. Hadn't he sinned enough?

He cast a glance at Jack sourly confessing to the priest who shielded his face in the cage of his fingers.

The priest put him in mind of Dame Marguerite and he suddenly remembered the solitary bead of her rosary still couched within his purse. The rosary. Something about it bothered him. He scarce had time to consider that night, what with Geoffrey in peril, the archbishop breathing down his neck, Sir Philip's treachery, and the evil he knew that the Summoner and Pardoner were getting up to.

All these worrisome thoughts clawed at his mind and they must have played on his face, for when Alyson stepped into the hall his expression seemed to stop her and she hurried toward him. "Crispin," she said in a quiet tone. "What is amiss? You seem greatly troubled."

He cast a curt glance at Jack, begrudgingly confessing, and turned away. "We must solve this inquiry as soon as possible and get free of this place, or it will surely destroy us."

She touched his arm and silently asked again. He moved away from the priest and the boy. "I am at a loss, Alyson. What would make a boy desire a nun, and a nun a boy, especially under such circumstances as these?"

She looked back over her shoulder at Jack. "Young Master Tucker and our Dame Marguerite? By Saint Catherine!"

"I am no prude. Certainly you must know that." She looked as if she would pull a face but thought better of it. He sighed. "And yet, such a thing turns my stomach. Is Jack such a paramour? Is she so willing to sin?"

"Peace, Crispin. What did you catch them at?" She pulled him back to the hearth and eased him into a chair.

"A kiss. And yet one kiss easily leads to another, and another, and then on to other sin."

"True. Judas did kiss Christ and from that received his everlasting damnation. But should it be so for young Jack?"

"I cannot abide it, Alyson. What would make so chaste a woman concede to it? Could it be the shock of the murder?"

"Ah me. I do not know. As you might have surmised, I am not a woman to succumb so easily to shock. But a frail thing like Marguerite? I do not know. Her past would seem to have prepared her."

"Yes. So you said. Her mother was with child when she came to the priory and Marguerite herself is a bastard. Was she treated ill by the Prioress as well?"

"She never said so. No, I would think not. She was glad to become a nun. She has said this repeatedly."

"Her surname is Bereham? Any relation to Barham? Does her mother hail from these parts?"

"Yes. So she said. But her mother is dead. I expect that became part of her decision to take the veil."

"A difficult life."

"Possibly. But look at me." She planted her hands on her wide hips. "I started out as a simple merchant's servant and married my master. The more I married the wealthier I became. And now they call *me* a lady, or near like it. It is a sore world indeed when servants become masters and masters servants."

"Indeed. How well I know it."

She blushed. "Bless me. Forgive my wayward tongue. I did not mean to speak ill of you."

He nodded and stared into the flames. "I know. Do not apologize."

She took his hand and he squeezed the warmth of her flesh in his. It did comfort him.

"She could seek solace from her family, if she knows them," he said. "But then again, they cast her mother out, so that is unlikely. She wishes to return to her priory."

"Oh aye," she said. "She was emphatic about that. Poor soul. It is the only home she knows."

He glanced over at Jack who had just finished with Gelfridus. Jack shot him a bitter look and shuffled up the stairs. *"Jesu,* but I suddenly feel old."

"Surely you cannot mean dalliance is only for the young?"

"No. But all this." He gestured loosely, aimlessly. "I am at a loss to understand it."

"Crispin Guest. Have you never taken a virgin's flower?"

For some unaccountable reason, he blushed. "Er, no. What has that to do with—"

"Then you cannot know the appeal to the young man. He can scarce be much of a man. Have you sat the boy down to discuss it with him?"

"Discuss it? Discuss what?"

"Blessed Mary and Joseph! Why! The ways of love! The boy has no one else to advise him, no father, brother, or uncle. That leaves you for the task."

Crispin shrank back. *"Me?* But *I* don't—"

"You cannot tell me you are not experienced enough to discuss such with him, for I will avow otherwise." She smiled and elbowed him.

His shoulders slumped. *God's blood!* He never reckoned on something like this. He'd almost rather face the torturers again. Well, if it's to be done he might as well get to it. Rubbing his face with a calloused hand, he rose. "Very well, Alyson. You have shamed me to it. God help me."

"God *keep* you," she said, smiling after him.

. . .

CRISPIN OPENED THE DOOR to his chamber slowly. Jack sat by the hearth, sewing a patch on one of Crispin's stockings. He didn't look up but scooted on his stool closer to the firelight. Sighing, Crispin closed the door, and sat on his bed. He watched Jack for a long time, saying nothing, letting the crackle of flames do the talking for him, until he knew he must speak. "Jack," he said gently.

"There's no need," Jack said tightly. "I done what you told me, and I shrived m'self. I'll do me penance and be done with it. Happy?"

He leaned forward, clasping his hands together. "You're a good lad."

"That's not what you said earlier."

"I misspoke earlier."

"Hmpf."

"Jack. It has come to my attention that the time has come to discuss, well, certain matters."

"What 'certain matters'?"

Crispin rose and tugged the stocking from Jack's clasp. He tossed it on the bed but Jack would not look up at him. He stood above that ginger head before he decided that wine was in order. He retrieved the jug from the sill along with two clay cups. He poured generously into each and handed one to Jack. Jack still would not look up and did not take it. "Come, Jack. Drink with me."

"I am not allowed," he grumbled. "I am on bread and water, remember?"

"As your master, I . . . temporarily reprieve you from your fast. Come now."

"So I'm still bound to you."

"I do not know. What am I to you? Besides a bastard."

He whipped his head up. "I never said such!"

"But thought it, I'm sure. Take it."

Jack stared at the sweating cup and slowly raised his hand to grasp it.

Crispin took a sip and returned to sitting on the edge of the bed. Jack stared into his cup but did not drink. "What matters would you discuss with me, Master Crispin?"

"Matters of the fairer sex."

Jack's head snapped up at that and he nearly spilled his cup. "W-what?"

"Tell me, Jack, how much experience do you have with women?"

"Experience?" The boy's face reddened almost more than his hair. "Well now. I don't rightly know—"

"Have you ever lain with a girl?"

"Now, Master! That is hardly a matter I'd discuss with you!"

"But this is the very matter that needs discussing. Come now. We are men here. Nearly."

Jack stared wide-eyed for a moment before he grasped his cup tightly and downed it in one. Crispin took up the jug again and poured more. Jack held the cup in both hands and chewed on his lip. "We-e-ell, I . . ."

"I trust you are schooled as to what parts must unite to—"

"God's teeth and eyes!" Jack shot to his feet. His face flushed as he paced before the fire. He drank down his second cup and wiped his mouth. "I know what goes where! Blessed Saint Margaret! That ain't talk for no decent folk!"

"If you can't speak of it then likely you shouldn't be doing it."

"I ain't doing naught! I just kissed the wench."

"She isn't a wench. She's a holy sister. And I beg you to remember that."

Jack continued his appraisal of his now empty cup.

"Well at least you know something," muttered Crispin. "But you obviously do not understand when you are reaching beyond your station."

Jack stopped and turned his head. His expression was mortified. Finally.

"Above my station? But she's a nun. She's a servant, ain't she?"

"She comes from better stock than that. They all do. And do I have to remind you again about vows?"

"She's a lady, then?"

"Yes. Or should be. True, she is a bastard and not recognized by her sire, but I doubt that even a learned thief would be suitable."

"'Slud," he whispered. "I didn't know all that."

"Indeed. Perhaps the next woman you kiss you might inquire."

Jack looked properly chastened. His eyes were wide when he looked up. "Am I in trouble?"

"Not from me."

"I mean . . . her priory. Can they do anything . . . to me?"

"No. They only have jurisdiction over *her*. The archbishop, on the other hand—"

"Jesus mercy!" He crossed himself. "You wouldn't tell him, would you? That priest, he won't tell, will he?"

"Jack, calm yourself. I certainly have no intention of telling the archbishop. I was jesting with you. And Father le Britton is prohibited by virtue of the sacramental seal—"

"Le Breton! Oh my soul!" He slapped his forehead. "That's three!"

"Three what? What are you babbling about?"

A hurried knock on the door drew Crispin's attention and Jack scurried to open it. Father Gelfridus pushed past him. "Master Guest! We need your help. Come, hurry!"

"What is it, Father?"

"It's the church. They won't let us in."

Crispin felt no surprise at this. So, the archbishop finally closed the cathedral as he should have done upon the heels of the first murder. "This is only correct, no? It must be reconsecrated—"

"No, it is not that. It is the masons. They have blocked the doors and won't even allow the holy brothers entrance."

"The masons?" He cast a glance at Jack, suddenly recalling Jack's words concerning the conversation between Dom Thomas and the stone carver. "I will come," he said and quickly snatched his cloak.

18

✥

THE WEST DOOR OF Canterbury Cathedral was blocked by a throng of townsfolk, some demanding entrance, others just curious at the commotion. Crispin wished with all his heart he still possessed a sword. He hoped a commanding tone would do for him what three feet of absent steel could not.

"What goes on here?" he shouted.

He smiled to himself to see the crowd part for him. There was something to be said for a noble upbringing.

He could see the door now. It had been wedged open by some of the townsfolk. Two broad-shouldered men stood within the entrance and one of them looked like the mason Crispin had seen the day before.

"That's Master Nigel," whispered Jack, elbowing his side. "The one I saw with Dom Thomas."

"Indeed." Crispin pushed his way up the steps, unmindful of the glares he received. "Master Nigel, what's amiss? Why have you barred the way?"

Nigel turned his wide, flat face, measuring him with keen, darting eyes. "And who might you be?"

"I am Crispin Guest. They call me the Tracker." There were a few gasps of recognition and even Nigel's features became graver. "The archbishop has charged me with keeping the peace in this parish . . . and there has been precious little of that of late."

"Aye," said Nigel with a leer. "If you have been so charged, you haven't been doing your job well. Two murders, I hear tell. And . . . other mischief."

"Is that why you guard the doors? Because of 'mischief'?"

"Well, we might make a little mischief of our own, good Tracker. We guard the doors as we have promised to do if the monks here refuse to pay their bill."

Jack lurched forward. "But—"

"Jack!" hissed Crispin and pushed him back. To Nigel, he said, "It is interesting that you should say so. I have it on good authority that you have already been paid these sums."

Nigel frowned and glanced at his fellows who were too far away to hear their conversation. He turned his back on Crispin to call a mason to the door. When a man arrived he spoke to Crispin again. "I will talk with you, Master Guest." Jack made a move to follow but the man looked down at him and shook his shaggy head. "Only the Tracker, if he is brave enough."

"Master Crispin is the bravest man in the kingdom!" Jack shouted, hands balled into fists.

Crispin laid a gentle hand on Jack's shoulder and eased him back. "That's enough, Jack. Wait for me here."

Jack, all former animosity forgotten, stood his ground. Crispin smiled inside but turned a solemn expression to the masons. His lone dagger was small comfort as he passed under the arch within the cool church. He glanced up the nave and saw more masons barring the way from the cloister. Nigel led him to a dark corner near the quire before turning to Crispin with his beefy fists at his hips.

His tunic was rough-spun and dusted with powder and bits of stone. His paunch spilled over the thick leather belt at his waist. His dark stockings had patches on each knee. Never had Crispin been happier to own a new coat and stockings, or he might have looked as poor as this man.

"Very well," said Nigel, his voice thick with intimidation. "What do you have to say?"

"Merely that you have been paid." He lowered his voice and glanced dramatically at the others. "Or is it a secret from your fellows?"

"You lie."

He straightened. "A poor game, this. For you know I am not lying."

Nigel grimaced and pulled his dagger. Crispin expected it and had his out first. His other hand darted forward, gripped the mason's arm, and slammed his hand against a pillar. The surprise of the action freed the blade from the mason's fingers. It clattered loudly on the floor and echoed throughout the empty church. Crispin pressed his own blade to the bull-like neck. The man's eyes widened when he stared down at the steel. "I don't like men pulling their daggers on me," he hissed close to Nigel's face. "It isn't friendly. It makes my own blade itch for blood. Should I scratch that itch?"

"No, Master," croaked Nigel. "It . . . it was ill-advised of me."

"I will put my dagger away and we will talk, yes?"

The man nodded and Crispin slowly withdrew the dagger from the man's neck and sheathed it.

"Now. This is what transpired. You received money from Dom Thomas to hold your tongue about something you saw." The man's brows rose up his creased forehead. "It matters little to me if you wish to share this boon with your fellow guild members. My interest in it is this: I want to know what it is you saw. Why is Dom Thomas paying for your silence?"

"It has nought to do with you, Tracker."

"Doesn't it? I wonder how your fellows would react should I tell them that you have indeed already been paid and choose to keep it for yourself. Could you feign forgetfulness, I wonder, and live?"

Nigel passed a hand over his sweaty face. "It's not what you think."

"I believe it is exactly what I think. What did you see? If it was murder and you failed to report it to the authorities then you are as liable as the killer—"

"Murder? *Murder?*" His sweaty face was suddenly pebbled with perspiration. "Blessed Mother! I am no party to murder!"

His voice rose in volume, alerting the other masons nearby. Heads turned.

"I have no part in murder!" he cried again.

Damn the man! Crispin saw his opportunity slipping away as curiosity turned to concern. Some came away from their posts and headed toward them. Soon the masons were gathered around the two, casting accusatory and threatening looks Crispin's way. Before Crispin could negotiate the situation, Nigel snatched up his own money pouch in a burst of inspiration. "Look! This man has talked to the good brothers and brought our pay! Let the monks come through, then, as our quarrel with Canterbury is at an end. We will return to our work. Come now!"

The men, acting like a shield around Nigel, cheered and moved as one to meet the others at the cloister door. There was more discussion, some arguments, but the monks were soon allowed in and the dispute appeared to be over.

Nigel looked back with a smirk. Disgusted, Crispin turned away.

He met Jack at the entrance again and the boy was beaming at him. "Don't be proud of me yet, Jack," he said with a scowl. "I was not able to extract the information I wanted from Master Nigel. And now I never shall." He recounted their exchange and Jack's face fell. "However," he said, "mention of murder produced a rather profound effect." Jack didn't understand. He steered the boy into the nave and bent close to Jack's ear as they watched the monks' shadows cross the Chapel of Saint Thomas at the far end. "Dom Thomas does not seem guilty of murder. I thought that would console you."

Jack nodded. "Indeed it does. A holy brother guilty of the greatest sin? Though I do not much like the man, I am relieved he is no killer. But what, then, did he need to pay extortion money for?"

"That I do not yet know. But I shall ferret it out some other way." He, too, was pleased that Dom Thomas, pompous as he was, was not guilty of murder, but it drew him no closer to finding evidence against Sir Philip. He shook his head. "Prioress Eglantine, Brother Wilfrid. Such heinous crimes. I wish I knew why—"

"Oh! Oh God's blessed eyes and ears! I *do* know why, sir!"

He stared at Jack as though he had sprouted wings. "What are you talking about?"

"It's that curse, sir," he said, grabbing Crispin's arm and searching the shadows.

"What foolish nonsense is this?"

"It's the curse, Master. What Edward Harper was telling me. The curse of Becket's bones!"

"I have never heard of such foolishness. I expected better sense from you. After the hours I spent teaching you—"

"But sir! First it was the Prioress, and her name was Eglantine *de Mooreville*. And then poor Wilfrid, and his surname was *de Tracy*. Don't you see, sir? They both have the same surnames as Becket's murderers. The saint is taking his revenge on their descendants. And Father Gelfridus is next! He's a *Le Breton*."

Crispin paused. He rolled the thought in his mind like dice in his fingers. Was there merit to such an idea? Was someone taking vengeance on the past?

"Why, Jack, that is a very interesting theory. But how could the murderer know that these three people would be at the same place and time?"

"If God wishes a thing done, then it is done."

"God is not killing these people!"

"Well *someone* is!"

"Who is this Edward Harper?"

Jack looked relieved at last. "I will take you to him, sir."

19

JACK LED CRISPIN UP through the nave, pulling at his arm.
But when they approached the cloister door, a monk stopped them.

"You cannot enter," said the tall cleric. "This is for the holy
brothers alone."

"Father Cyril!" Jack edged forward, grinning madly. He pushed
back his hood revealing his face . . . and tonsure.

Cyril glared at him until recognition washed over his features.
"Brother John, er . . ."

Sheepishly, Jack fingered his coat. "Ah . . . alas, no, Father. I
am Jack Tucker and this is my master, Crispin Guest."

Cyril eyed Crispin. "So it would appear. I have heard it from
on high that this person must be allowed anywhere he wishes." He
regarded Crispin haughtily and though his words allowed access
he did not step aside.

Crispin bowed to him. "I understand the rare privilege afforded
me, Father."

"Privilege," he muttered, eyes flicking toward a chastened Jack.
"Not so rare, it would seem." He stepped aside and Jack looked
back forlornly. Crispin felt a pang of regret for having used Jack so.

The cloister was large. The open greensward was filled with wind-rustled herbs and other medicinal plants. Jack seemed to know his way well after only two days within, but he expected no less from the clever lad. He followed Jack down the colonnade and into deeper shadows until they came to a gate. Jack pushed it open and a courtyard spread before them shouldered by several small cottages. A man with wavy white hair and white beard was hoeing in a little garden of carefully tilled earth.

The man looked up, squinted, and then straightened, leaning on his hoe. He waited until Crispin and Jack approached before setting his hoe against the cottage wall. "Do I have the honor of greeting Crispin Guest?" he asked.

Mildly surprised, Crispin looked down at a red-faced Jack.

"I told him your name, Master. I didn't think it would do no harm."

Crispin saw clearly in the old man's eyes that he knew his name very well. "Proper introductions, Jack."

Jack scrambled forward and threw back his hood as if doffing a hat. His tonsure gleamed in the sparse sunshine. "Master Harper, you knew me as Brother John and for that deception I am heartily sorry. My true name is Jack Tucker—" and he bowed low. "Here is my master, who is still my master. As you see, I am not a friar. I was sent to the cloister to help discover a murderer."

"And have you?" he asked tightly.

"No, good sir. Not yet. But my master will have him. He always does."

"So this is the famous trait—" He stopped himself and smiled grimly. "Tracker," he amended.

"Indeed," said Crispin stiffly. "And you are Edward Harper, pensioner."

"As you see me," he said, spreading out his hands. His clothes were not new but were a good weave and fairly expensive cloth. But they were well worn and bespoke his current status as pensioner, using only that which he needed to live. Crispin admired his willingness to live a simple life, to even tend a garden, for surely this man was a gentleman before his retirement.

"I am aggrieved you had to lie to me, young Jack," Harper said. "I liked your visits."

"Oh sir!" Jack dropped to one knee. "If I could have spared you I would have done so. I had no wish to lie to you. You seemed a right honorable gentleman."

"Arise, young squire. You need pay no homage to an old man. These simple furrows are now my lands with only crows for retinue."

Jack rose and dusted off his new stockings.

"It is clear you know of me, Master Harper," said Crispin. "Why did you not give the game away sooner?"

"I only just discovered. And it is an interesting game. For instance, am I given to understand that the poet Geoffrey *Chaucer* is imprisoned within these walls . . . for *murder*?"

Something squeezed inside Crispin's chest. He must see Geoffrey again today, though he had little in the way of good news to offer him. "This is true," he said carefully. "But it is not my doing. I do not believe him guilty."

"Truly?" Harper's eyes lit, eyes a cloudy blue like ancient ice. "Then perhaps I was in error about you, Master Guest. I thought perhaps you did it for vengeance."

"Master Chaucer is Master Crispin's old friend, good sir," said Jack. "He's trying to free him."

"Do you know Geoffrey Chaucer?" asked Crispin.

"Yes. I met him on several occasions." Harper thought for a moment, nodded his head, and then gestured toward his door. "Will you come in and take refreshment?"

With this shift in mood, Crispin took the offer gratefully. He ducked under the low lintel and looked around. Small, humble. What he expected. A pile of books and parchments lay on a table under the window.

"When young Jack here told me your name it sounded familiar, so I researched it. I wondered why such a boy would work for you . . . and be proud of it."

Crispin fingered the parchments. He recalled similar papers from his past as a knight. "You were a herald, sir."

"Indeed." He placed his hand on his breast and bowed slightly. The crescents of his fingernails were black with dirt.

Jack looked from one man to the other. "I don't understand, Master Crispin. I know *of* heralds but I do not know their calling."

But it was Harper who stepped forward. He proffered a parchment and unfolded it. "These drawings are the shields and blazons of our noble peerage. These books and parchments are my Ordinaries of Arms. I have kept a tally over the years, marking down as many as I could and writing also their ancestral lineage."

"Why?"

"Because, young Jack, when a knight competes at tournament it must be established from whence he comes; that he has a right to compete. Likewise, should he die in battle, he must be identified and this is achieved through his colors and blazon. Or if a man wishes to marry a woman they must not be too closely related, and these trees help me to see that."

Jack studied the carefully wrought pictures of shields with awe. "Then these are the noble souls of England?"

"And France and Flanders and a few other places."

Jack's face was scored with admiration. "Then you found my master in these pages."

Silently, Harper took another parchment, unfolded it, and laid it over the others on the table. Crispin peered down and followed the old man's gnarled finger as it climbed the page over shield after shield, finally coming to rest on one shield; one half blue, the other half yellow. A red dragon was set in its center; a dragon looking back over its winged spine and bearing no claws. Above the shield was a drawing of a great helm flanked by a red mantle and crowned with a swan. "And here is Guest. Shield per pale Or and Azure, a dragon passant reguardent unarmed, Gules. I see there were four children: Henry, Robert, Joan . . . and Crispin, this last the only surviving issue. The parents Henry and Johanna."

Crispin stared with prickly eyes at the stark recital of his past, little better than a headstone, just as silent and just as cold.

Jack turned to look at him. "You had two brothers and a sister, sir? I never knew."

"Yes. They died when I was quite young. I barely remember them." He didn't know why he said that. It wasn't exactly the truth. But it seemed to ease some of the hurt from Jack's features.

"I had a sister, too," said Jack without emotion. He leaned over the parchment. "Your father was a knight. A baron."

"Yes."

"Your mother—" Jack counted on his fingers, his mouth working it out silently, "died when you were six."

"Yes."

"And your father not long after—"

"This is all very interesting, Jack, but not to the point." He stepped back from the table. His hand trembled and to stop it he rested it on his knife hilt. Family. It had been important once, but now . . . He was the last. The only survivor. And he was a failure, for the name would die with him. Stripped from court, the colors of his shield were gone from the public rolls. His father, once so proud a knight who served a king, would be forgotten except on some dry bit of parchment read by an old pensioner, while his mother was no more than the memory of a horrific fall down a staircase witnessed by her terrified son, that "surviving child." What would she have said to him now, he wondered? Would she have hung her head in shame as these other families had done, those who had killed Becket? Was he any better than they were?

"You have filled this lad's head with nonsense of a curse," he growled. "From where does such foolishness arise?"

"It is not foolishness. I found evidence of such a curse in the priory's archives when I was helping the good brothers organize their records. Many strange incidents are recounted."

"Murder?"

"No. This is the most extreme circumstance yet."

"Master Harper," Jack interrupted, "there is a third descendant amongst the pilgrims. The nun's priest, Father Gelfridus Le Breton!"

"Bless me! You don't say?"

"No, he doesn't." Crispin leaned over the table and pressed his hands to the parchment. He felt their dry stiffness crinkle under his palms. "It is nonsense at best, a coincidence of names at worst."

"Then why are you here seeking me out?"

Crispin tore his eyes from the old man's and stared down at the drawings again, scanned the long dead names of his family that he had scarce thought of in so many years, and sighed. "Because in myth there is often a grain of truth and I need to know all I can."

Harper studied Crispin. "I expected a more foolish and impetuous man," he said. "I did not expect such a thoughtful and careful gentleman."

"I am that, Master Harper. At least, I am now."

"*Suus Pessimus Hostilis* indeed. 'His Own Worst Enemy.' Perhaps at one time."

"That's what *I* told him!" said Jack, grinning madly.

But Crispin's mind was suddenly elsewhere. When he turned to Jack he was filled with excited anticipation. "Jack, go get the sword."

"The sword?" But the gears finally rotated in Jack's mind and he snapped his fingers. "The sword! Oh, Master! You are ten times the man I will ever be!" Off he ran. His steps could be heard slapping the stone cloister walk until they slowly disappeared in the distance.

Harper pored through his parchments and finally went to his books. "Le Breton, Le Breton . . ." He flipped pages and found what he wanted. "Would you not call this an extraordinary coincidence now, Master Guest?"

Three of the four names? "Yes," he conceded. "I would have to say I would. And yet, the idea that a murderer could conspire to gather all of these together—"

"Perhaps the Prioress and her priest were lured here. Brother Wilfrid, of course, by virtue of his office, was forbidden from leaving the precincts of the monastery."

"But Father Gelfridus has been the nuns' priest for years. The planning of such a thing is staggering to the mind."

Harper shrugged. "Staggering it may be, but vengeance can simmer for years."

How well Crispin knew. What years had he wasted in the name of vengeance? But the task at hand was more important than his own sordid history. "Vengeance? The murders were avenged two hundred years ago. Who would seek vengeance now?"

"The answer to that, I believe, is *your* task." Jack was worried that Father Gelfridus would be the next victim. But a tingle down Crispin's spine told him that the priest was a more likely murderer.

Harper left his books and retrieved a jug from a shelf. "A poor host am I. I promised you refreshment and I have failed to offer it. Will you take some beer?"

"I thank you," said Crispin, still captivated by his thoughts as well as the colorful shields and achievements on the parchments and in the books. He took the cup offered and drank. The beer was flat and a little stale but he had drunk worse. "How long have you known about me?" he asked quietly.

"On the second day of Master Tucker's subterfuge. Our little friar named you as his former master and as I said, it was a simple thing to research. You were not long from court."

"You remained civil to him in spite of it all. For this I thank you."

"I knew he must be at the beck and call of his master, but I could not reckon the nature of his deception." Harper took a drink, looked at his chipped cup, and winced from the stale beer. "He spoke highly of you and of the learning you gave him. From the pattern of his speech I would think that he was more suited to the kitchens rather than the garb of a squire."

"Since I am no knight he is not a squire. But I saw no reason not to teach him. He came from humble beginnings. But he is sharp and learns easily."

"And you speak well of him. It is the measure of a man how he speaks of his servants."

"Jack . . . is a special case." But before he could say more, Jack himself returned to the courtyard at a trot and, panting, entered the cottage, bowed a greeting again to Harper before handing Crispin the wrapped sword.

"And what is this?" Harper's eyes ran over the object as Crispin unwound the linen from the hilt.

"This is the murder weapon, that which dispatched Prioress

Eglantine." The last of the cloth fell away and Crispin held up the pommel, showing Harper the red field with the muzzled bear head. "It would be most helpful, Master Harper, if you can find the name that belongs to this blade. It may help me drop the noose around the neck of a killer."

But Harper was staring wide-eyed at the pommel. His face had gone white.

"Master Harper?"

"I need no book or parchment to place this, Master Guest, for I know it well."

"Well then?"

"It is perhaps the worst of the four, the first to strike a blow against the sainted martyr. This, Master Guest, is the blazon for the fourth of Becket's murderers: the Fitz-Urse family."

20

"THE FOURTH NAME!" GASPED Jack.

Crispin's patience thinned. "Are you certain?" But it seemed foolish to even ask.

"Yes. Oh, yes. Since I first suspected and found the Prioress's surname and then Wilfrid's, I found the others. This is the most notorious of them all. I am not mistaken, Master Guest."

"Didn't I tell you, Master! Didn't I say!"

"Be still, Jack, and let me think." This was impossible! An incredible conspiracy of such unlikely circumstances that no mere mortal could have brought it about. No mere mortal . . .

He drew himself up and paced the small space. No. He refused to entertain the notion. Each time he was confronted with these supernatural events they could always be explained away. It was the mark of a foolish and unreasonable man who believed in superstitious happenings. No man with the logic of Aristotle could entertain the notion. *Some men are just as firmly convinced of what they think, as others of what they know.*

Logic, Crispin. Stick to the facts. "Then this sword belonged to the Fitz-Urse family. It may not be the same—"

"Surely you can see for yourself that it is old. The blade itself is not cared for. The scratches are aged. The enamel on the pommel—"

"Yes, yes. I have seen all this." He sucked in his lower lip. Then something else occurred to him. "Is the Fitz-Urse family motto *Fortis et Patientia*?"

"No, it is quite different."

Crispin deflated. "No?"

Harper consulted his papers. "I do not immediately recognize this motto. Shall I find it for you?"

Crispin nodded. "Yes. That might be helpful." Was someone indeed taking some sort of revenge, as far-fetched as it seemed? But was a Fitz-Urse a killer or an as yet unknown victim-to-be? "What happened to the Fitz-Urse family?"

"Much the same as happened to the others. The four murderers were excommunicated by the pope and forced into exile, a pilgrimage to the Holy Land. It is said they all died within three years of their quest. Their families faired little better. They were disgraced. Their fortunes failed. Many changed their names in hopes of changing their fortunes or at the very least hiding their past, and some were more successful at this than others."

"Can you find the Fitz-Urse family amongst your books and parchments, Master Harper? I know that heralds are paid for their services. I can pay your fee."

Harper waved his hand. The creases of his palms were still etched with dirt from his hoe. "I will take no fee for finding a murderer." He picked up a large journal and opened the thin leather covering. "I know that a century ago they dropped the use of the Fitz-Urse name and took another. But my memory is not what it once was. It will take time."

Crispin thought of Geoffrey in his cell. "Time, Master Harper, is a commodity we do not have in abundance."

"I will do my best."

"We are staying at the Martyrs Inn. And I thank you for your hospitality and your kindness."

"Not at all, Master Guest. It is good to feel useful again."

Crispin took his leave and after looking at the sword once more, he handed it to Jack. "Take this back to our room. I must see Geoffrey."

"Aye, Master. Are we any closer to knowing the truth, sir?"

"I wish I knew." He looked back at the little cottage as they crossed the courtyard. "Jack, how well do you know this Edward Harper?"

"As well as any man under such short acquaintance."

"He knows a great deal about this. Tales of a curse might be a stratagem to throw a man off the scent." Jack's openmouthed glare slowed Crispin but he did not stop. "It is not inconceivable, Jack—"

"Are you accusing Master Harper? That nice old man?"

"Nicer old men have been murderers before this."

"No. *No!* What cause would he have to—"

"I do not know." He shook his head and pinched his fingers over the bridge of his nose. "Perhaps I am grasping at straws. The very nature of this crime is enough to pummel a man's good sense. And now Sir Philip begins to seem less likely with this new information." He sighed. "Fear not. I do not intend to arrest Master Harper." But to himself he thought, *yet.*

Jack left to accomplish his task. Crispin still had the skeleton key to the church and monastery and was fairly certain no one had bothered to change the locks on the monk's cells, so he would be able to open Geoffrey's cell without assistance.

He walked slowly, thinking. After he talked to Geoffrey he wanted to return to Saint Benet's chapel and see the place of the Prioress's murder once more.

And he was beginning to get an idea about the fate of Becket's bones.

He reached the door to Geoffrey's cell, took out the key, and unlocked it. He stared at the shut door and then abruptly kicked it open.

Geoffrey stood by the archway, a stool raised above his head ready to cosh whoever came in. When he saw Crispin standing safely on the other side of the threshold he lowered the stool.

"Damn."

"That would not have helped your cause, Chaucer."

"I don't know about that. Freedom can help a man accomplish much."

Crispin stepped into the small cell. "And here I am close to freeing you for good."

Geoffrey rushed him. "You are? How? When may I leave?"

"Patience, Geoffrey. Not yet." He sat on the stool and surveyed the four walls. The last time he was here, Geoffrey had punched him in the jaw. He thought about returning the favor, but he reckoned being incarcerated for two murders was probably retaliation enough.

"I have an interesting tale to tell. It seems to concern the descendants of four murderers."

Chaucer sat on the cot. "What murderers?"

"Keep up, Geoffrey. Thomas à Becket's murderers, of course." Geoffrey gasped and hunched forward. "Madam Eglantine and Brother Wilfrid were both descendants of the killers, and, as it turns out, so is Father Gelfridus."

Chaucer shook his head in long sweeps. Crispin noticed that his carefully trimmed beard was getting shaggy and blending with a scruffy jawline. His hair was unkempt and his gown rumpled.

There was a certain amount of satisfaction with this, but after a moment it didn't sit well with him. What sort of friend was he to find joy in the misery of those he loved?

"This must be a jest," Chaucer was saying.

He shook his head. "And the best of all, the murder weapon belonged to Fitz-Urse, and so the fourth is among us. But I do not know who it is."

"This is incredible. Amazing. Why would such a thing be?"

"I do not know. But I will find out."

A new respect emerged from the poet's features. "You are very good at this," he commented softly.

"Yes. It keeps me fed."

"Not as well as it should."

Crispin made a noise in his throat.

"And so. How does this exonerate me?"

Crispin shrugged. "As of yet, it doesn't. At least, not to the satisfaction of the archbishop."

"But if there is another murder while I am locked in here—"

"Tut, Geoffrey. Would you wish that on poor Gelfridus?"

"No, no. Of course not." Chaucer dropped his face into his hands. "I make a very poor prisoner. If put to torture I fear I would spill all."

Crispin quashed memories of his own torture. *He* had said nothing, volunteered no name. But in the end, it had not helped him.

"Have you warned Gelfridus yet?" asked Geoffrey. "Or do you suspect him?"

"I will . . . talk to him."

"And Bonefey?"

He scowled. "He is a player. Of this I have no doubt. But is he the puppet or the puppeteer?"

"Speaking of puppets, those rascally fellows—the Summoner and Pardoner. I trust them not."

"Nor do I. I have issued them an ultimatum, though now I do not expect it to be carried out."

"You speak in riddles."

"I work in riddles."

Suddenly, it felt like old times; the two of them plotting, wrestling with an idea, some point of philosophy. He saw in Geoffrey's eyes that he sensed it, too. They both fell silent, regarding one another.

Finally, Geoffrey said, "I never believed you were guilty."

"I was."

"But dammit, Cris. Would you truly have killed the king?"

Crispin had wondered that himself over the years. He hoped that Lancaster would not have asked that of him, but now, knowing it was all a sham, made his guilt somehow worse. He sighed and shook his head. Too many years ago to ponder now. He had been three and twenty at the time. Young and idealistic. The world had been his, spread out before him like one of Harper's parchments. He had been in his majority, at the height of his strength and his wits—or so he had thought. To have been spared execution was both bane and blessing. "I was Lancaster's man. I would have done anything he asked of me."

Geoffrey cocked his head and studied his friend silently.

Crispin rose. "Worry not, Geoffrey. I will see you freed."

As he neared the door, he heard Geoffrey's voice softly say, "And who will free you?"

He resisted glancing back and stepped into the archway when he was suddenly surrounded by men-at-arms. He reached for his dagger but did not draw it. "What is the meaning of this?" he demanded.

"Step aside, my lord," they said to him, obviously having no idea who he was. "We are here for Geoffrey Chaucer."

"What?"

He saw Geoffrey through the doorway back away from the men who entered.

"What is this?" Crispin persisted. "Are you the sheriff's men?"

"No," said the one who seemed to be in charge. He was taller than Crispin and broad-shouldered and a little too formidable to take on. "I belong to the archbishop's retinue. His Excellency has called for an Episcopal inquisition."

"God's blood! He can't do that! This is not a heresy trial. This is the jurisdiction of the crown."

He pushed Crispin back. "Not anymore. His Excellency says this man confessed to Lollardism and murdered because of it. He must be brought before the bishops before he is executed for heresy."

"But—" He glared desperately at Geoffrey whose wrists were being bound by two guards. "He has only confessed to me. The archbishop does not even know the nature—"

"His Excellency says he does not need to hear it. Only that it is so. The hearing is only a formality. The execution is tomorrow. Now stand aside."

Breath caught, Crispin watched as the men ushered Chaucer forth. He stumbled once, looked back at Crispin, and followed helplessly.

21

CRISPIN WASTED NO TIME getting to Courtenay's lodgings, but the stern-faced chaplain said the archbishop was not there.

His voice was tightly controlled though his muscles were coiled for action. "Where is he?"

"He is unavailable, Master Guest. I suggest you return—"

Crispin lunged and slammed the defenseless cleric into the wall. He felt the man's bones jar against the stone. "Don't make me ask again."

The chaplain's rounded eyes watered from pain. "Please . . . have mercy!"

"I'm not in a merciful mood. God's blood! You will tell me or I shall grind you into this stone!"

"H-he is in the great hall . . . with his clerics. They are holding a h-hearing for the prisoner."

He pushed the man back and stomped through the corridors, turned the corner, and came upon the large doors to the great hall. They were closed, naturally, but there was no guard. He hoped they weren't barred.

Pushing them open he strode in. The archbishop sat in the

center of the head table flanked by the prior and sub prior and two other monks from Christchurch Priory. Chaucer stood before them as an inquisitor, the archbishop's chaplain, paced back and forth, speaking in a measured manner in such a way as to suggest his oration would go on for a long time.

Suddenly, everyone turned. He wished for the thousandth time he had a sword.

Courtenay jolted to his feet. "What is the meaning of this, Guest?"

"I would ask the same of you, Excellency."

The monks gasped. Courtenay slammed his hand to the table. "This is not to be borne! You are insolent in the extreme." He motioned for a guard and the man advanced on Crispin, his spear lowered toward him.

Crispin rushed forward, sidestepped the spear, and grabbed it. He swung the spear with the guard still attached and slammed him into the wall. The man staggered and released his hold on the weapon. Crispin turned it and brandished the point toward the assembly, effectively stopping the other guard from approaching. "I wish to address this hearing, Excellency." He did not lower the spear and kept his eyes darting from guard to guard.

"You are a churl, Guest," said Courtenay in a darkly pitiless tone. "I should have known. A traitor can never be trusted. Lancaster taught you your heresy and now we see the proof of it."

"Whatever you think of me, your Excellency, is your affair alone. But I am here to see justice done under the eyes of God. Geoffrey Chaucer is not guilty of these crimes. This was not his confession to me. If you condemn him then it is you who are committing a most heinous offense against God and Man."

The archbishop raised his arm and pointed a shaking finger toward the door. "Get him out of here!"

Crispin jabbed his spear toward the guard who seemed reluctant to take him on. "Your Excellency, I beg of you. Grant me one more day to prove his innocence. How can it be wrong to deny a man his chance at life? This body—this *holy* body—cannot mean to condemn a man unjustly."

"And you make your plea at the point of a spear?"

He tightened his grip on the weapon and measured both guards and the clerics. Most had risen in their seats and were anxiously watching the outcome.

Crispin had made many decisions in his life. Some had been terribly wrong, and some had proved his instincts. He had to rely on those instincts now.

With a hurried prayer, he tossed the spear aside and held up his empty hands.

He glanced at the guard. The man hesitated. It was enough. Crispin dropped to his knees. "My lord! Grant me this boon. I make this oath to you. I will find those guilty, and you will have been spared executing an innocent man." *Never mind that you have no right to do so!*

No one moved. No one breathed. He felt his heart hammering within his chest.

Courtenay was livid. But Crispin knew the man had no choice. No prince of the Church could turn down a plea like this. He could tell that the monks were moved and appeared more than willing to comply with his petition.

The archbishop licked his lips. The hand he pressed white to the table lifted and caressed the bejeweled cross pendant lying on his chest. "This is a matter of heresy, Master Guest," he said hoarsely. "Can you disprove that?"

Crispin paused, glancing toward Geoffrey. Of course. This was no civil murder trial. The Church would only deal in heresy. *Think fast, Crispin,* he told himself. "Of course, your Excellency. This rather *rushed* gathering would seem to benefit from the wisdom of your peers, bishops like yourself—" Courtenay's face darkened. "But since you felt the need to hurry the proceedings—fearing for the soul of Master Chaucer, no doubt—you must realize that the king's uncle would surely never harbor a heretic."

His words were well chosen, for he saw Courtenay blanch at the mention of the king.

"You have one day Master Guest. By sunset tomorrow, if you have brought no new evidence to me, then Chaucer hangs."

Crispin was about to argue but saw that it would do no good. "Thank you, Excellency. Thank you." He rose and only then did he dare glance at Geoffrey.

His friend's face was wet with perspiration. He felt a constriction in his throat. Chaucer looked frightened. He wasn't the only one.

Crispin bowed low to the assembly, threw his cloak behind him, and marched out. His mind worked furiously. Today and tomorrow. That was all he had to prove Geoffrey innocent. But what evidence was there? A charge of murder he could elude, but one of heresy?

He stopped. He *had* to get a message to Lancaster. It would certainly never reach him in time but he had to make the effort. He owed Geoffrey that much.

He needed someone with a swift horse.

Crispin hurried out of the cathedral precincts and then he ran. The Westgate. If the sheriff was there he had a chance . . .

He barely took note of the streets as he passed through them. He could be in London as any other place, though he did not know these streets as well as he did London's.

His gaze rose above the rooftops, searching for the round tower gate, and he turned the corner of many twisting lanes to keep in the right direction.

Finally, he rounded the last corner and the stone gatehouse loomed above him. The Westgate was surrounded by scaffolding while still under construction and he hoped the sheriff, or at least someone who could help him, was there.

"The sheriff," he told the guard, trying to catch his breath. The man only motioned him inside. Crispin looked around, saw a stairwell, and took it.

The first door he came to he peered within. A clerk sitting at a desk and penning careful words on a parchment looked up.

"The sheriff. Is he here?"

"Aye. He is within," and the clerk gestured to the closed door.

"I must see him. Now."

The man stood. "And who are you, sir? And your business?"

"I am Crispin Guest, and my business—"

"Oh!" The man seemed to know well Crispin's business and he scrambled to the door, knocked once, and entered, closing it behind him.

He paced. He couldn't stand still. Each moment that ticked by was another moment he wasn't using to find the killer.

At length, the door opened and Thomas Brokhull strode through. "Master Guest. What is it you require?"

"Praise God. Lord Sheriff, I need your swiftest messenger sent to London immediately."

"Why so urgently?"

"Because—" He suddenly noticed the clerk peering at both of them. The sheriff noticed as well, and led Crispin into his room. He closed the door.

"Tell me."

"The archbishop, like any wily fox, has taken advantage and has condemned Geoffrey Chaucer for heresy."

"What? He cannot do that! Even if it were an ecclesiastical matter he hasn't the jurisdiction to execute a prisoner."

"And so, too, would I think. But I do not put it past the man to use any means at his disposal."

"That is the crown's jurisdiction," Brokhull went on indignantly. "*My* jurisdiction!"

"Indeed. But can we argue the point later? The messenger, Lord Sheriff."

"Oh yes." He went to the door again and told the clerk to send for a man.

"Have you quill and paper?"

The sheriff offered his own desk for his use. Crispin circled to the other side, fetched a quill from its pot, and took the square of parchment offered. Hastily, he scribbled a note:

> *Your grace,*
> *I write this in haste without room for pleasantries. Your servant, Geoffrey Chaucer, is in danger of his life. He is accused of murders for which I know he is innocent but a charge of heresy will be his end. In all God's speed, send your emissaries to stop Archbishop Courtenay from this course. Urgency is utmost.*
> *Your servant,*
> *Crispin Guest*

He blotted it, sealed it with the sheriff's seal, and clutched it in his hand until the messenger arrived. When he did, Crispin all but pushed the sheriff aside. "Give this to the duke of Lancaster at Westminster Palace. In all haste. How fast can you ride to London?"

The man, wearing the tabard of the city of Canterbury, looked once at Brokhull and then at the window. It was almost noon. "With good weather and riding hard, I can perhaps make it by nightfall."

"Good then. Go. Go now!"

With a look of acknowledgment from the sheriff, the man left. Crispin listened to the man's feet thump down the stairs.

"Is there anything I can do?"

Remembering the sheriff, Crispin stared at Brokhull. "No, my lord. I work best alone. But believe me, if there was something you could do I would not hesitate to ask. I thank you for this."

"Well, there is one thing I will do. I will take my men and march to Christchurch Cathedral at once! This must not stand. Just who does the archbishop think he is?"

"He thinks he is the Primate of England . . . and he is."

"But he is not the *King* of England. And the king is the law. I shall do my best to remind him of that."

He nodded. He liked this fellow. He was certainly better than Exton or Froshe. And more useful. "I have been given a day, Lord Sheriff. Forgive me if I do not waste it."

Brokhull nodded and Crispin departed, making swift work of the staircase. The irony of the situation was not lost on him. Here, two hundred years ago, Archbishop Thomas à Becket opposed his king, claiming that priests and monks should only be tried in ecclesiastical courts, while the king argued that he alone was the law. And now Courtenay would reverse the sundial.

But at least Brokhull did not seem a man to countenance any perversion of the law. He might delay the execution in time for Lancaster's men to intervene. It would take that extra time, for even should the rider make it to London by late tonight, how would Lancaster's men get to Canterbury in time to stop Chaucer's execution?

He trotted back to the cathedral, hopeful that the sheriff might persuade the archbishop from taking further action, but uncertain if it could be done. True, the sheriff was the law, but the archbishop was the Church. When a man was threatened with excommunication and heresy, duties and loyalties could easily be forgotten.

He wiped his mind free of Courtenay's treachery. He needed to think, to concentrate. He had been so certain it was Sir Philip, but with circumstances being what they were, that certainty had eroded. He was so close to discerning the true killer he could taste it. Who? *Who?* Sir Philip had a grudge against Madam Eglantine but what of Bonefey and Wilfrid? And how did he obtain Chaucer's dagger? No, no. This was no good. One thing at a time. Was it for the bones? He didn't think so. Was it revenge? Was it this idiotic curse Jack would have him believe? Something about it was strange, personal, rabid. If God chose to take His revenge then it had been satisfied two hundred years ago. Even God ended his grudges in a timely fashion. No, this was human intervention. But to what purpose? The Prioress, poor Wilfrid, and perhaps Father Gelfridus. All religious. Did it have something to do with that? With the shrine?

He was drawing himself into circles and nothing was making sense. Becket's four murderers. God's blood, but that was the only thing that made sense! But how could that be!

He stopped. Jack was waiting for him in the cathedral's courtyard. After so heavy a heart, his spirits were suddenly lifted to see his protégé. *Protégé.* For so many years that word was like a curse. At least it had been to him, being Lancaster's protégé. But Jack was his now and he would not see the boy ill-used, especially by himself. He joined the boy in the shadows of the stone arches and merely looked at him.

Jack fidgeted. "W-what are you looking at, sir? Did I do something wrong?"

"No. Not at all. But Jack"—he laid a hand on the boy's shoulder—"if I were ever to order you to do something that you knew was wrong, I expect you to disobey me."

"Huh?"

"Just know that it will eliminate a world of mistrust and pain."

"Sir," Jack began carefully. "Master Chaucer. How . . . how did it go?"

His hand fell from Jack and they climbed the steps, entering the portico at the west door. "The archbishop has moved to take matters into his own hands. He has condemned him and means to execute him on the morrow."

"God blind me! Can he do that?"

"He forces the issue of heresy but he is breaking the law. I only hope the sheriff has his will of him, but I do not know . . . I earned Chaucer a reprieve, but only one day's worth. And it is already late." The sun was moving much too fast across the sky. "We must work quickly if we are to prove him innocent." He stared at the floor tiles, the sound of the masons hammering fading as he fell deeper into thought. "I think I should see Saint Benet's chapel again." They made their way together up the north aisle.

Apart from the masons and the occasional monk exchanging old candles for new, they were alone.

Except in Saint Benet's chapel.

A slim figure stood amid the shadows. A candle from the altar limned the person with an edge of gold. "Dame Marguerite," said Crispin, startled. He couldn't prevent a glance at Jack, who turned multiple shades of red.

"Dame," he said, softer. He was suddenly worried for the sake of all the religious within these walls. "Perhaps you should not be here."

She turned toward the statue of Saint Benet and then looked

again at the spot on the floor where the Prioress had lain, not too far from the place of Becket's martyrdom. "I needed to come to the church."

"But it is closed. It must be re-consecrated."

"Oh? I did not know." She pulled her veil about her like a cocoon. "I just felt . . . I should come. Here."

He said nothing. And then he remembered the rosary bead still housed in his pouch. Reaching in, he took it in his fingers. "Dame, this belongs to you. I know Mistress Alyson repaired your rosary"— and he gestured to the string of beads hanging from her belt—"but I hope this last bead can be added back." Small comfort but it was all he had to offer.

She opened her hand as if feeding a bird and he dropped the wooden bead into her palm. There was a bit of brown blood on one side of the berry-sized bead. This did not seem to affect her and she closed her hand over it. "I shall do my best," she said. She gazed at him squarely, even critically before she cast her eyes on Jack. She gave him a strangely alluring look that disturbed Crispin and made Jack's face blush even redder. She bowed her head to both of them and slowly left the chapel.

He watched her long shadow stretch until it blended with the others in the church. The sound of hammering thudded in his head.

"You don't think *she's* still in danger, do you?" whispered Jack.

"I do not know." Crispin stared at the floor worriedly, hearing her screams echoing in his head. "If she were, then why wasn't she killed that night? I wonder how . . ." He remembered a raven-black gown spread out on the floor with a scarlet pool of blood beneath it; rosary beads scattered like teardrops. He thought a moment, looking at the floor, eyes scanning to every nook and shadow. He raised his head and his search grew wider, encompassing the whole church. When he spotted his quarry he darted up the nave and accosted a monk exchanging candles. "Good Brother," he said to the startled man. He glared at the man's rope belt and huffed with disappointment. "Never mind," he cast over his shoulder, leaving the puzzled monk where he stood. He spied another quietly sweeping the paving tiles with a gorse broom. Crispin grasped his shoulders, and the monk, taken unawares, shrank back and dropped his broom. "Forgive me, Brother. But may I borrow your rosary?"

"My rosary?" His hand automatically slapped the beads hanging at his belt. It looked to be made of wood or possibly ivory. The berry-sized beads were similar to Dame Marguerite's. "Surely you can purchase your own from the many purveyors in the courtyard."

"I'll only need it for a moment."

The monk eyed him askance and snatched it protectively from his belt. "But—"

Crispin deftly liberated it. "Much thanks. Only a moment. I promise." He hurried back to the chapel where a perplexed Jack was still waiting. "Jack, I will need you to collect the sword one more time."

"But Master! I just went and put it *back* in our room."

"Jack."

Astonishingly petulant, thought Crispin as Jack huffed a weary sigh and dragged his feet out of the church. Crispin held the circlet tightly in his fingers and waited. Yes, he, too, had owned a rosary once upon a time, beads of filigreed silver. How ostentatious! He thought of them with embarrassment now. Shouldn't a ring of prayers be of humble materials? It was the one thing he was glad to have lost.

After a brief interval, Jack returned, lugging the sword over his shoulder. "Here it is, Master. *Again.*"

"Thank you, Jack. I will take it." He unwrapped the hilt first and held it aloft, letting the linen flutter off the blade. Candlelight shimmered along the cool length of steel. He stepped back and gave it an experimental swing. It whooshed as it passed through the air.

Jack leapt back. "Oi! Warn a man, eh?"

Crispin swung it again, getting a feel for the blade. Good balance, good weight. He turned to Jack and handed him the rosary from his belt. "Tuck this into your belt, Jack, and stand there."

Jack took the rosary, pondered the beads for a moment, and then draped it double over his belt as he had no doubt seen the monks do. He backed up to position himself as Crispin instructed.

"Now Jack, don't move."

Crispin swung the blade up and dropped it down, right beside Jack. The boy yelped and leapt back.

"I told you not to move."

"God's eyes and toes! What, by the blessed Mother, are you doing!"

"Visualizing. Now kneel and take out that rosary."

Jack looked for all the world as if he were going to his own execution. He gingerly knelt on the paving tiles and took the rosary in his hands. He stared uncomprehendingly. "Now Jack, for your own good, *do not move.*"

Jack nodded and closed his eyes.

Crispin swung upward again and, as close to Jack as he dared, chopped downward. Jack cringed as the blade whistled by him, but did not otherwise move.

Curious. He stared into the space that had once been Prioress Eglantine.

Jack pried open one eye. Once he saw it was safe, he opened them both. "What are we doing, Master?"

"'What we have to learn to do, we learn by doing.' But it doesn't make sense. Perhaps I am making too much of this. Take that rosary and return it to that brother there. The nervous one standing behind that pillar." Maybe it had nothing to do with anything. Maybe it was the key.

But one thing was certain. Neither Gelfridus nor Marguerite would remain safe until the killer was caught.

THE SUN WAS LOWER when Crispin searched the monastery and finally found Dom Thomas. The monk turned and saw him. *"Ecce iterum Crispinus!"*

Crispin didn't find it amusing. "I must have words with you, Dom Thomas, and there is little time."

"Yes," he said, more breath than word. "I have heard of the fate of Master Chaucer. I am at a loss as to my archbishop's thinking in this."

"Yes. It is of such things I must talk with you. I am in haste."

Dom Thomas looked up the empty colonnade and down the other way. "Very well. Come with me."

He led Jack and Crispin to a little room that served as his study. Parchments and leather-bound journals lay on a shelf on a wall next to a small arched window. He closed the door and stood beside his table. The surface was covered in parchments, an ink pot, and several quills stripped of their feathering, their sharpened tips stained black. "Well?"

"I'll be brief, Dom. Are you cheating the priory's books?"

Dom Thomas's jaw dropped. "What?"

"I do not have time for your theatrics. I am trying to save a man's life. Did you fix the books? I have sources that saw you pay bribery to the masons."

Dom Thomas darted an enraged glare at Jack who moved slightly behind Crispin. "I do not know what you *think* you saw," he began, voice chilled. "But I did no such thing. If you even breathe such a thing to his Excellency—"

Crispin lurched forward and grabbed the monk by his cassock. "Is this the truth?"

Chillenden's eyes enlarged, never leaving Crispin's. "It is the truth. I swear it by Almighty God."

He released the monk and stepped away. "Very well, then. I must tell you that I do not believe you guilty of killing Brother Wilfrid."

"Me?" He staggered backwards. His face seemed almost on the verge of tears. "I would never— He was like a son to me. I grieve over his death every moment."

"Yes, yes. I think I know what the mason saw and that you were keen to keep secret."

"How could you possibly—"

"I am paid to know. But never mind this. I will keep your secret for now if you will keep mine. I need your help, Dom. I cannot allow your archbishop to execute Master Chaucer. If you wish to redeem yourself in my eyes, there is something you must do."

Crispin explained it and then quickly took his leave. Jack scrambled to catch up to him. "Master. Master! Not so fast. Where do you go now?"

"Back to the inn. It is time to do a proper interrogation of Sir Philip. He is the key to this."

"He's the murderer, isn't he?"

Crispin strode quickly down the avenue. Sir Philip. If he had to, he'd *beat* a confession out of him.

As they neared the inn a man wearing the city's tabard looked up and trotted forward. *Now what?* He stiffened, expecting the worst.

"Are you Crispin Guest?" asked the man.

"Yes."

"I have bad news, good sir. The man I was watching—Philip Bonefey—"

"Well?"

The sheriff's man lowered his head and shook it. "I do not know how it happened. I do not know what to say—"

"Spit it out, man!"

He nodded. "I am aggrieved to say that, somehow, he escaped. I do not know where he is."

22

CRISPIN'S HEART SANK. WITHOUT Bonefey and the information he suspected the man was harboring, his chances of proving Chaucer innocent were nil. He stood in the courtyard, the sun sinking lower, the sky darkening. He thought furiously, or tried to, but his mind was a frustrating blank.

Something was pulling on his coat. He swung back his arm to strike it away when he realized it was Jack. "Master, what are we to do now?"

"I don't know, Jack!" he said a little more harshly than he intended. He paced in a small circle while Jack stood to the side, wringing his coat hem in one hand and clutching the sword with the other.

This was impossible. Impossible! Geoffrey's life hanging from a thread; the only and best suspect gone. Why was God treating him so? Hadn't he done his penance for forswearing his king? Was there no end to it?

"*Why!*" he cried out, fists in the air. If he could climb the cathedral and reach God himself he would do it and ask Him personally.

"Th-there must be something we can do for Master Chaucer," said Jack softly. "There must be some way to prove it was not him."

"And weren't you keen to prove it *was* him not too long ago?"

"Aye, sir, I know. I am heartily sorry for that. I did not have all the facts. Someone clearly snatched Master Chaucer's dagger from him and did the deed. But who, Master? Sir Philip?"

His mind snagged on one word: facts. *Did* they have all the facts? It wasn't for the bones. He knew *that*. Then if not the bones, why? "We *don't* have all the facts. The sword, Jack. We don't know who it belonged to."

"I just assumed it was Sir Philip's."

"He has his own sword. But Master Harper was researching that blazon for us. Perhaps we had best revisit him to see what facts he has uncovered."

It was not much, but it was something. Crispin turned on his heel to head back to the cathedral. He went straight to the priory gates and rang the bell before his impatience made him slam his fist repeatedly to the door. "Open up, I say!"

A monk drew the door open a crack. "Why do you disturb the peace of this priory, sir? It is late."

"Get out of my way." He pushed the door open and the monk fell back. He had no time for apologies and stomped forward. Jack scurried in quickly behind.

Crispin paid no heed to the monks he shouldered out of his way, nor the angry words and gestures they invoked toward him as the monks threaded in the direction of the chapel for Vespers.

His eyes were fixed on the arched colonnade ahead and to the little door that led to the courtyard where the pensioners lived. No one said anything more to him as he passed through the cloister. He thought about sending up a prayer for forgiveness as he trespassed but swallowed it back. There would be time later for shriving.

He trusted that Dom Thomas was doing his part. Crispin would do his.

They reached the courtyard at last but Harper was not out hoeing his garden. Of course not. It was Vespers already. Crispin had barely registered the sounds of bells chiming above him and the line of monks heading to the chapel to perform the Divine Office. He hoped Harper was in his cottage with his books and not with the monks.

He stalked up to the door and knocked. The door immediately opened and Harper greeted Crispin with a grim expression. "You're back. Good. I have the answer you are seeking."

"God be praised." Entering, he stepped right up to Harper's table. The old herald was directly behind him and reached forward to open a parchment. He moved a candle forward, its light casting a warm glow over the piece.

"You see, Master Guest," he said, pointing to the parchment.

Before Harper could speak, he pressed his hand to the man's arm, silencing him. He didn't know what to say. His mind raced like a stallion in a meadow. He could not have fathomed this, but slowly, it began to make sense to him.

"Master Harper," he said, his strained voice strange to his ears. "May I borrow this?"

Harper looked over the paper and frowned. Clearly, he did not like to part with his Ordinaries, but when he looked up, Crispin could see the conviction in his pale eyes. "Yes, of course. If it will help."

"It will. And Master Harper, I thank you. You have saved a man's life." The herald bowed. Crispin folded it up, carefully following the creases, and stuffed it in his belt. "Come along, Jack."

Jack waved his farewells to Harper and ran after his master's long strides. Crispin didn't want it to be true, but he didn't see how it couldn't be. It all fell into place. Except for Wilfrid. But he'd have to ask . . .

When he got to the transept door, he entered the church. The masons had given up their work for the day and Crispin's troubled soul fell into the quiet and solitude of the lonely spaces of vault and column. He walked up the nave, stopped before the rood screen, and turned on his heel to face Jack.

"What is it, sir? Do you know who owned the sword? Did Master Harper—?"

"Yes, Jack." He couldn't help it. His eyes fell from the boy's. How was he to say? He tugged the parchment from his belt and opened it. He pointed to the red shield with the muzzled bear head. Then his finger traced downwards from the shield. "This was the Fitz-Urse line. The murderer Reginald had no issue, but his brother Richard did; a daughter named Mabel and a son Warine. Then Warine had an issue named Gilbert. But as you see here, by the fourth generation, they changed their name."

He took a breath and glanced up at Jack.

Jack looked back at him, puzzled. "And what is that surname sir?"

Crispin lowered the paper to his thigh. "Bereham."

It took a moment, but Jack's face slowly changed from puzzlement to pale incredulity, and finally to reddened outrage. "That's a lie! That's a filthy lie! Let me see that paper!" He snatched it from Crispin's hand. He gazed over Jack's shoulder, following his finger tracing over the stiff paper, resting here and there on a name until he reached the sixth generation. Margaret de Bereham was Crispin's age and there was a line struck through her carefully penned inscription. A note was written to the side probably by Master Harper some years ago. Crispin recognized the look of such slightly browned ink. It read: *Gave birth to bastard daughter and was banished from the family. May God have mercy.*

Jack dropped the parchment and walked like an old man to the rood screen, dragging the sword behind him. His fingers curled around the rood's carved wood and he stood a long time facing it. Crispin didn't know whether he should go to the boy or better to stay away. "Jack," he said softly.

Tucker slowly shook his head from side to side, but he did not turn to Crispin. His voice sounded wrung from him, taut, fighting back tears. "Why did it have to be *her*? Of all people. Why, Master Crispin, did it have to be her?"

Crispin licked his suddenly dry lips. "I do not know, Jack. But this sword most certainly belonged to Dame Marguerite. She . . . she must have known the nature of Prioress Eglantine's name and bided her time. Or . . ." He shook his head. "I know not why. But it explains the broken rosary. An errant sword swipe could not have cut through it without harming her. But if she had lifted the sword herself and caught the crossguard on her own rosary in her belt, it would have snapped it."

"That is so clever of you," said Marguerite.

Crispin and Jack both spun. Dame Marguerite stood behind them in the darkening church. She cocked her head and looked at Jack. "He is a clever man, isn't he?" she said to Tucker.

"Dame Marguerite," whispered Jack, anguish breaking his voice.

Footsteps. From around a pillar, Chaucer and Dom Thomas trotted and suddenly stopped.

"Cris! This monk—"

"Master Crispin?" asked Dom Thomas, taking in the tableau.

"Silence! Both of you!" Crispin swept his hand up, gesturing for them to stay as they were.

"I have decided something," said Marguerite, face white within her surrounding veil. She seemed little put off by the presence of two more, and in fact took little notice of them. "I shall leave the Church and go with you, Master Tucker. Yes, I think this is best."

"Marguerite." He took a step closer to her.

Crispin clasped Jack's shoulder and pulled him back, stepping forward in his place. "Dame Marguerite. That sword." He gestured to the one in Jack's hand. "Did it belong to you?"

"Of course. I am of the family Fitz-Urse."

Chaucer and Dom Thomas gasped but wisely stayed silent.

"It is Bereham now. *Fortis et Patientia*. The Bereham motto. 'Strong and Enduring.' So foolish a thing, truly. Strength and endurance, aye. My mother had it in abundance. She was a Bereham but she was shunned from the family. They gave the sword to her. I do not know if it was a jest or whether she was supposed to use it on herself for disgracing the family so. Or perhaps they simply wished to rid themselves of the reminder of their dreaded past."

She edged closer to Jack. Crispin shoved the struggling boy behind him.

"Did you kill the Prioress?"

She smiled. It was the same as her pitying smiles. It chilled him to the bone.

"Yes, of course. She needed to die."

The words, so gently spoken, could well have been mistaken for something else. But Jack's gasp behind his back told him it was true. Crispin felt the boy's fists at his spine and Jack suddenly burst forward. Tears streaked his face.

"But why, Marguerite?" he cried.

She turned dull eyes on Jack, where they softened. "Because she was most cruel to my mother. Is God not love? Isn't that exactly what my Lady Prioress preached? And yet. There seems to be so little love in the world. My mother was not loved by her family and they sent her away all because of a babe. An innocent babe. And my Lady Prioress showed little love to her, treating her cruelly, giving her much penance and hard work, all because of this babe. She was a lady once. My mother. She died a peasant. And she died saddened to her soul. She was not loved. But *I* loved her. And I swore to her as she lay dying that I would avenge her. And I have. But I am sorry about the monk."

Jack closed his eyes. His lashes were dark with tears. Without opening them he asked, "Did you kill Brother Wilfrid?"

"I regret that I did. You see, he knew the nature of my name. He works in the treasury and the rolls of the church, so he said. He knew my name and knew it used to be Fitz-Urse. He was going to tell. And then everyone would have known it was me."

Crispin wanted to be far from this place. But it had to be done. Questions needed to be answered. "How did you get the dagger?" he asked.

"Master Chaucer was leaving his room when I noticed he had quill and parchment. I begged him if I could borrow a portion of parchment to send a missive to my priory. He was kind and allowed me to write my note in his rooms. But he is also careless. For he left his dagger behind. I took it. It was a pretty thing with gems upon it. The Prioress was fond of pretty things. She had beautiful sleek greyhounds who ate meat and gnawed good bones better suited for soup, while my mother ate rough bread and stale cheese. I'd lost my sword, you see, so I took the dagger in compensation."

He glanced back at Chaucer and his face was white and grim. "But how were you able to smuggle the sword into the church?"

"I told my Lady Prioress that I had forgotten my rosary and I went back for the sword in my things. I have kept it carefully hidden in my trunk. We are not allowed to own anything of our former lives, you see. But I knew I needed my mother's sword. It was all that was left. And I killed my Lady Prioress, and I killed him. And I have confessed it, and so I am absolved."

And Father Gelfridus was the beneficiary of that! He now understood the priest's agitation. A murderer *did* confess, just not the one Crispin thought. The priest was not allowed to say. To even warn anyone.

"I cannot allow you to go free, Dame. And I certainly would never allow you to go away with Jack. You are my prisoner now."

She frowned and looked down. She shook her head. "No. I think not."

"You have confessed it, Dame, before witnesses. You must pay for these crimes."

"But I have confessed it to a priest. I was absolved. I am a nun and I have killed my prioress and a monk. Surely it is a matter for God."

"For God, yes. But first for the hangman."

Her eyes suddenly took on a wild expression. She looked at Jack, his face marred with tears, and then caught sight of Chaucer and Dom Thomas cringing in the near darkness.

Like a frightened sparrow, she darted away into the smothering shadows.

Everyone moved at once. Crispin cursed. "Be still! I cannot hear in which direction she has gone!"

"That way!" pointed Chaucer.

But Dom Thomas lifted his arm and aimed at another direction. "No. It was there!"

"God's blood! Everyone go off and search!"

Crispin looked back at Jack. The boy slid to the floor, the sword clutched in his hand. He left him alone. The boy needed to grieve.

He heard Chaucer retreat toward the quire and Dom Thomas

down the nave to the west entrance, but Crispin headed toward the north aisle, ears cocked and listening.

He made his way up the north ambulatory, spying around corners and pillars, but he saw no one. Darkness had fallen, and the church was draped in deep shadows and a few flickering candles. Starlight shone through Saint Thomas's miracle windows.

He crept up the pilgrim stair and carefully entered the Chapel of Saint Thomas, scanning over the many silent tombs. The candles around Becket's shrine had been extinguished. No need for candles when the relics were not there.

When he turned back, a shadowy figure stood at some distance. Startled, Crispin squinted. Who was it? He recognized the odd shape of the miter on his head. It was not a tall miter as he usually wore, but a shorter version. His face was a dark silhouette. "Your Excellency? What are you doing here?"

The archbishop said nothing. He raised an arm and pointed toward the Corona tower door. Crispin looked. The door hung open.

"Much thanks," he called over his shoulder and ran for it. He reached the door and gently pushed it open. The stairwell was empty. Crispin felt like a fool, but decided that "better a live fool then a dead one" and pulled his dagger. Slowly, he climbed the stairs, sliding his back along the stone wall. The dark stairwell was cold from a draught swirling down from the open door above. He could see stars through the opening and finally reached it. He peered around the doorpost and spied the nun standing by the battlements, looking out across the city.

"Dame Marguerite."

She did not turn. "Look at all the houses down there. See the little candles in the windows? Is it lovely having a family, all homely together, I wonder?"

"I am sorry for the cruelness of your life, Dame, but it is never a matter for murder. Surely you could have left the priory when you came of age and found your own husband."

"Who would take me? No dowry, no name. I am no one."

Crispin flinched. Yes, how cruel the world could be to those without a name. "And so, too, did I lose all. But I have made a life."

She turned then and studied him with deadened eyes. "You find criminals and bring them to justice." Her voice was unsteady.

He nodded. "I do."

"Am I a criminal?"

"I fear, Dame, that this is so."

She seemed to consider this. "Will the sheriff hang me?"

He hesitated. "Justice . . . must be served. Would you see another die in your place? Master Chaucer was accused of these crimes. He was slated to die tomorrow for them. Would you see that happen to an innocent man?"

"Master Chaucer? And he is such a merry fellow. I would not see that happen."

"And so. You will have to accompany me to the sheriff and tell him your tale."

She sighed and turned back to the sparkling city with its torches and candlelight glittering on the evening air. "I shall never have a family. Not a proper one. I wish . . . Alas. Wishes are sometimes like prayers, are they not? They are as lost and as futile."

"Prayers are not futile, Dame. God listens to us."

"He listens, but does He act?"

Crispin fingered his dagger before sheathing it. "I am no theologian."

"No. You are a man. I am a woman. And I have sinned. Death is the only course for sinners, no?"

"Dame . . ."

He should have suspected; he should have been better prepared, but it happened so fast.

Marguerite gave him a sad smile before she pivoted on the stone, stepped up between the merlons, and flung herself over the edge.

"*No!*" Crispin leapt and slammed hard against the tower floor, grasping at air.

Her gown fluttered in the wind, lifting her for only a moment, before she fell into the blackness of the night. She made no sound in her descent.

He strained his neck looking up at the empty place where the nun had stood, feeling the uneven paving dig into his chest. He gradually drew himself up, dragged his feet to the edge, and looked down, but the tower's foundations were lost in darkness.

There was a scramble at the stairs and Jack's white face appeared. "Where is she?"

"Jack . . ."

The boy looked quickly around and made an abrupt run for the edge. Crispin grabbed him and held him tightly. "It's too late, Jack. It's too late."

Jack gripped Crispin's coat. He struggled, but it was only for a moment. All at once he slumped and sobbed into Crispin's chest. He held the boy tighter, hoping to make it better, knowing he could not.

23

THEY MET, ALL OF them—Crispin, Jack, Chaucer, Dom Thomas—in Courtenay's study. The archbishop was not pleased to be summoned out of Vespers, but Crispin insisted, and with the sheriff and his men nearby, it was easy to persuade him.

"What is *he* doing out of his cell?" Courtenay pointed at Chaucer. Geoffrey, mustering his dignity even with several days of beard growth on his cheeks and a dirty gown, spoke for himself.

"Your Excellency, God Himself has released me."

"Is that so? I think, rather, it is a disobedient monk." He swiveled his glare and landed it squarely on Dom Thomas.

The monk did not cower, and for that Crispin held a new respect for him.

"Your Excellency," said Dom Thomas, "I did what was right and proper. Master Chaucer was not guilty. We have seen the proof of it this night."

"Proof? I see only another death. A suicide, you say? I should lock you up, Crispin Guest. You have brought nothing but trouble to us."

"I have brought you truth, Excellency. A quality this parish has sorely lacked."

"You dare—"

"*Enough!*" Crispin's voice stilled the others. He brought his scowl all the way to the foot of Courtenay's chair. "I have had enough of your lies and trickery. You didn't bring me here to guard the bones of Saint Thomas. You called me here to discredit the duke of Lancaster! And when Geoffrey's dagger was found in Brother Wilfrid's throat, you found a better revenge. You thought to execute Lancaster's pet, never thinking, never dreaming that lives were in peril. What sort of shepherd are you?"

Courtenay said nothing. He squirmed on his chair.

Crispin straightened his coat. "I will explain events here as I reckoned them, and then I will be leaving this place. Canterbury does not feel as welcoming as it once did." He turned to Geoffrey. "Master Chaucer lost his dagger by mischance. He left it in his room where Dame Marguerite easily found it and took it."

"The poor soul," said Dom Thomas. "We heard her confession," he said to Sheriff Brokhull. "There is no question she was the killer of both her prioress and our brother monk. But why did she kill her prioress?"

"Cruelty," said Crispin. "She lived under the Prioress's roof and witnessed every day the cruelty the Prioress inflicted against her mother. Every word of scorn, every touch of the rod, must have chipped away at Dame Marguerite's sanity until she became the sad and confused woman we encountered today. I am certain Prioress Eglantine thought she was serving God's will by treating the sinful woman as she did. But after penance, there must be a time of reconciliation and healing. Surely that is what God intended."

"You speak with your own authority, Master Guest," said

Courtenay. "You know nothing of the hardships that one endures in the confines of a monastery. Discipline must be maintained."

"Indeed. Saint Benet devised the rule under which your own monks as well as Prioress Eglantine's nuns live. But even he cautioned that those who have power over other souls must make a reckoning on Judgment Day. Prioress Eglantine's day . . . came early."

Courtenay scowled. "You walk very close to the line, Master Guest. But let us put an end to this discussion. Our poor daughter Marguerite was insane when she committed these crimes and died by her own will. We will pray for her soul, but she may not be buried in consecrated soil. The matter is at an end. Your duty has been discharged."

"Then I am a free man," said Chaucer, smiling at the sheriff.

"There is still a matter of heresy," said the archbishop.

Geoffrey scowled. "My lord! I am a loyal son of Mother Church. But I am sworn to serve in his grace the duke's household. If Lollard he is, it does not make it so for me."

Courtenay glared at him, chin burled. "Very well, Master Chaucer. The charge of heresy is dismissed. But mark me, should you set foot on Canterbury soil again, the eye of the Church shall be upon you."

"Your Excellency, should I ever be fool enough to venture to Canterbury while you live, I will be in sore need of the Church's benefit." He smiled at Courtenay's expression and rushed to take Crispin's hand, shaking it vigorously. "Cris! By God! Tracker? No indeed! You are a Miracle Worker!"

"Nothing of the kind," he said with a rush of heat to his cheeks. He stepped away from Geoffrey, stamping down the pleasure he felt in his chest.

"My treasurer will fetch you the remainder of your fees, Master Guest. If you will, Dom Thomas?"

"One moment, Excellency," said Crispin, stopping Dom Thomas as he turned. "There is still the matter of Saint Thomas's bones."

"Oh, er . . . that is a matter we will content ourselves to solve on our own, Master Guest."

"There's no need," said Crispin. "I know where the bones are." He hooked his thumbs in his belt and stepped forward. Amid all the horrors of this inquiry, he felt an uncommon satisfaction at the expression on the archbishop's face. "Shall we repair to the Chapel of Saint Thomas?"

He could tell Courtenay was about to say no, but Brokhull spoke up. "I for one would be pleased to see an end to this. Lead on, Master Crispin."

Crispin bowed to him. He didn't wait for anyone to follow.

It was quite late now. Dame Marguerite's body had been recovered and the monks had taken her to their infirmary. Crispin had suggested calling upon the help of Alyson again and she had come, exchanging with Crispin the saddest look he had yet seen her jovial face wear. She said she would keep vigil with the nun's remains until dawn and Crispin left her to it. He had asked Jack if he wished to join her, but Jack had silently shaken his head. No doubt there was much on Jack's mind, and Crispin did not wish to interfere with the labyrinth of emotions the boy had to face on his own. Jack had chosen instead to accompany Crispin, strangely holding the unwrapped sword tight to his chest yet again.

Crispin situated himself by Saint Thomas's empty shrine and waited while the others gathered, carrying candles. But Crispin was only interested in Courtenay's face. The man was angry but there was something more. He had seen that expression many a time on countless culprits. The man was caught. And he knew it.

"I know it is late, but I shan't keep you long," said Crispin. "I worried over many things when I began to make my inquiries. I worried that a murderer and thief had escaped and absconded with these most precious relics. But I soon came to understand that the one had little to do with the other.

"Dom Thomas was seen paying extortion money to a master mason who had seen something. Was it murder? I was soon disabused of that notion when I put together the facts. No, what the mason saw and what Dom Thomas was no doubt ordered to do, was remove the bones of Saint Thomas before I ever arrived. I do not blame your loyal monk, Archbishop. A man is only at the power of his superiors. Had he the presence of mind, the fortitude at the time, he would have refused to follow your orders as petty and small-minded."

"Now see here—"

"Protest if you will, Excellency. It does not change the facts! He was ordered to remove the bones before my arrival."

Brokhull shook his head in amazement. "If that is true, Master Guest, then where are they now?"

Crispin walked several strides to the tomb of Prince Edward. "I regret to say, that the bones of the sainted martyr are housed in the late Prince Edward's tomb."

"How could you have possibly known?" gasped Dom Thomas.

"Only later. I recalled being shooed away unceremoniously from his tomb not once but twice. The lid of the casket is slightly askew. And I found the finger bone of Saint Thomas between his own shrine and Prince Edward's tomb. Obfuscation notwithstanding, this is the only possible answer." He looked sharply at Courtenay. "Am I right, Excellency?"

Courtenay sucked in his lips but said nothing.

"It is true," sighed Dom Thomas. "Poor Wilfrid. It was too great a burden to lay upon his young shoulders. To keep such a secret!

He was greatly troubled by the deception. I should have taken my conscience from him. Too late."

"You talk too much," growled Courtenay.

Thomas raised his head. "I should have spoken earlier. I am ashamed at how I used all of you. You can be assured I shall do much penance in recompense."

Crispin nodded. But he saved his iciest glare for Courtenay. "Have *you* nothing to say?"

The archbishop remained his aristocratic self. "Well, naturally I moved the bones."

Silence followed this pronouncement. Crispin snorted. *He's playing it that way, is he?*

"I feared a Lollard threat," Courtenay said, red-faced. "I felt it the wisest course to protect the bones."

Still no one spoke. Crispin doubted anyone believed the archbishop.

"At any rate," said Crispin after a long pause, "I have you to thank, your Excellency, for helping me find Dame Marguerite when she escaped from us."

"Me? I do not know your meaning."

"In the cathedral. You pointed out where she had gone. To the Corona tower."

"Are you mad? I was at Vespers."

Crispin shook his head. "But I saw you there. You were wearing a short miter and you pointed. From there."

They all looked to the edge of Saint Thomas's shrine where Crispin indicated.

"But I tell you I was at Vespers with my monks. They can all attest to that."

"But then . . . what bishop did *I* see?"

As soon as Crispin said it, coldness crept over him, starting at his temples and trickling downward.

Dom Thomas was the one to say it though Crispin well knew they were all thinking it. "It was Saint Thomas!"

"No," said Crispin, the words coming to his lips without thinking them. He refused to believe it.

"What other explanation could there be? The saint himself, who witnessed all these terrible things. Oh my Lord and my God!" Dom Thomas fell to his knees. "Forgive me for this deception. Blessed Thomas. Forgive me!"

FAR TOO MUCH HAD happened that night. Crispin retired to his bed and Jack, as white as a ghost himself, settled on his own cot, though Crispin doubted the boy slept.

Brokhull came early to the inn the next morning. Crispin left Jack huddled by their fire to speak to the sheriff. He carried with him the sword of Fitz-Urse.

Crispin greeted him with a bow, but Brokhull's greeting was more to Crispin's liking: He offered a full jug of ale and two cups. They sat together by the hearth and downed a cup each before the sheriff spoke. "All is well, Master Crispin. At least, as well as can be with tidings such as these. Three religious dead." He shook his head and his face was lost again behind his beaker. He wiped his mouth with his hand. "Saint Thomas's relics have been restored to their rightful place, thanks to you. I do not know what the archbishop is paying you, but I am certain it is not enough."

"My payment will be better served by leaving this place and returning to London, for I sorely miss it," he said, even though such a thought had been foreign to him before.

"Are you certain? I could use a man with your talents. I would pay you well."

"That is something to consider. Though London is my home."

"Tracker, eh? Does it satisfy you?"

"In its way."

"I can see that a man such as yourself would be better served with no master. Perhaps . . . I envy you."

"Me? Do not envy me, Lord Sheriff. What you see is the sum total of what I have."

"Then what I see is a man well armed to take on the world."

Surprised, Crispin merely drank another. He looked at the sword at his feet and handed it to the sheriff. "Lord Sheriff, I surrender the sword of Fitz-Urse to you."

The sheriff sneered at the weapon. "You do not own a sword, Master Crispin. Why don't you keep it?"

Crispin hefted the blade a moment, but then offered it hilt first to Brokhull. "True, I own no sword, but I fear this one would be a poor replacement. It has ill-luck attached to it, to be sure. And more ill-luck, I do not need."

The sheriff nodded and reluctantly took it.

Harry Bailey thumped down the stairs and when he caught sight of Crispin he hurried down the last several steps and joined the men by the fire. "Master Crispin. Lord Sheriff." He sat with a heavy sigh. "Bless me! I have never in my life experienced a pilgrimage such as this."

"Nor, I hope, shall we ever again," said Crispin darkly.

"I will drink to that," and he poured himself a beaker and drank it down.

The innkeeper brought a platter with cold meats and bowls of steaming broth. They thanked him and partook of the food.

Crispin sipped at the broth. "By the way." He set down the

bowl and wiped his lips. "Have our friends the Summoner and Pardoner returned?"

Bailey shook his head. "No one has heard or seen a wisp of them."

Crispin snorted into his beaker. "As I thought."

The sheriff drew his bowl from his lips. "Were there others you would have me pursue, Master Crispin?"

"Not for the moment."

Harry Bailey edged forward, an earnest look on his weary face. He seemed much older of a sudden, and Crispin realized what a great strain this whole affair was for all concerned.

"How is young Jack? It was apparent to me—to all of us—that he was enamored of the youthful nun."

Crispin sighed. "He will recover. As must we all. He is young and resilient."

They fell silent, no doubt reliving their own first loves. Crispin worried about Jack, but young men suffered disappointments and trials all the time. Jack was certainly no stranger to either. Of course one's survival was easier to cope with than one's passions. Dame Marguerite would be burned into his consciousness for years to come. It would help mold him into the man he was swiftly becoming. Crispin only hoped it would make him stronger and not tear him down.

"Whatever happened to our dear Franklin?" asked Crispin.

The sheriff harrumphed. "Sir Bonefey?" He waved with a pullet haunch. "My men apprehended him on his way back to London. Do you still want him?"

Crispin considered. As annoying as the man was, he had done no actual harm. "No. But I fear I must apologize to him. I treated him with little courtesy."

"Never fear that. If he would not declare it to you, he certainly feared the king's justice. He eagerly confessed his entire plot. To serve the Lollards, he conspired to steal the bones with the help of your Summoner and Pardoner. Of course, Dom Thomas ruined that plan with his own plot. Or rather, the archbishop's."

Crispin snorted at the machinations of the nobility. Had the archbishop simply left it alone . . . But alas, Prioress Eglantine and Wilfrid would still be dead. "And his Excellency. What of him?" Crispin sipped his ale and watched the sheriff with steely concentration.

"I cannot bring charges. He is the Archbishop of Canterbury. If he wishes to relocate the relics in his own cathedral there is nothing for me to say to it. As for his calling his own Episcopal trial, well . . . That is a matter I do not wish to trouble the king with. Or Rome. The cathedral is being re-consecrated. There has been no mention of a theft but the bones will be paraded about Canterbury tomorrow in celebration."

"I shall be gone by then."

"Indeed," said Bailey. "So should we all. We must return to London. We have tarried here long enough." He set down his beaker and rose. "I'm certain the others would agree with me. Come with us, Master Crispin. Verily, you could do with the company."

Crispin felt the abrupt weariness of the week's events and agreed with Bailey. To return to London with an assembly was certainly more companionable. And it might be better for Jack as well. He was about to say just that, when a man burst through the inn's door, shouting at the top of his lungs.

Everyone jumped to their feet. All Crispin could think was, *What is it now?*

"There's murder, Lord Sheriff!" cried the man, little older than Jack, and more ragged. "We have a man cornered. There are witnesses! Come, please!"

The sheriff was almost out the door the moment the man mentioned "murder." The others followed. Crispin cursed Canterbury. It seemed they simply could not escape death this trip.

Brokhull led the way to the crowd of shouting townsfolk who had seized someone. When the sheriff arrived the people parted for him and Crispin saw what the trouble was.

He wasn't much surprised.

Peter Chanticleer was being held tight by two men while the others shouted at him. His long gown was covered in blood.

"What is this?" the sheriff demanded.

"I killed him," said Chanticleer, chin thrust proudly. "He cheated me! He was a foul, loathsome churl and I killed him. And I shall not repent of it, though I know I will hang." His lips trembled. "God will find forgiveness for me for ridding the world of that vile Summoner."

Crispin nodded to himself as Brokhull took his leave of him to lead Chanticleer and the others away.

A fitting end for two wicked men.

The Miller was right, though. The Devil *had* come to roost in Canterbury. Crispin was glad to leave it.

24

THE ROAD SNAKING AWAY from Canterbury was a ribbon of mud. The solemn troupe left the city behind and good riddance to it, but they hadn't left it very far when they encountered mud-splattered riders with the livery of the duke of Lancaster. With all the emotional turmoil of Dame Marguerite and Becket's bones, Crispin had quite forgotten he had requested the duke's help.

Chaucer rode forth to meet them. Crispin wasn't close enough to hear their exchange but with emphatic gestures and, Crispin suspected, rosy embellishments, the tale was told. Geoffrey gestured once toward Crispin and the two men fixed their eyes on him for a long moment. They spoke to Geoffrey a few moments more before turning their mounts. The horses kicked up a cockerel's tail of mud as they galloped away back toward London.

Chaucer rejoined Crispin with a smile. There was a spot of mud on his cheek but Crispin did not tell him of it. "That was my rescue. Cris, I'm touched."

Crispin rolled his eyes at Geoffrey's expression. But he was relieved he had not needed Lancaster's men.

For the rest of the long two days back to London, spring rains continued to drizzle over their quiet company, and often the weary travelers had to dismount and walk their horses through the worst of the mire. Crispin had led Alyson's horse over the stickiest of muddy places and she smiled that gat-toothed grin at him in gratitude, the first smile in at least a day after the terrible events in Canterbury.

It was two days of watching Jack sitting straight-backed on his horse, sinking into a dull and unfamiliar quietude that worried Crispin.

But it was also two days of reacquainting himself with his friend Chaucer, and he was glad of it.

Geoffrey regaled him with stories of court and of his own adventures as the king's spy, though he kept those stories close for their ears alone. They laughed together. *Crispin* laughed, and he felt the sharp pang of regret rasping behind it, because he knew this renewed camaraderie could not last. So he clutched at it like a cherished object, keeping it in his heart for now, a heart almost as broken as Jack's.

London's spires and rooftops came into view, masked by thin layers of smoke and mist. They reached the Tabard Inn and dismounted their horses in the courtyard, the remaining company of Thomas Clarke, Alyson, Father Gelfridus—who had stayed by himself for the ride back—Edwin Gough, Harry Bailey, Geoffrey Chaucer, and finally Crispin and Jack. They were certainly not the jovial party that had set out from this little inn a sennight ago. All had been sorely tested and they entered the inn for a last beaker of ale and to bid their farewells.

"Drink, my friends," said Bailey, lifting his own horn. "We will drink to the grace of God for delivering us safely home, to the souls that did not return with us, and to a brighter morrow."

Everyone lifted their cups in solemn silence. Bailey's wife watched curiously from a doorway.

Jack turned slowly toward Crispin. "Can we go home now, Master Crispin?"

"Yes, Jack. Let us say our farewells."

He shook Clarke's hand and thanked him for his candidness. He gripped the Miller's strong arm and wished him well. Father Gelfridus glanced up at him with guilty eyes but Crispin clutched his shoulder reassuringly. "Father priest, do not look so saddened. I knew full well you could not divulge what you heard confessed under the sacramental seal."

"I know I have fulfilled my office." He rubbed his hands and clutched at the crucifix dangling from his neck. "But I prayed for guidance. I failed that lost soul."

"She was lost far too long ago, Father. You might have been her next victim."

He shook his head. "And such would have been a blessing compared to the feelings I must carry with me now."

He nodded to the priest. There was little left to say to that. He watched the priest move away, shutting himself within his rich cloak. Crispin wondered what the man would tell the priory when he returned to it. Crispin didn't envy him.

A touch. He turned and gazed into the glowing countenance of Alyson. She smiled. The grin was frayed by the sadness of recent events. "Ah, Crispin," she said. Her fingers slid down his arm and entangled with his own. "You are a fine man and a clever one. You and I, eh? We are a pair of mules, are we not? Stubborn to the last."

He chuckled in spite of himself. He regretted very much that they had not had one more night together.

"I tell you what you must do," she said, her smile broadening. "Marry me."

Crispin jerked with surprise. "What?"

"Marry me, man. You'd be number six. And you'd be happy, too."

He sorted through his shock and tried to form words. "I . . . it's a generous offer."

Instead of being insulted by his hesitation, Alyson gave a full-bodied laugh. "All my husbands, young and old, died before me. I'll warrant that you do not eagerly rush to that! Aye, it's a genuine gospel puzzle, that is. Whose wife would I be in heaven? And you don't relish standing next to those fellows. Well, bless me, I don't blame you. I tell you, Crispin. You are a lusty and vigorous bedmate!" She said the last a little too loudly and the Miller, Edwin Gough, chortled. Crispin glanced guiltily at Jack who was doing his best to pretend he hadn't heard.

"I have never been presented with so magnanimous a suit," he said. "But . . . I regret to say that I am not ready for such a commitment."

"Alas! Such a loss. You would have liked it well, Crispin." She reached up and planted a moist kiss to his cheek. "Then fare you well. God keep you. May the saints watch over you." She patted the spot she had kissed, and swept from the inn, calling her goodbyes and advice to the others.

Finally, there was only Crispin and Chaucer left. They thanked Harry Bailey and left the inn together. Crispin's heart felt heavy, for he knew that he and Geoffrey would now part, perhaps never to cross paths again. Geoffrey mounted alongside him and the three of them rode out of the courtyard together. Crispin said nothing as they traveled across London Bridge, but finally had to speak. "I must return these horses to Newgate. And then I'm returning to my lodgings. I suppose . . ." He sniffed the heavy air of London, feeling a strange pang of familiarity and regret that he was home at last. "I suppose that this is where we part."

Chaucer stared at him forlornly. He wound his reins around his gloved hand. The horse shook out its head, jangling the bridle. "Oh." He bit his lip and furrowed his brow. "Curse it, Cris. I have seen so little of you. And now I owe you my life."

Crispin yanked his hood lower over his forehead, hiding his eyes. "You owe me nothing. We are friends, Geoffrey. Whether . . . whether we see each other again or not."

Chaucer considered this and stared at his saddle pommel. "We will. You can be certain of that." He wheeled his horse about and Crispin watched his mount saunter away into the dense crowds of Thames Street.

AFTER THEY RETURNED THEIR horses, Crispin and Jack walked silently back from Newgate down the Shambles. Looking up, he caught sight of the pot hanging from a hook overlooking the tinker's door. Home. He hailed the tinker Martin Kemp, who was showing a customer his work. The man smiled back in greeting.

Crispin trudged up the stairs, weary in body and spirit, and abruptly pulled up short when he saw his door ajar.

He motioned for Jack to step back, drew his dagger, and kicked the door open.

A figure turned from the cold hearth. He was shadowed at first, but when the door opened wider and shed new light, Crispin nearly dropped his knife.

"Your grace!" He dropped to his knee to the duke of Lancaster and hastily sheathed his knife. Rising, he stepped in, pulling Jack along, and quickly closed the door. "My lord, why are you here?"

And suddenly, Crispin felt his face go scarlet. Lancaster was seeing for himself the conditions in which he lived. The incongruous spectacle of the velvet-gowned duke standing in his lowly residence made him cringe with shame. "Why are you here?" he asked again, desperately.

Lancaster looked Crispin over before his eyes settled on Jack. The duke pulled out the one chair and sat. He laid his gloved hands on the rough surface of the table. Ruddy spots tinged his cheeks over a dark beard. "Well? Have you no wine?"

Crispin blinked, woke himself, and went to fetch his jug, hoping it still contained something drinkable. His heart clenched when he saw there was very little left in the chipped clay jug. He raised it and must have looked so stricken that the duke waved him off. "It doesn't matter. Sit with me."

Crispin slowly extracted the stool from its place beneath the table and gingerly sat. Out of the corner of his eye, he noticed Jack making himself as small as possible in the corner.

The duke wasted no time. "I received your missive and dispatched a representative as soon as possible, but you had already left Canterbury."

"Our business there was done. We encountered your riders and told them . . . told them . . ."

"Indeed. They arrived a day before you did and told me all."

Crispin picked at the edge of the table with his fingernail. "I was only doing my job. It is what I do."

"Yes." Even though he would not look up he could tell the duke was studying him attentively. "You are still angry with me."

Should he lie? It didn't seem to matter. "Yes," he answered.

Lancaster chuckled. "Subtle as always, I see."

"You used to value my honesty."

"So I did."

"And I yours."

"Now Crispin. I never professed to be honest. Honesty in a prince is not his most highly prized commodity. It can, in fact, be to his detriment. I suppose the last time a monarch was truly honest was our own Saint Edward the Confessor. And look where it got him? Invasion by William the Conqueror."

He rolled his fists on his thighs beneath the table. "History lesson duly noted. Why are you here?"

"Very well." He settled back. "You have saved the life of my very valuable servant and have recovered the honor of my house that would have been scandalously damaged by that cur Courtenay, had his plot succeeded. Secreting the bones of Saint Thomas in my own brother's tomb! The gall of the man!"

Crispin said nothing. *Why are you here? WHY ARE YOU HERE!* he screamed in his head.

"Deeds such as these require more than mere compensation."
What?

"Indeed, I could pay you in coins, but . . ." He looked around the shabby room. His brows said it all. "Instead, I wish to offer you a post in my household."

Crispin's fists whitened under the hiding shadows of the table. "But . . ." The king had been explicit about his orders. No one was to succor him. No one. True, he had saved the life of the king and Richard had offered him back his knighthood and riches . . . if he would ingratiate himself in front of all the court. He had naturally refused and this had set Richard off on another tirade. He had told Crispin—shouted at him—that he would never be trusted, never be allowed back at court. What was different now?

"I know what the king declared," said Lancaster, seeming to read his mind. "But this is a humble post. We would rarely see you. Something similar to what Chaucer sometimes does for me.

Small jobs requiring a man of your skills. The compensation would be quite a bit more than you expect now."

"None of these jobs would have anything to do with treason, would they?"

Lancaster leapt to his feet. "By God, Guest! I should strike you down!"

Crispin slowly rose. It did not do to sit while his lord stood. "It has been tried before. But I am like a cat. Nine lives."

"How many left, I wonder?"

He shrugged. "No doubt Geoffrey gains from such employment. Though I rather thought he was spying for the king." Lancaster's face revealed nothing. "Well," said Crispin. "King, crown; uncle, nephew. Little difference it makes."

"You tread too fine a line."

"Between life and death? Yes, it seems I am always treading that line, my lord." He moved to the hearth, retrieved the tinder box, lit the small bits of straw, and tucked them under the peat. It only smoldered at first before the dark chunks of dried peat caught a flame. "I do not feel I can trust you, my lord. I would have thought you'd know that by now."

"Crispin! You were like a son to me!"

"And you sacrificed me. No angel stayed your hand as they did for Abraham when he would have slain Isaac. No, my lord. I have had a taste of the king's justice. It is not to my liking."

"I offer you a chance at your rightful place again."

"And he will not take it."

They both turned toward the voice at the back of the room. Jack straightened his coat, the one Crispin had bought for him. "He has said his peace, your grace."

"And what is this place you now inhabit, Crispin, when servants speak for their betters?"

"A place of trust," Crispin answered, never moving his gaze from Jack's. "Where the master will *never* sacrifice the servant for himself."

Lancaster gathered himself as if he might strike down the both of them, but as quickly as his anger blossomed, his resolve seemed to wilt and he took a step back. "Will you never forgive me, Crispin?" His voice was unexpectedly soft.

He looked up at his lord then, the man who raised him, made him a knight. But as Geoffrey so succinctly put it, he was also a man who, by rights, could just as easily take it all away. Did such a man truly owe Crispin anything?

"On this journey," said Crispin, "I have seen how the sin of vengeance can seep into the heart of an innocent and shred that life till the soul is left in tatters. I have no desire to see my own soul degenerate to such a state." He felt Jack's eyes on him, felt the warmth from his gaze. "And though I . . . I may find it hard to forgive, your grace, I find that it is not . . . impossible." He lowered his eyes, unable to bear the expression in Lancaster's steady gaze. "Give me time, my lord," he said softly. "Perhaps in time, our debts to one another will have been paid."

The slump of the duke's shoulder and his drooping lids showed a more subdued demeanor. He gave a curt nod.

"Though I thank you for your kind offer," said Crispin more lightly. "Today seems to be my day for propositions."

Lancaster, now ill at ease, measured him, the room, and finally Jack. "What is your name, lad?" he said to fill the silence.

Jack straightened his shoulders. "I am Jack Tucker, sir. Apprentice Tracker."

The corner of Lancaster's mouth twitched, but he did not smile. Instead, he nodded to them both and gathered his cloak about him. "Then I must say my farewell, Crispin." He took a step toward the door, paused, and without turning, said, "Whatever you may think of me, I was only doing what was best for the kingdom."

Crispin looked at the floor. "So was I."

Lancaster inclined his head. He grasped the door latch and was quickly out the door.

When it closed at last with a final click, Crispin collapsed into his chair. "I have done a very foolish thing. Again."

Jack touched his arm. "No, sir. You stood up for yourself. I am proud to have witnessed it. 'The ideal man bears the accidents of life with dignity and grace, making the best of circumstances.'"

He blinked. "Why, Jack. Is that Aristotle?"

"Aye, sir. It seemed fitting, sir."

It also seemed to be Crispin's day for blushing. He settled himself on the chair, leaning on the table's surface. "It is fitting to you, as well, Jack."

Jack shrugged. "I have had hardships, it is true. And there will be more along the way. That's a certainty. But this is your day, master. You told that duke. You showed him what your mettle is. No matter what others may say, I think your family would have been proud of you this day, sir."

"Family. I think you are my only family now, Jack."

The boy smiled. "If only that were so. But I am pleased to be your apprentice, sir. That is good enough for me. Far better than I could have hoped for."

Crispin nodded. But the boy started him thinking about his family.

"Jack, fetch my rings." He knew that the lad knew where they were. Jack hesitated and then went to the loose floorboard beside the wall under the window and brought out the little cloth bundle. Jack handed it to Crispin and he took it. Unwrapping the package, the rings fell into the little well of his palm. Two rings. One belonged to his father and the other to him. He held the gold band to the light of the opened window and studied the signet carefully created on its face. The arms of Guest.

He held it in his hand for a moment longer, feeling its weight, before slipping it on his finger.

Author's Afterword

Ah, I wish Becket's bones were still around (Henry VIII had them destroyed when he took over the Church of England, or so it is believed). I wish they were safely tucked away in Prince Edward's tomb. But wishing doesn't make a thing true, so it's best to leave Edward's tomb alone, all right?

Though the characters in Chaucer's *The Canterbury Tales* all revealed specific themes and lessons of morality, I'd like to think that some might be based on actual individuals. The original number of pilgrims in his story was thirty-four, including Chaucer, but I chose to cut that amount down considerably to a much more manageable number. The descriptions come directly from the text, with some added help from the Ellsmere Manuscript with its extraordinary illustrations of all the characters.

So who was real and who was fiction in this piece? Well, certainly Chaucer is real, though he was planted firmly in this fictional play, one he might have been heartily amused to be involved in. He indeed worked for Lancaster as a spy, as a comptroller for the ports, and as a poet, of course. And his sister-in-law was the duke's longtime mistress, Katherine Swynford, whom Lancaster eventually married after his second wife died.

The Archbishop of Canterbury, William de Courtenay, was also a real figure and did have animosity for the duke of Lancaster as was described herein, with a strong dislike for the Lollards.

Dom Thomas Chillenden was indeed the treasurer and eventually became the prior of Christchurch Priory. And just what did he say in Latin to Crispin when he said, *"Ecce iterim Crispinus"*? Translated: "Lo, Crispin again." It's from the first-century Roman poet Juvenal who also coined "bread and circuses," and means "we're back to *this* again!" Been wanting to use that phrase for a while.

I've also been wanting to get to Chaucer in my series. I grew up with *The Canterbury Tales*. I was probably the only American five-year-old who could recite the first few lines of the Prologue. In Middle English, no less! I just assumed school kids in 1960s Los Angeles all knew the story of Chaunticleer. They didn't. I had a children's version of *The Canterbury Tales*, which I pored over during my childhood with its Bosch-esque illustrations. I have it still. Later, of course, when I was older I could enjoy the *Fabliuex* of the Miller's Tale and the finer points of the Wife of Bath's Tale. I haunted the Huntington Library in San Marino, California, when I was a kid and later as a teen, where they have, among other wonderful things, the Ellsmere Manuscript on display.

In this book I have strayed from a firm point of view through Crispin's eyes and offered a look through Jack's. I hope, dear Reader, that this didn't throw you and that, indeed, you found a new pleasure in the reading, having a rare glimpse into Jack's psyche. I love Jack. He's Peter Pan, the Artful Dodger, Huck Finn, and every other smart little boy we've ever known who just needed a chance to prove himself. Where would Crispin be without Jack? Jack is growing up, though, and in no other previous novel has this been more apparent.

There is more murder afoot, sly deceptions, a mysterious relic, an irresistible femme fatale, the return of Geoffrey Chaucer, and more stirring adventure in Crispin's next tale, *Blood Lance*.

Glossary

CANONICAL HOURS Also called the Divine Office, these are specific hours for certain prayers by monastics, though the church bells that called each canonical hour helped divide the day for the laity as well.

CHAPERON HOOD A shoulder cape with a hood attached.

CHAPLAIN In the context of *The Canterbury Tales*, the Prioress' chaplain is a personal assistant rather than a confessor.

CHEMISE A shirt for both male and female, usually white. All-purpose, used also as a nightshirt.

COMPLINE The last canonical hour of the day.

COTEHARDIE (COAT) Any variety of upper-body outerwear popular from the early Middle Ages to the Renaissance. For men, it was a coat reaching to the thighs or below the knee, with buttons all the way down the front and sometimes at the sleeves. Worn over a chemise. Sometimes the belt was worn at the hips and sometimes the belt moved up to the waist. This is what Crispin wears.

DEGRADATION This is when knighthood is taken from a man, usually because of treason or other crimes against the crown.

FRANKLIN Ranked below the gentry, he is a freeholder of land.

HOUPPELANDE A fourteenth-century upper-body outerwear for men or women, with fashionably long sleeves that touched the ground.

INDULGENCE A remission of punishment (in Purgatory, for instance) after sacramental absolution.

LATTEN An alloy resembling brass.

LIRIPIPE The long tail on a hat or hood.

MANCIPLE Servant responsible for supplying provisions for a college or inn; in this case for law students.

NEWGATE A city gate in London as well as a prison.

NONE One of the canonical hours of the day, about two pm.

PARDONER A purveyor of indulgences, a pardoner of sins.

ROUNCEY A riding horse.

SENNIGHT A period of seven days, a week.

SHRIVE/SHRIVEN To make confession in the penitential sense.

SORREL Chestnut brown color, commonly used when referring to horses.

SUMMONER Official of ecclesiastical courts who calls upon religious offenders to attend.

VESPERS One of the canonical hours, sunset.

WHELP A young dog.